Halfkinds
Volume 3:
Alphas

by Andrew Vu

Recoil Books

ISBN-13:
978-0988520622 (Recoil Books)

ISBN-10:
0988520621

All Rights Reserved by Andrew Vu

3

ALPHAS

Table of Contents

Chapter 1 - Lucy

Collection

<u>January 29, 3061 4:01 PM</u>

Working on example all day, need break. Progress improving, splicing trials no longer complete failures. Am glad with results thus far. Step away from equipment to get snack. Hunger building, dinner soon. Might work late, not sure when next meal will occur. See what is in kitchen.

Lab is messy, need clean later. Since moving into facility, been able to adjust surroundings for use. Have set up several stations for work. One station for research, another station for testing. Have quarters in another section for sleep. Kitchen for eating. Shower and bathroom for hygiene. Enjoy setting. Is private, away from commotion.

Been working and living here for past few years. Fits preferences. Walls white like HORUS. Halls long, facility expansive. Have small differences. Lighting not bright as HORUS. No lab techs. Only scientist here is self. Cannot have inferior minds working with me. Must have focus and concentration to do this on own.

Has taken long time to reach this stage. No one else to support me. Been doing all work on own. No lab tech, no research assistance. Setting is in solitude, unlike at HORUS. Had Lionel Changer to guide me, fellow humans to look for help. Has made work harder to complete, slowly but surely getting there.

Disappointed taken so long. Did not anticipate splicing be so difficult to discover by self. Seeing why

Changer decided to go through birthing route. Too many idiosyncrasies involving DNA splicing; birthing process much more natural and fluid. Odd. Most think splicing easier than birthing to create hybrids, but it is opposite. Generic code delicate, cannot force hand.

Changer might have also done this because more cost-effective. Have wasted abundance of resources and credits pursuing genetic splicing method. Not to worry. Changer has made enough credits for multiple lifetimes, have access to accounts, will not be a problem for foreseeable future.

Changer did not have patience. Splicing is possible. Takes time, but possible. Changer did not want to wait. Gave up after some attempts, then took easy route by going with birthing method. Method too messy. Too many strings attached. Must get those to cooperate who don't want to cooperate. Changer used prostitutes. Leaves too much of a trail. That is how he got caught. Alliance was able to discover HORUS thanks to evidence left behind by Maya Lawton. When loose ends kept open, Alliance will come.

Loose ends must be eliminated. Splicing allows this. Less dependencies, only dependencies on self.

Currently walking by living quarters. Also messy. Must remember to program cleaning drone while working. Forgetting to do so.

Another reason abandoned birthing plan to focus on splicing is splicing allows chimeras. Hybrid only two animals, chimera many. Ultimate goal remains the same—to create ultimate species to eliminate competition. Still remember time when humans reached utopia. Many advances made, progress only going up. Then stopped thanks to intelligent animals. Became too smart, too dangerous, competed for resources with humans. Development regressed. Quite disappointing.

Propose that if only one dominant animal like old times, progression can rise again. However, only method for this is genocide. War costly, destructive. Alternative solution is to unify all intelligent animals. Status quo returns, only one dominant species, the chimera species. Finally, achievements would evolve once more, like pre-Event times. May take hundreds of more years, time needed. As long as goal in sight, then not worried. With persistence, things will change.

Excited to start task of combining several different animals. Curious to see what results emerge. Winged human type with claws and reptile strength jaws one possibility. Quadruped wolf type with leather skin and sapien-level intelligence another. Combinations endless.

Now in kitchen. Check containment units. Still have some fruits left unconsumed. Am fond of sweetness from bananas. Perhaps from chimp traits? How typical, do not like to fall into such stereotypes.

Ultimate goals discussed with Bastion. Balked at idea. Eventually led to falling out from Bastion. Has no vision, only focuses on living in shadows. Wants to protect family, thinks plans attract attention. Afraid I will endanger Lawton and daughter.

First, time with Lawton, Bastion was harmonious. Enjoyed it there. Felt part of family, like HORUS. Lawton accepted me. Relationship started rocky. Circumstances that we met stressful. However, started to admire her determination. Had endured much in life, yet continues. Hard for me to do same.

Demise of HORUS traumatic. Am logical person, could not find reasoning behind destruction. Understood Alliance saw us as enemies. Massacre at their hands was violent response. Saw much death and destruction within few hours.

Common perception is that self lacks empathy. Was reputation obtained during life at HORUS. Part of this is true. Find it hard to reach emotional connection. However, does not mean that demise of mentor did not affect self.

Had grown up all life with Changer. Was father in sense. Felt gratitude for all lessons taught me. Goals different, but respect mutual. When we left, sadness broke into psyche. Could not explain the feeling. Was first time ever experienced such things. Felt as someone had injected depressants into system. Felt as if failure occurred, as if something taken. Was harrowing experience.

Worst part was did not go away. Haunted memories years after. Focus and work suffered, had hard time completing tasks that posed no challenge to me prior. Drive to continue work halted.

Could not deal with trauma, did not know who to go to. Lawton still resented me at times. Bastion was less help. Was too focused with Lawton to care. However, despite resented feelings, still approached Lawton for guidance. Knew how to deal with tragedy when self did not. Am more intelligent than most beings on Earth, yet did not have knowledge to deal with remorse.

For first time in life, discussed emotions and new feelings regarding loss. Was nice, felt human. Lawton also surprised with sudden need for help. Able to get past resentment. Perhaps due to connection made coupled with lack of contact from other beings, bond was formed.

In turn, helped Lawton fulfill goal of becoming mother. Had already decided to abandon birthing process. Changed mind specifically to help Lawton.

Approached me, said wanted to be a mother. Warned her effects synconium may have on body. However, wanted to continue goal of perfect species. Birth to new hybrids necessary, only three remained. Helped Lawton on her journey to give birth. Bastion suitable male donor. Perfected birthing implants for use, applied them to Iris Lawton.

Owed to her for helping get through difficult time. Needed repaying.

Also was able to study Lawton, understand powers, understand physiology. Still had Changer's data to go off of. Have built off ideas in ways Changer only dreamt of. Ideas for new implants, improving hybrids process, so on.

Synconium poisoning was eliminated. Gave birth to healthy girl, Ivy Lawton. Lawton also healthy, still is. No signs of future poisoning. Was able to create safe prototype two years after fled from HORUS to private facility. That's when realized additional complication from birthing. Lawton can only have so many children. Then wait whole generation for next group and next group and so on. Too slow to cultivate hybrids this way. If done artificially, can produce at rapid pace.

After Ivy Lawton born, link continued to nurture. Honestly enjoyed Lawton's company, vice versa. Regret did not last longer.

Finishing fruit. Putting scraps in receptacle. Returning to lab, must make stop to check subjects.

As stated, had long-term goals. New experiences did not mean abandonment. After birthing process perfected, focus on splicing began. Research, purchases of equipment, documentation, planning started. Kept to self, only occasional interaction with Lawton, Bastion, and Ivy. Caused Bastion to become curious.

Found out about plans. Became infuriated. Feels trust betrayed. Made clear that work unwanted on island. Under assumption that Changer's work, my work, ceased. Wanted quiet life with family. Did not want Alliance pursuers. Living under radar only way to ensure privacy. When found out about plans continuing, banished me. Stated that hybrids not fit for today's world. Noted Changer's work brought destruction, purpose of hybrids lost among controversial beliefs. Stated best thing for hybrids is leave alone.

Disagree. Hybrids created for purpose. Given special gifts, cannot squander. Prime example, Lawton. Has power to see future, psychic abilities. Changer believed she was key to plans. Would be disgrace to Changer's ideology if such power wasted hiding from surface. Hybrids made for more than that.

Conflicting values too big for small island. Banished but glad to leave. Did not want to deal with arising conflict from Bastion. Bastion weak. Did not want to continue Changer's goal, my goals. Done with hybrid creation, was family man. Called plans silly, has more important things to do. Says vision robotic, sociopathic, insane, evil. Plans anything but evil; plans for greater good. Could not see eye to eye. Eventually left island in Pacific and developed own base of operations. Have not been on island for years, been at current facility since. Have no intention to return. Facility is home now.

Island also not suitable for development phase. Not enough resources, faced possible sabotage from Bastion. Current facility far away from Bastion and Lawton, space unlimited, expansion always possible.

In subject room. Viewing surroundings. Walls grey, air cold. Room is large auditorium with many prison pods. Inside pods lie vagrant animals. Cats, humans, rhinos, frogs, every intelligent species known. All locked up. Some in stasis, others yell because confused, angry, demand answers. Do not know how they arrived in facility. Most taken unknowing of how, where, why.

"Someone, something, help us!" one tiger yells.

"What happened? I got knocked out and now I'm here!" yells human.

"You, you monster. I don't know what you are, a chimp or a human, but so help me, when I get my jaws on you, I'll tear you to shreds," screams one crocodile.

"What are you going to do with us?" pleads eagle.

Questions irrelevant. Will not answer. Do not have time, have more important things to do. Simply concerns of splice materials.

As stated before part of reason left Bastion's island. Facility too small. Large space needed to house subjects like these. Splicing needs donors. Species DNA, genetic code, cannot be harvested from thin air. Thus, need to get hold on specimens to harvest building blocks to splice method. I receive and experiment on such animals.

Gather animals that not missed. Vagrants, lowlifes, society members that waste world's special gifts. Feel no remorse for abductions. Feel no remorse for sacrificing animals to obtain samples that are building blocks. Splicing possible thanks to contributions, captives help greater good.

Bastion would not appreciate. Would think is prison. Holding species against will in pods, cells. Disagree. Not prison, laboratory. Testing, research phase complete. Plan going according to schedule. Currently in production phase. Harvest must start soon. Specimen area crowded now, but after get what self needs, will be empty.

Repeat, this not prison. Simply place where specimens rest until reaping. Prison negative term. Implies wasted life. Lives here valuable. Cannot spare single one, need all.

Long ago, humans have places like this. Animals stored, observed, study. Put in cells much like here. Fed and given sustenance. I do same. Humans called such place zoo. Same concept applies. Animals captured for scientific study, experimentation, observation. Only difference is in old days, animals non-intelligent. Here are intelligent. Such fact is irrelevant, purpose remains same.

No, this place not prison. It is collection.

Chapter 2 – Bastion

Separated

<u>March 9, 3061 8:25 AM</u>

I'm feeling chipper this morning, and I know why. Ever since I marked the date on my calendar, I've been looking forward to it for some time. We've been trying to do this thing weekly, but now it's turned into monthly. She says she's busy, that her mom has her doing a lot of errands and that it can't be discussed with me. It's too bad she's been training less. My daughter was developing into a very capable fighter.

The last five years have been tough to digest. It seems like only yesterday when I held Ivy in my hands for the first time. I couldn't believe I was a father. A child wasn't something I even considered while under Lionel's rule. I didn't think it was possible. Our existence, the halfkind, hybrid one, was already a marvel unto itself. The journey to our creation was difficult, and I believed the journey to allow us to create would be an impossible challenge. Lucy pulled off a miracle developing birthing implants for Iris that were completely safe. I'll give that to her.

Since Ivy's birth, things have been going up and down like the waves that crash on this island's shores. It started off rough. In a matter of days, Iris had been kidnapped, watched her friend died, lost her hand, and was banished on an island with us. And she hated us for it, blamed us for all her losses. She wouldn't talk, even though I tried to make it as easy as possible for her.

I cooked for her and made sure she had all she needed. I supplied her with anything to make her life comfortable, thanks to our access to Lionel's private accounts. But it wasn't only the material things that I gave her. I was kind to her and took care of her when she didn't want to take care of herself. She wouldn't eat, wouldn't sleep, she was a mess. And no matter how many times she rejected my offers of help, I persisted until she had no choice but to receive it. It was the only way to get her on the right track so she wouldn't devolve into a depressive insanity. I wanted to make sure this place was her home even though she didn't want it to be.

She had to stay. There was nowhere else to go for her. She couldn't return to her life in the Wolf's Den without Fenrir Snow. Going public was never an option either. The only place she could seek refuge was here on this private island in the Pacific Ocean. She wouldn't be safe anywhere else.

Life wasn't easy for me either. Iris wasn't the only one who lost something. I lost a home too. The hybrids and scientists I called my friends were dead. And of course, my father, Lionel Changer, was executed by Alliance monsters. I went through the scenario a million times, trying to think of why it happened, trying to fathom how I lost so much so fast. Even to this day, I still can't come up with an answer, and that pains me deeply. Yet I didn't and still don't dwell on it. I needed to remain strong for the others who relied on me.

That first year there was a lot of tension in the air. However, over time, things cooled down. It was a day-by-day process where small bits of Iris's emotional armor were chipped away. Her resistance lessened, and she came to accepting that this place wasn't so bad. I suppose it's hard to stay angry forever. You can stay mad, but eventually, it gets tiring.

My caring attitude toward her also helped ease her in. Iris got to know the real me and subsided the fury that boiled inside. I treated her like a queen. My civility made her realize I was a decent guy.

More surprisingly, she made a connection with Lucy. Even more shocking, Lucy was the one who approached her. It appeared my colleague had developed some serious PTSD and was unable to deal with the events of Operation HORUS. Her lack of social skills made it hard for her to cope with things alone, and she sought Iris for help. Iris probably hated Lucy more than me, but her kind heart let Lucy in. Lucy's vulnerability tugged at Iris which allowed her to see past the deranged, robotic mind that Lucy possessed. They became friends. Out of gratitude, Lucy spent all of her time perfecting the birthing implants so Iris and I could be parents. That is how strong their bond is. I haven't talked to Lucy for a while, but the only person still alive that she has fond memories for is Iris.

I can't say it's the same for me.

I was happy. Iris was happy. Even Lucy, as hard as she was to read, seemed happy. We lived together like a family. But as I mentioned before, our journey was like a wave, and eventually waves come crashing down.

I suppose during those first few years, I was just on an emotional high the whole time. I was completely in love with Iris. I was too quick to see the sunny side of things that I didn't question if those feelings were reciprocated. However, upon further observation, they weren't.

She didn't show the same enthusiasm for our relationship as I did. It was always the small things. When she smiled, it looked unnatural, as if it were forced.

When I regaled her about my time growing up in HORUS, she'd listen politely, but always had her hands fiddling with something else. When I told her I loved her, she responded the same, but in a tone that was slightly sullen. She'd always find something to do to distract her from us, whether it was tending to Ivy or saying she needed some time to herself. Everything she did appeared to be false, yet I was too deluded to question that her gestures were disingenuous.

I was weak. I let it happen. I didn't want to think the worst, that despite all I had given to her, she didn't love me. In these last years, I realize I cannot run from the simple truth anymore. The idea that we will be together forever is just that, an idea. It's not reality, only what I wish were so.

Sometimes I wonder if the reason she stayed with me was for the sake of Ivy. The one thing I could see she was passionate about was motherhood. After the first two years on this island, Iris had enough time to think about what she wanted in life. I think part of her was lonely. She had us, but there was only so much we could fulfill. Her face didn't light up when she was around Lucy or me. Rather, it was kind of empty. I could tell she wondered what her purpose was in life, what the trials and hardships she went through meant. Her life was one of doom and gloom, and she needed something to brighten the dark void that consumed her soul. Ivy would be that bringer of light.

I don't want to admit it, but she might have fooled me into love. It was the only way I'd agree to help Iris in her quest to be a mom.

No, she couldn't have been that manipulative. She knew I loved her. Yet it makes too much sense for it not to be true. My daughter needed a father, despite whatever lack of passion there was in her mom and dad's relationship. To her credit, even if she didn't love me, Iris kept it together for Ivy's sake. And she's allowed Ivy to be a part of my life. My love may be estranged from me, but I still have a relationship with my daughter.

There are some days where I think about it and wonder if the way things turned out is really my fault. There were a bunch of other factors that also contributed to the crumbling of our relationship. It was one-sided because she still had feelings for another creature. She loved Fenrir Snow and still does to this day. I can tell that even though eighteen years have passed, his death continues to hit her hard. She spent three years living with him, and when she talked about it, she always looked back on those memories fondly. It wasn't a subject that she brought up often, however. Perhaps it hurts her too much to bring up those good times. Iris tends to keep the most painful things to herself. That's how I know Fenrir's demise burns a hole in her heart after all these years.

Things haven't changed for me either. Even under such unfortunate circumstances, my love for her burns brightly. I loved her the first time I knew of her existence, the only other cat hybrid on this planet. Her opinion might be different, but she and I are kindred. I know it, and I won't stop until I win her back, until she sees the truth she denies.

I knew how deeply Fenrir's death had wounded her, and it caused some of the conflict between us, but I never saw who would be the true wedge between Iris and me. She was the person I expected the least to meddle in our affairs. But I can't ignore the writing on the wall. Lucy was the one who influenced Iris to push me away.

I was stunned to see how her and Iris's friendship had bloomed. On paper, they are complete opposites. Iris is articulate, kind, and gentle. Lucy is... none of these. When we first arrived on this island, they mutually hated each other. Yet, friendship works in odd ways, and through a series of their shared events, they were able to harvest one.

At first, I only saw this as a positive. I was tired of Iris always showing an angry face at Lucy, tired of playing the peacekeeper. It was draining to make sure they got along. With that burden lifted, I enjoyed it. In fact, I would say it was the closest to having a true family. I was looking forward to a future with them.

Lucy had other plans though. She wanted to continue Lionel's work. I wanted nothing to do with the sort. I was done with the science game. Life is too short for plans of grandeur, and it leads to nothing but trouble.

Look at all the attention HORUS had brought unto itself. The last thing I wanted was for another Alliance squad to storm the shores of our beautiful island. I had a family to worry about, and I wasn't going to let Lucy and her rogue experiments jeopardize our safety. It was time to give up that life.

I forbade her from doing anything of that sort on our island, and she reluctantly agreed. She went on about her business, and I had no reason to believe she wasn't being honest in her actions. That was my fatal mistake. I trusted her too much.

At the time, my family and Lucy lived in opposite corners of the island. She left me alone to do my thing, and I left her alone to do hers. We were still civil with each other, and Iris even sent Ivy to be schooled by Lucy. She was smart, after all. But civility faded away because I slowly started to worry about what she was really doing.

I forbade her from working on any experiments and she also hated me for forcing laws she deemed were silly. She asked who was I to impose the rules?

I didn't care about her protest. I knew she was up to something. It's her nature to be a scientist, and she couldn't let go when she was on the verge of several breakthroughs. Her talent could not be denied. She was and still is the biotic genius Lionel groomed her to be. To throw that potential away was unacceptable to her.

I extinguished her life purpose because one false move, one slipup, one unnecessary risk would have the Alliance on our asses post haste. Lucy and her maniacal plans couldn't attract danger.

She broke the rules anyway. One day, Ivy came home with something from her lesson with Lucy. Ivy thought it was a gift, but when I saw what it was, I became enraged. It was something unspeakable, and it proved to me what I had suspected all along. Lucy's genetic dreams were far from over. It was just the beginning. That's when I banished her.

I expected Iris to be infuriated with Lucy. She was not. She was actually pretty mellow about it. In fact, one could say she was almost sad to see her go.

At first, I didn't understand why. Didn't Iris understand Lucy was a danger to us all, to Ivy? How could she sympathize with such a backstabber?

As I thought about it, I understood a little. Up until that point, we had been living in seclusion on this island for years. That's a long time to live without interacting with others. The only creatures Iris had to talk to were Lucy, Ivy, and myself. If I was considered Iris's husband, then Lucy was considered Iris's best friend, her only friend. She'd gotten accustomed to her company and had already lost so many companions in her life that seeing one more go devastated her.

That was why our relationship went the other way. She blamed me for pushing Lucy out and never let me forget it. I explained my reasons, but it wasn't good enough. Iris started to resent me after that day.

She grew more and more bitter because of her loneliness and requested many times that I find somewhere else to sleep. We didn't talk much, and she turned away several of my attempts to apologize.

Worst of all, she influenced Ivy. She put ideas in her head that I was responsible for her unhappiness. Ivy was still fairly young and was easily impressionable. Naturally, she listened to her mother and slowly but surely harbored negative feelings toward me. Ivy's dislike isn't complete. Even now I still call her my daughter and I spend time with her when Iris lets me. But Ivy doesn't return those feelings.

We lived awkwardly, still sharing the same space but acting like strangers. Eventually, five years ago, Iris grew tired of this and banished me away to Lucy's old quarters. This island isn't big, but it's large enough so there are underground facilities scattered throughout it. Iris lives on her side, I live on mine. The only party who travels between both ends is Ivy when she comes to see me.

It's been five long years and there isn't a day that goes by where I don't feel depressed. I've rarely seen Iris since. I ask myself the same question over and over— why have things turned out this way? I only had good intentions. I only cared about keeping my family safe. I wish Iris could see that, I wish she understood. She's too trapped by her resentment of me to see clearly, but she's been trapped in resentment her whole life, thanks to this world that simply can't accept what she is.

I still love her. She can ignore me for days, years, centuries, but I will continue to hold a glimmer of hope that we will be united. I want to make our family complete again, to return to those days when we were happy.

But first, I have to work on the small things.

"Guest has arrived," says my artificial intelligence.

"Let her in," I respond.

The doors open above, and I see Ivy descend on the lift. She's fifteen now, and she looks beautiful, a spitting image of her mother. She's strong like Iris and just as precocious. For a teen, she's matured into a confident young hybrid. I couldn't be more proud to call her my daughter.

She wears some gym clothes and carries a bag with her gear.

"Ready to train?" I ask excitedly.

"Yeah, sure," she says apathetically.

I've been looking forward to this day. It's baby steps, but we'll be together again one day, a nice, happy family.

Chapter 3 - General Rox

Prototype

March 9, 3061 8:45 AM

Eastern Russia, cold, blistery, barren, even as spring approaches. It's a good thing I'm indoors. I arrived about thirty minutes ago. Fortunately, I'm only here for business because there aren't any sights to see.

Arkady Research Prison, home to the most brilliant and dangerous minds the Alliance has captured. Confined in this facility are genius-level thinkers who have committed intellectual crimes against our government. We have geneticists, hackers, weaponizers, embezzlers, roboticists, programmers, biologists, and botanists, just to name a few. What they've done is broken several Alliance laws: conducted illegal genetic engineering, programmed unsanctioned artificial intelligence, hacked into classified documents. Only a handful are violent criminals, but they are criminals nonetheless.

At the Alliance, we don't like to waste things, especially superior intellect. We recognize that these convicts are valuable resources with potential. Why should they rot in a prison pod? No, we're better than that. We'll have them working for us so we stay ahead of the scientific curve. Their wonderful minds will still be developing great things. The only difference is it will be legal.

Each prisoner gets their own living pod and has access to whatever equipment they need. We outline their jobs for them and have them working on projects that both suit their skill set and serve our needs. We treat them civilly. They get three meals a day and adequate leisure time. They also get clothing, health coverage, and hygienic needs taken care of. It's quite the deal.

When they are working, we have strict rules and plenty of guards to ensure they don't go rogue. There's also an in-house consultant to make sure our prisoners are working on things correctly since not all of us have the scientific knowhow to understand what they do. Any attempts to stray from their goals leads to stasis or death. And for those inmates whose potential has peaked and offer no other value, well, we find ways to let them off the job. The greatest minds don't stay sharp forever.

The reason I am here today is to supervise one such convict. His name is Mark Allen, the only hostage we took from Operation HORUS. He worked under Lionel Changer, the reclusive, wealthy, human-loving hate machine who was a revolutionary in biotic implants and biological engineering. It would have been nice if we could have gotten him instead of this crony to work for us, but he was a mad man who had to die for his crimes.

Changer was a visionary who fully utilized his vast knowledge in biology and robotics to transform the implant field. His work at Implantus already allowed humans access to cutting-edge tech that improved their bodies, making them stronger, faster, more durable than ever before. He did so with nanotech that integrated itself to a host's physiology, grafting to its target whether it be a muscle, bone, or brain. He called these machines biotic implants. They opened our minds to what was possible, the knowledge that was lost after the Event.

During our raid on his facility, I had my soldiers extract whatever information we could obtain in hopes of replicating his research so we could apply it for Alliance purposes. All of the separate species' governments agreed to this, the High Dog Council, the Human Council, the Gorilla Government, and so on, as they believed a benefit for the Alliance is a benefit to us all. The only group that remained hushed was the Brotherhood of Wolves. Though they won't admit it, their leaders within the Alliance circles are still sour grapes after they were reprimanded from Operation Halfkinds some years ago. They felt the blame they incurred for its failure was unjust and have been passive-aggressively hostile during Alliance matters since. That was more than twenty years ago. They need to get over it.

Changer used his biotic implants for genetic recombination and medical purposes. We plan to do the same. We've already achieved feats of science to help the greater good. Colorblind species are no more. Voice box grafting so different animals can communicate with each other. An increased lifespan. However, with Changer's research, we'll go even further. It's a long-term project the Alliance is very excited about.

I'm not in charge of the medical applications though. We already have some top-notch engineers working on it in a different unit. The reason I'm in Arkady Prison is to focus on the other use that Changer's data allows— military use. We're looking at physical enhancement implants. Implants can be weaponized in the sense that it will make our soldiers invincible. The responsibility I've been handed is to reach toward this goal.

Since it's a lower priority, we only have our one prisoner working on it with a support staff. He has the edge because he's directly worked with Lionel Changer during his time at HORUS.

Mark Allen doesn't appear to be a very impressive specimen. I've met with him a few times and nothing has caught my attention. He's always looked like a run-of-the-mill lab jockey to me.

It's his appearance that makes me come to this conclusion. His hair is messy, his posture is slouched. He mumbles through explanations and talks with a nervous tone. He lacks confidence. When he speaks, he sounds like a virgin who's talking to a prostitute for the first time. I don't like the man. He's fodder, easily disposed of. However, my superiors insist he is useful because they think he has the secrets of HORUS locked in his head. Quite frankly, I disagree with them.

To be fair, he has shown some promise. He was able to read Changer's notes and understand them, and he has been developing a final project, the same one he will present to me later this morning. However, it's taken him too long to do it. Eighteen years and he's finally reaching a conclusion? That's pitiful.

There's not much I can do. I suppose he is adequate for now. Besides, we have all of Changer's data, the blueprints for his future work. Mark Allen is no Lionel Changer, but with this kind of information available, he doesn't need to be. He just needs to be a caretaker of development, a man who can decipher Lionel's schematics. Once we have him doing that, then our men can take over.

He plans to demonstrate what he's been working on this whole time. I am aware of what he's created and have seen the test exercises they've completed. So far, I'm impressed, but the true examination will occur when we send them out in the field. That is why I'm here, to see if they make the grade.

I shouldn't let my personal opinions get in the way of my goal today. I am to confirm field-testing of his project and make my remarks. If my assessment is good, we'll continue development. If it's bad, Mark Allen won't have much of a future here.

I walk through the halls of the Arkady facility. It's a clean facility, though the construct isn't state of the art. Arkady has been around for quite some time, built about one hundred fifty or so years ago. The walls are a depressing grey, and the building is cold and musty. I see several cracks here and there. Everything is so indistinguishable that I'm not even sure what material comprises this place.

They didn't skim on security though. Armed guards patrol the area like soldier ants and there are operators to monitor prisoner movement. They appear intimidating, stern and cold. Good. I can't see them, but I know there are plenty of hidden sensors and weapons in case some crazy inmate tries to escape. They're everywhere, in the rooms, on windows, even in vents in case some of our smaller residents try to make a break for it.

I approach the containment cells, which are much more state of the art than the rest of the building. The Alliance doesn't cheap out on providing these intellectuals the greatest equipment, as long as they produce some results. It's a small price to pay if we get to harvest technological gold.

Each prisoner is held in a small laboratory with a translucent screen so outsiders can look at what they're doing. There are various animals in different cells, each working on a variety of things. I walk by one cell that has a pig furiously working on his compcube while an armed guard carefully monitors him. I see another cell with a rhino messing around with a drone. Sparks fly from the machine, but the rhino looks unfazed. With an enforcer in the room, he's too focused, too afraid to do anything else.

I arrive at Allen's compound. His cell has a compcube that he works from and large display screens and holo interfaces. I see tools and documents scattered about, datacubes, gizmos and mechanical parts, lenses and electronics. Like all the other inmates' dwellings, it's like the lab of a mad scientist.

"General Rox," he says as he stands up in attention. I enter his cell with the guards at my side.

I look up and address him.

"Allen," I say sternly, "you've been expecting me, I assume."

"Yes… yes, sir," he says nervously.

He worked for Lionel Changer, but I'm unsure if Mark Allen believed in Lionel's ideology. If he did, to him, I'd be some lowly dog who doesn't deserve the position I'm in. He'd scoff at referring to a canine as his superior. But I don't sense any of that. I sense a frightened prisoner scared to make a mistake. That's probably how he's been most of his life, a weak-willed individual who always reports to someone. No initiative, no gall. Simply a spineless follower. He's been gone from Changer's crew for an extended time, any human supremacist ideals have probably died within him long ago. With nobody guiding him, there's nowhere for it to live.

"I've heard your prototypes have done well in enclosed testing," I say.

"Um… yes," he says. "They demolished the drones and completed the gauntlet in record time."

"Excellent."

"Do you want to know the specs?"

"We'll discuss that when I see them. The main reason I am here is to determine if they are ready for field-testing."

"Field-testing? You mean you want to send them out there?"

"Yes."

"To do what?"

"We'll talk about it on the way to the prototype room. That's where they are held, correct?"

"Yes."

"Good, then my guards will escort us."

My agents, a chimp and a human, approach Allen and attach energy cuffs to his wrists. He does not struggle. He merely complies in a sheepish manner.

We walk side by side on our way to the prototype room, with my guards walking closely behind us. Allen is wearing a standard issue jumpsuit. He looks around at his surroundings meekly, as if he's being led to slaughter. It's been a few good minutes, and he hasn't said anything.

Finally, he talks.

"So what is this field-test you have prepared?" he asks. "Are you allowed to talk about it with me?"

"Yes," I say. "You'll need to understand the details in order to assist me on my request. This will essentially be the final test before we deem your work is a success. After that, the United Species Alliance Science Division will be more involved."

He looks curious by my statement.

"So does that mean I'll be able to help them?" he asks anxiously.

To Mark Allen, this means a step toward freedom. If we allow him to work with high-ranking Alliance scientists, it is a statement of our trust in him, that he'll be able to leave Arkady. He's hoping this is a sign that he's close to completing his sentence.

"Now's not the time to talk about that," I say, shooting him down.

He looks disappointed.

"Sorry about that," he apologizes.

"Anyway, we're sending your prototypes to Shogun," I say.

"Shogun? You mean the quader city?"

Quader is a term to describe a place that has few humans. Humans are bipedal, most other species are quadrupeds. Hence the term quader. It's a stupid term though, because gorillas and apes are bipedal, but cities filled with them are still described as quader.

"Yes, Shogun, located on the southern tip of what was known as Japan, built on top of the aftermath of the Event by the species who relocated there," I say.

"I see. Isn't that place, kind of a, um, crime capitol?" he asks.

What Allen says is true. I haven't been there for a while, but it's not like I have reason to. It's a place managed by degenerates. Illegal activities run rampant, and the under-budget police force has no handle on it. It looks highly developed. New buildings and tech litter the town like diamonds in a coalmine. But it's only there to hide what lies beneath, the shady corners and dangerous creatures that make it their home.

"It is. That's why we're sending the prototypes there, but for a very specific mission," I say.

"What mission is that?"

"In the past months, there has been a huge increase in the amount of missing creature reports. Before that, there'd be a few here or there, but officials have noted a spike in cases. Naturally, there's been a public concern on why this has happened."

A showing of apprehension flushes Allen's face.

"So creatures are just getting plucked on the streets?" he asks.

"That's the case. I wish they had legalized identification tags long ago, but we all know that was shot down in seconds," I say. "Stupid privacy issues."

"Is there a link to any of these missing cases?"

"Yes, we've deduced that most of the abductees have had some run-ins with the hundreds of gangsters in Shogun, so we suspect they're involved somehow. Not surprising considering the city we're talking about. Some owe them money, others are small time rivals. Either way, I wouldn't say the victims are completely innocent bystanders. These crime bosses are no joke either. Most are ruthless beings with no morals who have made their bones at the price of another's head. The task will be difficult and perilous, but it will also be the perfect way to test the prototypes' capabilities."

"You're going to send the prototypes to investigate?"

"Yes. Before your work on them, they were natural trackers. A case like this will be well suited for our subjects."

We pass through a hall and are only a few minutes from where the prototypes are stored.

"I see. Well, I think they are ready," Allen says.

"They better be," I reaffirm. "There are a few suspects we think are involved, and we'll want the prototypes to interrogate."

"Who are we talking about?"

"The Van Faye family."

"I heard they're bad news."

What Allen says is no exaggeration. If there was ever a dynasty among the filthy and corrupt in Shogun, it is the Van Fayes. They were one of the first inhabitants of Shogun and have heavily influenced its development into the crime mecca it is today. They're a conniving bunch, with family members often going after family members. Currently, the sole leader of the Van Faye family is Two Van Faye, elephant queen of the underworld. She has the cops and the local government wrapped around her trunk. She's an ambitious one who is trying to expand her criminal empire outside of Shogun. Her goal is to eventually control all of the crime country known as Fan Zui Bin. She might have the guts to do it. But she's also delusional, and in the grand scheme of things, she's small potatoes.

"Indeed, they're not to be taken lightly, but from what I've seen of your creations, it shouldn't be out of their scope," I say.

"I agree. We're here," he says.

The door opens and I enter a humongous room, no laboratory, filled with glowing lights and high-tech structures. It's messy, the ground is covered with industrial cables and pipes. Power cores are dispersed here and there. There are secured compartments where various experiments are held. Many are new drones that some other prisoners have created, some are biological experiments. It's a gallery of what could be and what will be, but our group simply sidesteps them and walks to Mark Allen's holding station.

We stand in front of a sliding door, which will lead us to a smaller room that holds the prototypes. One of my guards steps up and enters the code as we stand back. The other unshackles Allen. A glimmer of light hits my eyes and I'm briefly blinded by the glare. As my eyes focus, I look in front of me and see what lies in the brightness.

There stands two wolf-like creatures, robotized and powered up. They are heavily armored from head to toe with synthetics. One is in a dark shade, the other has a lighter, slate-colored tone. Their eyes, two diamond-shaped openings, glow on their steel-clad faces. They are soulless. No expressions can be seen on their armor, and I'm sure the faces the lie beneath are just hollow. I'm a hardened soldier, and when I look at these two creatures, I sense they are nothing but non-discriminating killing machines.

"Here are your prototypes," Allen says. "Blackwolf and Silverwolf, also known as the Alphas."

Chapter 4 – Mark Allen

Alphas

<u>March 9, 3061 9:29 AM</u>

I can't believe eighteen years have passed. Every day I've been at it, attempting to understand the notes that Lionel left behind. His work isn't easy to comprehend, and I'm not the master of biotics he was. I was only some young researcher who got caught up in this situation. I'm no revolutionary, but the Alliance is expecting me to be one. I'm scared what might happen if I fail.

I remember when I first met Lionel. I was a naïve guy, fresh out of the university where I focused on bioelectric engineering. I had the same problem that billions of new grads have had for centuries—I needed a job. That's when I received an anonymous message about such an opportunity.

It didn't state who was hiring, where the job was, or what I'd be doing. All it gave was a private communications link for me to contact. I was extremely skeptical at first, but I figured I had nothing to lose. I gave them a ring. I was put on the link with a very friendly person. They asked what my qualifications were and told me about an opening in their research department for biotics. They also told me what they'd be paying upfront, and needless to say, I was impressed. I quickly booked an interview. I was informed a representative would come to escort me.

A few days later, a person arrived and notified me the interview would be held in a secret location. Again, I was suspicious, but before I could do anything, I was hit with a stunner and knocked out.

I woke up a few hours later in a conference room a bit dazed, but alert. A man in a lab coat walked into the room, and I was star struck. This was the famous Lionel Changer, a man that had dropped off the face of the Earth. I was so shocked that I wasn't even curious about how I arrived there and didn't wonder if I was in any danger.

He interviewed me himself and gave me the rundown. I wouldn't have contact with the outside world during my employment at HORUS and would live underground. That put me on high alert. However, necessities would be provided to me and the credits offered were more than anything I ever dreamed of. And I'd be working with the man who was practically the father of modern biotics. The perks greatly outweighed the negatives, and within a week, I was a member of HORUS.

Daily life was interesting enough. I was assigned to biotic testing and worked with some very nice people. It was an entry position, so I didn't get to do much, but I didn't expect to since I was fresh out of college.

Not all was great, though. There were some folks who, honestly, were downright nutty. I quickly learned that many of my colleagues had a pro-humanity philosophy. Some were fanatics. I never really bought into the ideology Changer promoted. I was simply a spoke on a wheel, doing the work I was assigned.

Despite that, I liked my time at HORUS, but I wasn't there long. About a year into my career at HORUS, the Alliance sent their soldiers and I was captured. I should be thankful that I wasn't killed like all my friends and colleagues.

When the Alliance seized me, they thought they inherited the next Lionel Changer. Boy were they disappointed. Yet they saw potential and gave me a choice: be sent to Arkady and attempt to continue Changer's work or be stuck in a prison pod. It wasn't much of a choice. They gave me his data and shipped me to Russia with the expectation that I could master the implant field.

My progress was slow at first. I basically had to cram all the knowledge that Changer possessed into my brain during those first few years. We're talking about a lifetime of work. I got frustrated many times and was fearful I'd be sent to a pod if I failed. But I persevered and kept at it, gradually absorbing all his work to a point where I understood his schematics and documentation. I was ready to start the project of replicating his implants so it could be applied to military personnel.

Of course I couldn't build my prototype on a living soldier. The Alliance wasn't interested in offering their best and brightest to be my test rat. But they also weren't going to make me work empty handed either. They already had a couple of hosts on which I could test my newly acquired implant skills.

They were wolves, two of them, part of some famous wolf military family called the Snows. The Alliance had found five of them in the hidden transportation bay at HORUS. An explosion had gone off, claiming the lives of some of the wolves and what the Alliance thinks is Iris Lawton, Bastion, and Lucy. Their bodies weren't found among the number of creatures Brock West slaughtered, but both Bastion and Iris's blood and bits of a dismembered hand were found within the blast zone. The

Alliance assumed the unaccounted had disintegrated from the explosion.

Miraculously, there were survivors in the remnants of the transportation bay. Eli Winde, a member of West's team, extracted the two that were found alive. I use the word alive in the loosest terms, because when the Alliance discovered them, they were a wreck. The bodies were charred from top to bottom, fur completely burned off. Their basic functions worked fine. They could breathe and cardiac systems were intact. Overall, though, they were in poor condition. I sometimes wonder how the hell these two survived such a blast.

Their minds were blank slates. They were vegetables. No independent thoughts, no reactions to stimuli, nothing but complete, hollow shells. The two wolves were in between life and death, stuck in limbo.

The Alliance persevered and kept them alive. Though their brains were damaged, deep inside the bowels of their psyche lurked two masters of war. The Alliance needed someone to gain access to these minds. The Snow family had quite the reputation, and our leaders didn't want to squander such potential. That's where I came in.

My goal was simple: to create implants that could repair the damage done. Basically, to bring them back from the brink of death. The logic was that if I successfully make the brain-dead combat proficient, the door would be open to apply my work to those in military service. Then, those soldiers would be unstoppable and the Alliance would have an army of super-teched agents.

I quickly went to work on the two wolves. I started with the inner repair, focusing on muscle enhancers to restore any lost tissue, and a layer of outer casing implants on their vital organs for durability. I also injected some immunization implants to boost their healing factor and increase their condition. They went from being on life support to being capable of functioning on their own.

These modifications weren't immediate, and at every stage, testing needed to be done. The Alliance also gave me some valuable team members to assist me during this process. That's how we spent the majority of the past years, developing on one area and testing, developing another area and testing. It was a long, slow, drawn-out process, but we saw the fruits of our labor every step of the way.

Their skin was too burned up and stretched too far to effectively utilize my biotics. Usually implants were only used for internal purposes. Instead, I grafted armor on their exterior to remedy this problem. One is in a dark-black shade, the other in chrome silver. Hence the names Blackwolf and Silverwolf. The armor also adds a level of aesthetic that will no doubt strike fear into our enemies' hearts.

Their physical bodies had been repaired, but sadly, I couldn't restore their brain function. Their minds remained empty. I spent more years focusing on neural implants, but everything I researched led to disappointment and failure. The brain is a delicate organ, and I didn't have the skill to understand how biomechanics could integrate with it. Also, the destruction done was too extensive for me to repair.

I was able to fix enough of the damage to the point where they retained motor function and can rely on their instinctive wolf nature. They could control their bodies on their own, and with the other implants, they would be agile and quick to respond. In fact, their physical prowess surpassed anything they could do in their former lives. However, they lacked the ability to think critically. They had no free will. Behind their eyes were the same voids that populated their souls when we first harvested them. To put it colorfully, they were robotic wolf zombies. The only purpose they had was to kill.

I had an alternative solution to this issue that allowed a certain level of control. Though my implants couldn't restore their mental capabilities, I could get it to a state where another party could be in charge of the wolves. These implants received vocal commands, processed them, and applied action to the vessel body, in this case, the Alphas. It worked how any standard AI did, except the subject would be a living organism. In a sense, Blackwolf and Silverwolf were glorified drones.

After I applied these mental implants, my work was complete. We started material testing on them, putting them through obstacle courses, simulated battles, and other various examinations while a trained operative barked out commands. The Alphas passed every test with flying colors. With a keen mind in control, enhanced bodies, and their innate instincts combined into one, they were unstoppable.

I am proud of what I've been able to accomplish in the past eighteen years. I went from a kid fresh out of the university to a prisoner to a biotic expert. I've said I'm not Lionel Changer, but with my accomplishments as my proof, I'm on my way to matching his genius. I've recreated life from the near dead.

General Rox has seen the footage of their carnage, and needless to say, he's been impressed. Today marks a very special day because this is the first time he's seen them live, dog to wolf. And, as he has informed me, they'll be going on their first field-test. I am excited to see how my work will thrive.

He stands on four legs, inching toward the Alphas. They are on standby mode, so they don't move a muscle.

"I must say, Allen," General Rox says, "these two look quite impressive."

"Thank you, sir," I respond.

"So how do these things work?"

"That's a broad question. Should we start with the specifics?"

General Rox takes a brief sniff to get a better sense of what these creatures are.

"Sure," he says. "Why don't you start from the beginning?"

"Okay," I say. "I'll begin with energy generation. As you can see, their armor is powered. The glowing, diamond-shaped eyes are a giveaway."

"I see. But I don't see a power source on them."

"That's true. That's because it's internal. Their armor feeds off the natural electricity conducted within their bodies. I have installed some implants that harness and amplify the energy output and integrated the armor to receive it. Thus, they are completely self-sustaining units."

"But they're both living organisms. Don't they require a food source in order to survive?"

"We have feeding tubes installed in their armor for that. They only require minimum sustenance in order to function."

Rox looks pleased with both pieces of news.

"The Alphas are also very durable," I say. "Their armor is made from jupiternium."

"Isn't that the stuff they use to make hovertanks?" he asks.

"Indeed it is. Pure synthetic alloys able to take blasts that can level small crafts. Not much will cause a dent to them. However, the armor is disconnected to allow joint movement, so it might be possible to separate or even remove fragments of armor piece by piece, if one is diligent enough."

"Well, I guess you don't want to sacrifice mobility for armor."

General Rox peers directly into Blackwolf's eyes and shakes his head. He's testing to see if it will react, but it does not.

"Blackwolf and Silverwolf also have enhanced healing powers thanks to some additional implants," I say as I recapture his attention.

"How enhanced are we talking about?" General Rox asks.

"Well, if for some reason they are hit with a blast that gets through their armor, they can heal in minutes, maybe even seconds."

"So you're saying if I stripped them of their armor and shot one of them in the torso, the wound would close up immediately?"

I nod.

"That's amazing!" General Rox says. "Right now, there's not much on the market that can do that. I can only imagine what your implants will do for my soldiers. And you and the Alliance-assigned science team were able to develop this and other implants from Lionel Changer's notes?"

"Yes. It took a long time, but we did it. Eli Winde also provided some input on tactical elements," I say.

General Rox continues to pace around the specimens, investigating every aspect of their cold bodies.

"So now that we have their specs out of the way, tell me, how can I utilize my agents?" he asks.

"The Alphas are controlled by voice command," I say. "Tell them an action and they will do it."

"Really? Is it possible to test it out right now?"

"Uh, sure. Give me a second."

I walk toward a control panel and pick up a tablet. A holographic appears in front of me and I fiddle with the schematics. The glow from Blackwolf and Silverwolf's eyes turn from bright white to dark red.

"I've changed them to sentinel mode," I say. "You can tell by the shade of their eyes. Now that they're activated, you can bark your orders."

"Excellent," he says. "Alphas, walk ten feet forward."

On cue, the two wolves march in unison. They take a few steps until they make it to ten feet, not a single inch over or under.

"Remarkable," General Rox says.

"That's not all," I say.

I mess with my controls again and out pops a video interface. I swipe my hand so the holographic slides in front of Rox.

"This is the point of view video interface directly linked to their optical implants," I say. "Essentially, on the screen, you'll see what they see."

"Interesting," General Rox says. "Blackwolf, move your head left."

Blackwolf moves its head left, and in synchronization, the point of view presented on the screen moves with it.

"A direct view of their vision will allow the user to gauge their mission firsthand and provide a realistic combat setting," I say.

"Excellent idea," General Rox says. "Speaking of combat, what do the Alphas have in terms of weaponry?"

"I'm glad you asked."

I use my controls, and plates of the Alphas' armor slide open, exposing six cannon barrels.

"The weapons research guy you brought in was very helpful with installing these on Blackwolf and Silverwolf," I say. "He suggested to put switchers on them."

"Yes, that's a wise decision," Rox says. "With switchers, the wolves won't be limited by barrel size. They'll be able to change ammunition size and type. Bombs, cannons, plasma, basically a slew of weaponry fired from the same gun."

"Yes, and their weapons systems are tuned to both the artificial intelligence implants I installed and voice command. The Alphas can survey the situation and use their judgment on what firepower is the best fit for their task, much how a drone would. Or you can always take over and direct them yourself."

"Excellent."

Two coils made from light and energy spring forth from the sides of their armor.

"They also have these," I say. "It will allow them to grip and latch onto objects, since their paws give them limited capabilities when it comes to handling things."

"A pain I know too well," Rox says.

"Yes, but that's not all."

I use my controls once more, and Blackwolf starts to float in the air. It takes General Rox by surprise until he realizes what has happened.

"You put hover technology on them?" he asks curiously.

"Yes, I figured flight would aid them on certain missions," I say.

"Fantastic!" Rox says. "I've seen enough. It appears they are ready. We'll set up a control station so you can help guide them during the mission."

"Me, sir?"

"Yes. You know them and will handle their operation. However, I'll be here to give supervision and talk strategy. It will be a team effort."

"I see. Thank you for the opportunity."

"Don't thank me yet. We haven't done anything. My superiors will be keeping a sharp eye on how the Alphas preform. If all is successful, they may start integration to real soldiers as soon as possible. They are excited by the potential of having their elite forces installed with this newfound power."

I do a mental gulp. From what Rox said, it's very likely that my fate will fall on the outcome of this mission. And the biggest bosses of the Alliance will be watching. It's nerve-racking.

"So where do we begin?" I ask.

"After the Alphas are prepped for operation, we'll send them directly to Shogun," Rox says. "I have a contact there that will give us a briefing and provide us with a starting point to this investigation."

"And when will this meeting take place?"

"A few days from now, March 13, in the afternoon. Winde will be joining us as well. Do what you can to get ready. There's no telling what we'll encounter."

"Yes, sir."

"My guards will escort you back to your cell. For now, this review is over."

One of his agents re-cuffs me and escorts me back to my room.

As I walk back, I feel a mix of emotions. Happiness, fear, hope, anxiousness, dread, and excitement flow through my body like a mad rush. I'm looking forward to seeing how my creations will do, to prove my worth as a scientist, and redeem my name that had been dragged through the mud thanks to Operation HORUS.

However, I'm also scared of what will happen if I fail. Does it mean an automatic trip to stasis? And does that mean the eighteen years I've spent toiling away on my creations amounted to nothing?

In the end, I hope this all pans out for me. General Rox seems very impressed. As he hinted, success could lead to a lighter sentence, even freedom. That would be nice. I'll finally be able to leave Arkady and live a normal life. I've been here for so long, working like a slave, and now I'm close to the end of this hellish journey.

The Alphas will help me reach the light. They will be my ticket out of here.

Chapter 5 – Fenrir Snow

Snowfall

<u>December 19, 3040 6:00 PM</u>

Boy am I tired. A month has passed since Operation Halfkinds, and here I am struggling through the sleet. I've been dragging over one hundred pounds of supplies. Worst part is the hover mechanism has totally crapped out, so I've been doing things the old-fashioned way.

I turn around and make sure no one is following me. I'm not being paranoid. Operation Halfkinds ended on suspicious circumstances. Then again, that idiot Leons unknowingly helped me cover my tracks. Nevertheless, I'm worried that the Alliance has caught on to my ruse. Smuggling these items through Wolf's Den territory already raises a lot of suspicions. If someone sees me, they might report it. This is precious cargo and what I'm doing is highly illegal. In fact, it's so bad that I might get the death penalty for it.

The sled contains a big box of food, clothes, and one industrial-sized insta-item, all for Iris Lawton, the helpless halfkind. She's a strong one, mentally at least, but she is not used to this cold climate. I thought the cabin would have warmed her up, but a lifetime living in the Vegas desert has probably ruined any resistance she had to this frigidness. She's pretty lucky I've got her back.

Shoot, I've even let her have access to my credits. I have plenty to go around. I've been living on my own since Eve passed, and my countless missions have scored me a nice stash. It's odd, though, that I trust her enough to give her access to my account, even if it is limited. Then again, what is she going to do? She's only a naïve, sheltered creature. I doubt I'll have to worry about her plundering my savings.

I don't even know why I'm doing this. I saved her. What else is there to do? She's safe here in the Canadian wilderness, the exiled lands of the Wolf's Den.

On the other hand, I know that's not enough. Even though she escaped with her life, they'll come after her. The Alliance will hunt her down until she's dead. I'm her only chance at survival. I can't bear the guilt of knowing that I left her and she perished. Saving her is not good enough. I need to see this through.

It's the least I could do. That mission, Operation Halfkinds, it changed so much about me. Before it, my depression had sunk to an ultimate low, and I wondered if there was a soul left in this hollow body. I hated what I became, a murdering machine, and went through the motions as the night played out.

Still, I resisted breaking my duty, even after I killed Lombardi Lawton. I watched the others slaughter the Lawtons like chickens. It was only when I saw Apollo Bradley point the barrel of his gun at Iris Lawton's head that I decided to act.

I am ashamed of this. I should have acted sooner. So many died before I changed my mind. Iris could've had siblings that lived past the ordeal.

But she didn't, and for that, I am sorry. I guess that's why I'm doing this, to make it up to her. It's what any decent wolf would do.

I have my doubts now that some time has passed. I haven't talked to my family since I came back. I can't. It'd be suicide. How could I tell them that I betrayed the

Brotherhood's trust? How could I tell them that I helped a fugitive escape? How could I tell them that I purposely failed a mission?

They would never understand. They'd think I was insane. In fact, they would have turned me in as a traitor. I know them. They're too loyal to the Brotherhood, especially Fang. Sad to say, I can't trust my family with these secrets.

I wish I could. I think I've been distant from my family ever since Eve died. I barely visited or talked to them since her death. I buried myself in my work. I didn't have time to reconnect. I wanted to. In fact, I want to now. If it wasn't for this Iris Lawton business, I'd call up each and every one of them—Raymus, Danzel, Patrice, hell, even Fang—and catch up like old times. I want to show them my new lease on life.

I'm being foolish. As I think about it, even without the Iris problem, I know that wouldn't happen. Things are too different now between my brothers and sister, it can't be like old times. I'm simply fantasizing.

I suppose I have to accept these kinds of things for the goodwill of Iris Lawton. I don't know what to make of her and wonder if she is worth this kind of sacrifice.

She is quite an interesting character. Despite all she's been through, she remains hopeful. I guess it's her youth that helps her. She's only seventeen, turning eighteen soon, and sometimes it seems she doesn't really understand her situation. An older mind would be panicking at the thought of being on the run, but Iris lives it day by day. I can tell she tries to focus her mind on other things. She makes little crafts to pass her time and watches the streams on the compcube I've given her.

These actions make me question her ability to comprehend grief. If I had lost my loved ones the way she has, I'd be devastated. Actually, I was devastated. I remember when Eve died I was in a slump for five years and never looked forward to the future. Iris appears positive of her situation, and it boggles my mind how someone can seem so optimistic about the shitty situation they're in.

I think I misjudge it though. I notice some things about her that make me wonder if she's holding her grief inside. When she talks, she smiles, but if I look longer, her lips trail off to a more dour look. She stares out the window from time to time. She's probably wondering if that's all she'll be doing her whole life, living inside, trapped, only being able to see a world she'll never be a part of.

Her voice speaks in a cheerful manner, but also one of caution. Sometimes I can't tell if what she says is genuine because the tones are so different. I feel for her, I know what it's like to hide behind a mask, a false representation of self, when inside all you want to do is keel over and die.

But I must say, Iris Lawton is quite charming. She is brave in the face of new conflicts. Look at the way she interacts with me. I am a killer, even now, after my "retirement." She knows this. Yet she is never afraid to voice her opinion. If she hadn't pushed me, I don't think I would have been as proactive about helping her. I find that kind of courage interesting, curious, alluring.

I'm just not sure how this arrangement will work out. She's a halfkind and has a target on her back. If I continue to help her, I'll have one on mine as well. That's a risk I'm not willing to take. Eventually, down the line, I'm going to have to figure out what the long-term plan is.

I don't want to babysit her forever. We'll separate at some point. I'll teach her how to survive on her own and how to stay underground from the Alliance's watchful eyes. She seems smart. I think she can learn. And when the lesson is over, we'll part ways. I'll feel redeemed for all the crappy things I've done in my life. If I can change this girl's destiny for the better, then I can say I walked away from a mission with my head held high.

I can't think of that right now, though. We'll come to that when she's ready. Until then, I suppose we'll have to see how things work out. But honestly, when she's ready to move on and I've taught her how to remain safe, that'll be that. I don't see this partnership lasting very long.

Chapter 6 – Ivy Lawton

Workout

March 9, 3061 10:12 AM

"Okay, Ivy, are you ready?" my father asks me.

I look at the empty dirt trail ahead of me. The road is covered under a canopy of tropical trees. It's a hot morning on the island, and the humidity causes me to perspire even before I take one step. The gauntlet's purpose is to test my agility and reflexes. I've done this obstacle course many times, but it's unpredictable, and the tension makes me nervous.

"Yes," I say.

"Remember, your goal is to get to the finish line in under a minute. There will be turrets popping up from different locations, firing force blasts in an attempt knock you off your feet. They won't kill you, but it'll make you fall, like if someone pushed you in the middle of a run. But you have the patchpads, so you'll be okay," he says. "Use what you've learned to sense where and when they're coming so you can dodge them. On your mark… Get set… Go!"

I sprint forward as fast as I can. The churning of my legs creates small puffs of dirt that float in the air. Leaves rustle from the swiftness of my body. I can feel the wind hit my face, which causes a cooling sensation that is most welcomed in the sweltering heat. There's a small log in front of me and I hurdle over it.

While I run, my senses are fully alert as I try to detect an incoming blast. The turrets will pop up, and the sound of their gears moving will give me enough of a warning for me to react before they fire their shot. However, the window of time between turret initialization and firing is incredibly small. I can't hesitate and need to be in an evasive position immediately. One mistake, and I'll be eating the dirt.

The first cannon rises from the ground, and I stop my dash. I can hear the brush clearing and sense the blaster warming as it stands erect. I concentrate hard and focus. There's no time to look and in these brief moments I must use my time wisely in order to know from where the shot will fire. The sound of the mechanism's movement echoes faintly through the air, and I use my instincts to determine its location. Ten meters south, to the left of me.

Boom!

The noise from the detonation reverberates throughout the canopy and careens in my direction. My body moves like it's been possessed, my legs rocket me forward before my brain thinks about it. Once in the air, I curl up and prepare for the landing. I quickly tuck my head toward my legs and gracefully roll frontward as my body makes contact with the ground. A burst of soil flies into the air. Just like that, I dive ahead, a summersault landing, and a missed shot have transpired in seconds.

My father has taught me to rely on impulses, act before thinking when it comes to life or death. It's the process of having full trust in your instincts, to make the decisions your brain takes too long to process. He has perfected this. His ability to react is lightning fast and his body moves like water. These exercises have helped him hone such a craft, and one day, I will be as good as he is, if not better. It's all a matter of training.

I quickly hop back to my feet and continue my race to the finish. I'm already halfway there, but suddenly, I hear a whizzing sound...

Pow!

Without warning, I'm hit on the right side of my arm. It feels like someone's whacked me with a wooden board. I instantly lose my balance in the middle of my sprint and tumble over on my left side. Fortunately, the patchpads do their job. The two small, white adhesive strips on my arms inflate open, creating a soft padding for me to land on so I don't break any bones. I'm not hurt, but the wind is knocked out of me. My pads close up, back to their original form. I lie there tired and despondent.

I'm angry, not because I've been flattened to the ground, but rather because I failed. I became careless after the initial evasion. I hate losing and am every bit the perfectionist as my auntie is. I strive to succeed. This course has been frustrating to conquer because the blasts fire quickly and can come from anywhere, making the level of difficulty much harder. Sight becomes useless, and I haven't had many workouts like this.

My father walks to me and offers his hand.

"Tough break," he says. "Why don't you take a breather?"

I flash him a disgusted glance and bat away his hand.

"Stand aside," I say as I get back to my feet.

"You look tired," he says. "I think you should rest for a few minutes."

"Unlike you, I don't quit. I fight until the end."

He responds to my comment with a shameful face, and I walk away from him, back to the starting line. Once there, I take a few deep breaths and I get myself in a runner's stance. My father has the controls ready in his hand. He resets the program and the turrets go back into hibernation. However, cranking and churning sounds vibrate the ground below us. The cannons are repositioning themselves so I can't anticipate, based on my last run, where they'll spring up. A few seconds later the movement stops.

"The program is primed," he says.

"I'm ready," I say to him.

"Okay, take your mark... Go!"

Once again, I start the task, galloping with full force toward the goal. I barely run ten feet when a blaster erupts from the ground to my left, firing a force shot my way. I hurdle over the shot, but I'm still not fast enough. It clips my left foot, and I spiral in the air. My patchpads expand once more, but I land hard on my chest.

My torso is sore as hell. The spinning in the air and the sudden thud walloped my body. The damage done is twice as painful as my previous attempt. I roll to my back in agony and look up at the sky to calm myself. The canopy is spinning, and my vision blurs in and out as I heave oxygen into my lungs.

My father approaches me and sticks his head in my view.

"You can't say no this time," he says as he smiles and offers his hand.

He is right. I'm too exhausted to even try on my own, so I begrudgingly grasp his arm and he pulls me up.

"This course is damn hard," I say.

"Don't worry. Your mother had the same problem," he says.

He's correct. I remember before I left this morning, mom asked me what the agenda was. I mentioned I'd be running the blaster course, and she chuckled to herself. She told me I'd be in for a day of frustration and revealed that she never completed the run in its entirety. Mom mentioned Aunt Lucy had designed it and installed all the underground devices herself. In fact, most of the machines and hardware on this island are the result of my aunt's ingenuity.

From what she told me in the past, mom used to train quite often with my father, back when they lived together. She was a quick learner and had all this hidden potential that she never realized. It took some time, but it got to a point where she was as physically fit as my father and could match up with him toe to toe. Of course, my father is also an excellent physical trainer and is the reason for her swift progression. Their inherent gifts have carried over to their offspring. I haven't been at it as long as mom, but I'd say I've impressed both of my parents with my capabilities.

Obviously, Mom doesn't train with dad anymore. That was a long time ago.

"Yeah, she told me," I say, responding to his earlier reply.

"It's funny, even though Lucy built a lot of the obstacle courses we use today, she would always avoid this one during our workouts," he says.

"Workouts? I didn't know Lucy trained with you."

"She doesn't seem like the type, huh? But yes, she did. In fact, she got pretty fit and became as adept as your mother. You'd be surprised that it's not all brain with her. She's quite agile and stealthy. Then again, that was years ago. I'm not sure what she's like now."

"Yeah, I wonder why."

My father looks away from me and changes the subject.

"Well, that's enough with agility," he says. "Let's move on to strength training. Here are your weighted gloves."

He hands me two black gloves and they fit snuggly over my hands. The gloves are rubbery, made from some kind of synthetic that can adjust its weight. They're thick, padded, and have some switches and grooves on them.

"One hundred pounds," I say.

The gloves get heavier and heavier, causing my hands to sink to the floor. I slowly pull them up to do a curl, struggling the whole way. I started out with twenty, then thirty, then fifty, working my way up to one hundred. I think this is my limit, but there's always room for improvement. I know father can get up to three hundred easily. Mom does these at home, and I've seen her go up to two hundred or so. I have to work my way up.

This is usually the routine when I train with father. He focuses on three areas: agility, strength, and endurance. Each category also has sub-categories of focus. Agility includes hand-eye coordination and reflexes, strength extends out to muscle control and quickness, and endurance is all about stamina and keeping in shape. Sometimes they go hand in hand with each other.

There are a variety of methods we use to increase our potential in each. The gauntlet is great for reflex training and endurance, the gloves obviously build up our strength and toughness, and to maintain our fitness, a nice, long run is always good for the body. The island is scattered with structures we utilize for training.

Why do we undergo all these arduous routines? "Just in case" is always the answer. We have enemies in this world. Actually, the world is our enemy. When the Alliance first knew of my mom's existence, they sent a team to kill her and her family in Primm. She escaped but was the only survivor. Then they stormed and destroyed father's and Aunt Lucy's home. My father, mom, and Aunt Lucy were hunted down and escaped to this island, the same place I've been living in my entire life. Both my mom and dad have warned me about the dangers the outside world holds for us, that if they found out our existence, they would try to wipe us out like they did before.

My father has taken this threat seriously and has trained both my mother and myself, and Aunt Lucy apparently, so we can properly defend and evade our pursuers if the time ever comes to battle them. Not only do we keep our bodies finely tuned, but we also engage in combat training. My father is an excellent fighter and has taught my mother well in mastering the martial arts. The scar on his chest happened when he fought a bear and lost. He vowed to never have that happen to any of us. I think now he could kick anyone's ass. I learn from both mom and father, so I'm pretty capable. Mom might not train as much as she used to, but she can still pack a wallop if she wants.

Both my mom and father have firearms in their homes and are proficient at shooting. Both have trained me well in using this weaponry, and I'd say I'm a pretty good shot. I imagine Aunt Lucy also has these skills. We have a sizable armory that could take out a small invading army. If the Alliance wants to send their cronies, let them. I'm ready.

Lastly, all three of us have biotics implanted in us. Muscle enhancers to increase our natural strength and reflexes, amplifiers that heighten our senses, basically the kind of tech that's not even on the market. They were gifts from Lucy before she left this place.

"I'm done with strength," I say to father after I've completed a few reps.

"Already?" he says in an astonished tone.

"Yeah. I'm going to start my jog. Here."

I take off my gloves and hand them to him.

"Do you want me to come with you?" he asks.

"No, I'm going alone," I say.

My father looks a little disappointed with the news. "Okay. I'll be here continuing my strength exercises."

"Do what you like."

My legs move and I speed by him on an opposite trail going uphill. Within a minute or so, he's out of my view.

I jog through the path and make way into the sunlight, away from the canopy. My nose is hit with the aromas of fresh plant life and a cool sea breeze. I'm at the top of a hill, overlooking the beautiful coast of the island. I stare at the azure Pacific Ocean while my legs continue to travel ahead. There are a few clouds in the sky, but a shower of warm sunrays engulfs my body. The view is mesmerizing and it's the one part of this island that I don't take for granted.

The environment is what I need to clear my head. There are so many things to think about. There was a time when I wasn't always so icy to my dad. I was his angel, his prized possession, part of the family that he swore to protect. And he and mom were together then. We were one happy bunch. He even got along with Aunt Lucy and I saw her often. Yes, those were good times.

But they don't last forever. I was only six when Aunt Lucy had to leave. I remember the last time I saw her on this island. I cried and cried and cried, I didn't understand why she had to go. I hugged her, clutching hard, hoping it'd be enough for her to stay.

"Don't go," I said while weeping.

"Experiencing sadness," she said. "Bond strong. Regret must go as well. Tears not needed. Will miss you."

She looked as me, then looked at mom while father gave her a scowl, and she left this place forever.

At first, I was angry with her. I thought she left because she was tired of us, tired of living on this island, tired of me. But eventually, mom told me the truth. It was his fault she was gone.

I learned it when I was older, when mom's and father's relationship started to fall apart, Lucy was doing things father didn't like. So he banished her, like a king, like a tyrant. How could he have done that knowing how much I loved my auntie? I was younger at the time and asked him straight up why he did it. All he could blabber about was that Lucy was a bad creature, that she was putting us in danger, that she was evil. She was my aunt. She wasn't the horrible being he said she was.

My father is a coward, plain and simple. He wants to keep us safe, but in doing so he's making this island a prison. Being locked up here is his ultimate plan. I am trapped. I have been trapped here for my entire life so far, and I don't see anything changing.

Aunt Lucy was as much a family member to mom as she was to me, and mom didn't take father's banishment lightly. That's what began the fallout. They argued all the time about a slew of topics: why Aunt Lucy had to leave, what we were going to do in the long run, why we should or shouldn't hide any longer.

At first, I tried to stay fair and not take sides. Yet I couldn't get over the sting of losing Aunt Lucy, and I quickly sided with my mom. She was right, he was wrong. My mom knew Aunt Lucy was looking at the bigger picture. My aunt wanted to create a new generation of hybrids so we could earn our place in the world instead of cowering in fear. She wanted to fight for the future. My father would rather run away from this like a scared child. I can't look at my dad without thinking how weak he is.

Even though they're separated, and even though she hates his guts, mom hasn't left. We're here on this island, playing by father's rules. But I'm not sure how long that's going to last. For now, this place is still our home, and I'll continue to train. We don't have anywhere else to go, but that's a short-term problem. She'll make the decision to go, and I'm looking forward to the day when we leave this place.

Mom is rather tightlipped about the future. I know about her precognitive abilities, but she tends to keep those things to herself. She always says it's a burden to know what's going to happen, and she doesn't want to share it with others. I respect her decision. When the time comes, she'll tell me what she wants me to know and that will be that, but I'm not going to press her on it.

I love my mother. Things might have changed between father and me, but my mom will always be dear to my heart. She's smart, caring, and knows what is best. She respects my desires and needs, which is more than I can say about father. He wants to control me, mom wants me to live.

My relationship with mom has strengthened, but with my father, it's gone downhill. I hate him. It's kind of ironic too. When mom and father first arrived on this island, he was the one who was the fighter, the leader. My mom was the naïve youngster. But my father is spineless, wanting to live a life in the shadows. And he's a dictator, kicking Aunt Lucy out and making these rules that he upholds strictly. We may have a life that is safe, but it's unfulfilling. Mom has been living in fear all her life. It's now her time to make her move. And I plan to help her, whether it's being by her side or pushing her in that direction.

An hour has passed and I'm close to finishing my loop. I return to the umbrella that is the jungle canopy, away from the sunlight to the shade, back where I started. In the distance, I see my father sitting under a tree. I slow my pace until I'm walking and control my breath until I'm no longer heaving in air.

"You're still here," I say to him as I cool down.

"Yes, I was waiting for you," he says. "I didn't want to abandon you."

"Don't worry, you're not."

I go straight to my bag and gather my things. This workout is over. My father looks at me hesitantly. It seems he wants something.

"Well, what are you doing today?" he asks. "Want to get lunch?"

I think I know what he wants. Father-daughter time is rare these days. These sessions are as close as he gets to bonding. I purposely try to tiptoe around the issue and avoid looking him in the eyes.

"No, I already have plans," I say.

"Oh. How about tomorrow?" he asks.

"Also busy."

We stand there in an awkward silence, each of us unsure of what to say. After a few seconds, I break the ice.

"Anyway, I'm heading home now," I say. "Thanks for the workout."

Mournfully, he accepts his fate.

"Okay, I'll see you later," he says. "Say hi to your mother for me."

"Yeah, whatever," I say dismissively, but before I go, I turn around to ask him one question. "Hey, dad, are you proud of me?"

He's caught off guard by it.

"Um, of course," he says, stumbling through his answer. "Are you okay? Something on your mind?"

I pause a bit before I speak.

"No, it's nothing," I say. "Sorry to worry you. I'll see you later."

I walk in the other direction. I keep my head forward and refuse to turn back. There's no point. I already know the sight behind me, a sad sack of a hybrid that refuses to face reality. He gave up the fight a long time ago, and in return, we gave up on him.

Chapter 7 – Iris Lawton

Midnight

April 3, 3046 11:58 PM

I'm in bed and I can't sleep. It's one of those nights. I'm a light sleeper, and my heavy belly doesn't make it any easier. On the other hand, Bastion is knocked out cold. He can sleep through anything, lucky guy. I get out of bed and walk to the kitchen area to get a snack.

We got a fresh batch of fruits and veggies insta-itemed in earlier this evening. I go through the new choices, pick out a plate of apples, oranges, and pears, and walk to our nearby dining table. I sit down and look out the large window that's placed in our wall. It's a view to the ocean, several tens of feet below the surface. Of course, it's too dark to see anything right now, but during the day, I get a clear picture of the ocean life that hugs this island. It's quite majestic and is one of my favorite places in this facility.

There are several pods scattered about the island. Lionel Changer's backup facility is structured differently compared to the headquarters the Alliance obliterated three years ago. The one in the Bay Area was a large, centralized sprawl housed underground. The one on this island has miniature units buried underground. Some are in the center, surrounded by dirt. Others are housed on the perimeter, below the surface like this one. Thus, our pod is connected directly to both the island and the ocean, allowing this wonderful view.

Each complex serves various purposes. Some are science facilities, others are medical bays, and one is a transportation bay. It's organized similarly to the main headquarters. Each pod has its own living area, including some beds, food storage, kitchen, showers, and bathrooms. Bastion and I currently reside in one of the storage pods, which houses the armory and supplies accumulated over insta-iteming.

The facilities are connected via teleporters, allowing easy travel between stations. There's also aboveground access. The island itself is extremely remote and off the radar. The only inhabitants are us three and some wildlife. I'm farther from civilization than I've ever been before, farther than Primm, farther than the Wolf's Den, farther than the original headquarters. All I have are my compcubes and streams to connect to the outside world.

This whole island was built by Changer long ago by the wealth he amassed over his lifetime. We have direct access to those credits to fund our lives. After we survived the Alliance's ambush, Lucy immediately transferred Lionel's accounts, which were mostly illegal anyway, to private ones, allowing our purchases to be untraceable. Credits are something we don't have to worry about probably ever again.

We are the only inhabitants of this island. There was no one here when we first arrived; the structures were empty. I'm surprised Changer built this place without staffing it, but I guess it was a backup plan in the truest sense.

Our lives have been quiet for the past three years. We live in seclusion, hidden from society's watchful eye. Of course, this is nothing new for the three of us. We've been doing this dance our whole lives. Lucy and Bastion lived in secret at HORUS since their births. I've bounced from home to home, hiding in fear. This life on the island is no different. We are isolated from the rest of the world because there's no other option.

For now, though, this is the way I prefer it to be. I rub the bulge on my stomach comfortingly. My child's safety is a priority, and I don't mind living in the shadows to protect what I hold dear.

Besides, things aren't that bad here. It's a life of leisure. I eat when I want, sleep when I want, and have found ways to satisfy my curiosity. There's a lot one can accomplish when given enough time. I learned things from Lucy and have become an adept engineer. Occasionally, I assisted her with her fine tunings, and overall, I enjoyed the experience. Crafting items was like solving a large puzzle. It kept my mind focused, occupied, and fresh. I was exposed to opportunities I didn't have before.

The island itself is quite beautiful. It's practically untouched and is small enough to sway away interest from anyone who might stumble upon it. Before I was pregnant, I'd been training with Bastion to my physical peak. With my newfound prowess, exploring the land was a daily adventure. This wasn't like Primm. I actually roamed around in this free land and discovered so many natural treasures. I was exposed to an environment that was new, exciting, and I enjoyed it immensely.

Still, most days I have my moments when I look back on my past, at my time at the Wolf's Den, and reminisce. I don't miss my cabin, nor do I find myself yearning to return to the woods. No, instead, I think about those happy moments with another loved one I've lost. Fenrir, I miss you.

I gaze at my hand. You couldn't tell by looking at it, but it's completely fake, personalized for me by Lucy. I've had it for a while now, but it still doesn't feel natural. Though it practically is the real thing, when I move it, it's like I'm controlling a machine instead of my hand. It's my souvenir from Fenrir's final confrontation with his family.

His last moments replay in my mind over and over every day. Me holding on to him, shielding him from his crazed sister, the valiant push he gave me into the teleporter, the bomb popping into the air, his sister's bewildered dash to escape, and the bright flash of an explosion blinding my eyes. That sequence of events will stay in my mind until the day I die.

His death is a collection of tragic memories I have stored from a lifetime of hardships. Why does it always come to that? Why have I lost so much? It's hard to find meaning in all this senseless death.

That's all I could think about those first few months here. I was overcome with grief and didn't have the will to live. I hold Fenrir in a very special place in my heart. I felt safe around him. The worries I had about the outside world subsided. I didn't think about it when I lived with him. I suppose it was because I was happy. My troubles floated away.

I met a wolf who was completely devoted to protecting me. My experiences in Primm soured my trust in loved ones. However, something about Fenrir told me things would be okay with him. I was once fearful of the future. I wondered if I'd ever have a shot at happiness. It didn't seem likely. How could one find a way to live peacefully if they were shackled by the chains of oppression? But living with Fenrir gave me some hope. We coexisted peacefully and became each other's support

system. That right there was enough to prove my doubts
wrong.

I will never forget my time with him, and when I
remember it, I become infuriated. He was taken from me.
In fact, all of my loved ones were. The Brotherhood—
hell, the Alliance—they are responsible. I can't do
anything now, but one day, the world will know of my
existence, and the leaders of this world will be powerless
to stop me. I don't care if it takes a lifetime. My loved
ones and I will live without persecution.

Fenrir's death happened so quickly, so abruptly. It
shocked my core, and my life spiraled down further. I
didn't take care of myself. I wanted to waste away
because I was too tired to deal with life. Hope,
motivation, those things take energy, and after Fenrir's
death, I was deflated. Day by day, I broke apart. At the
rate I was going, there'd be nothing left to fix.

There were days where all I did was lie in bed and
cry. I wanted his warm body next to mine, to comfort
me, to tell me I was going to be okay in the strange
situation I found myself. But the only thing I had to hug
was a pillow. The room was cold and empty. I was
alone. Fenrir would never be by my side again.

Sometimes I thought about suicide. It was a solution
I feared but the only one that made sense. I couldn't
endure any more loss. I couldn't run away from it either.
Misfortune was drawn to me like a moth to a light. I
couldn't escape the rotten hands fate dealt me no matter
how hard I tried. I felt the only life I could lead was one
filled with cruel circumstances. The only way out was
death.

But then I remembered my brother Curtis, who
seemed to only exist in another lifetime. I was becoming
like him, a creature so torn by the sorrow he endured that

suicide wasn't an act of rage, but one of peaceful release. He hated life, and when someone is so angry with it all, their mind goes into dangerous places. It was a path I didn't want to travel. I was becoming like that, and it scared me.

I needed to do something to change this. I was still enraged at Lucy and Bastion for what they did to me, but I realized that mentality wasn't healthy. I was stuck on this island and had nowhere else to go. If I was to live with these other hybrids, I had to get along with them. I couldn't stay isolated.

Bastion naturally welcomed my newfound friendliness with open arms. It didn't surprise me at all. In fact, I expected it. His infatuation with me was quite obvious. Even when I first met him, I knew he had a thing for me.

On the other hand, I'm utterly shocked how Lucy's and my friendship has blossomed. I'd only known her a short week when she and Changer forced their implants on me. The process was traumatizing and painful. Because they did it when I was unwilling, I held a grudge against Lucy for those first months. I thought she was a monster, a freak who didn't have a shred of empathy for her fellow hybrids.

It was weird to even attempt to open up to her, but then an even stranger incident occurred—she opened up to me. She talks like a robot and may only have a pellet of emotion within her, but what happened during the Alliance raid deeply affected Lucy's psyche. Her steel wall of logic and remorselessness was penetrated, and she needed someone to talk to. Despite all her scientific reasoning and focus on her goals, she still was part human and could only contain so much grief.

She talked to me about the odd feelings she'd experienced, things she never felt before. Grief, sorrow, depression. The death of her mentor hit her hard. At first, it was difficult to piece together what she was trying so say. Her blunt style of speaking and lack of tone forced me to decipher her speech like reading a code. Yet I did my best to advise her through the motions. After the following months, I understood what she was feeling. Lucy didn't exactly break down or pour out her heart to me, but she told me enough that showed me her trust. I was her therapist, and we developed a bond.

My hatred of her wore off. How could I not sympathize with her dilemma? I saw she was as fragile as the rest of us, capable of feeling the emotional pain I've felt all my life. I could relate to her despair. That's what allowed our friendship to blossom. I assisted Lucy with a problem she couldn't solve on her own. I don't think she ever received that kind of help her entire life. Certainly, Changer didn't provide it. He only saw her as a genius, not a being capable of such sentiments. Bastion couldn't offer it either. I'm probably the only one who cared for Lucy in that manner, and I could tell she was forever grateful.

In return, Lucy helped me immeasurably with her technological genius. For starters, she repaired my blown-off hand, enhancing it to pristine condition. She also developed implants that made all of us stronger, healthier, and in the long run, will increase our lifespan. She fulfills any request I may have post haste, whether it's an upgrade I need to my pod or general improvements to the facilities. And she only answers to me, not Bastion. I suppose I have taken the role that Lionel Changer used to fulfill for her, the one of her leader. Lucy's loyalty is without question.

That's why I felt comfortable when I told her, "I want to be a mother." I lacked purpose. Living on the island made me examine my life thus far. The only experiences I've had were being on the run. The goal of my life shouldn't be to survive, it should be to live. Motherhood would allow me that, the one thing the Alliance wouldn't take from me. So much life had been lost. It was time to get some back.

But I was unable to give birth, and I knew Lucy had the specs to complete birthing implants for me. She simply needed to modify Lionel's designs for my anatomy, and she'd already started work on that before I asked. That wasn't the problem.

"Synconium poisoning still issue," she told me bluntly.

"Yes, I know. It's the same poisoning that took my mother's life," I said. "I don't want that to happen to me. But I trust you, Lucy. I know you can make things right, fix the synconium problem. I believe in you."

She looked at me, touched by my positive words.

"Okay," is all she said in response, but I knew she would get the job done.

A few months later, Lucy completed the work and I had a fully functioning, safe version of the uterus implants my mother had. I was ready to have a child. All I had to do was find a partner.

In a sense, I feel bad that Bastion was the only option I had. I knew he loved me, but I didn't love him. He was nice, he cared for me, but I didn't have those feelings. Nevertheless, I needed him in order to have my child. So I pretended he was special to me to ensure I would be a mother. He thought we were in love, but it was far from it.

However, I got what I wanted. I became pregnant. When I found out, it was the happiest news I've ever received in my life. I was going to have a child!

Bastion is happy as well. He's looking forward to being a dad. I need him around. My child has to have a father figure, and I know Bastion will love the little one we'll raise. Things haven't changed, though. I still don't love him, and he still thinks I do. My love will always be reserved for Fenrir. But I can't deny the guilt I feel. Is it wrong to use someone, to lead them on for your own purposes? I just don't know.

It's not ideal, but it'll work.

I rub my pregnant belly as I devour my plate of fruits. I find peace in this quiet moment and should appreciate it, for I know the future is coming, and I'll have to fight for my baby. The Alliance, the Brotherhood, bring them on. I have trained and prepared to keep my little one safe.

My powers have grown since the raid. I tasted my first glimpse of it that night, and after three years, my control has improved considerably. At this point, I can voluntarily look into future events, about a week beyond the present. If I want to know what's going to happen in a few days, all I have to do is think about it and my mind will tell me. So far, my accuracy has been off the charts. I've never been wrong.

I've also gained the ability to look into alternate futures, various possible future events that could happen based on the actions of the present. Thus, my power is infinite. I can delve into the timeline and see when it diverges and the outcome of each tangent. I always know what the resolution is and choose the optimal one. It's like I have the power of a god, choosing my destiny at will. I was reluctant to accept the implants Lucy installed in my brain, but I must say, they have done wonders for me.

It's not perfect, though. It's true I can pick my fate, but only in one-week chunks. I can't look far into the future yet. Anything beyond a week comes in random flashes, just like before. Thus, the scope of my decisions is limited to seven days. Perhaps I take a course of action I thought was favorable based on what I saw in the days ahead. However, in the long run, that choice may not be the right one. Time is unpredictable. What seems correct one day may be a fatal mistake another. I must look into my visions wisely and use my best judgment to choose the correct actions.

I also don't have a grasp on the other mental gifts I possess. I guided Fenrir to my location using a "mental radar" of sorts. However, since then, I haven't experienced anything like that. Perhaps it's because I had a close bond with Fenrir, one that I don't have here. Sure, Lucy and I are close, but it's nothing compared to what I felt with my wolf friend. Lucy hypothesized the connection we made opened up some kind of physic gateway, allowing me to do what I did. She's uncertain, though, and it requires further time to study. But it's not a focus now because I have bigger things to worry about.

Lucy still believes I hold the potential for greater things—telepathy, telekinesis, even mind control. She believes I'll be able to pass my gifts to my children. I'm not sure about that. I'm the only one I know who can look into the future. The dozens of other hybrids, both my family and the ones raised at HORUS, showed no signs. I don't want to sound arrogant, but I believe I'm one of a kind.

Perhaps my son or daughter will be special like me. It's hard to say. I wish I could look further into the future, not just a week or so. One day I will. It's only been three years, and I've improved greatly. Only time will tell how far I can push my limits. I'm looking forward to that day, to the chance of reaching my peak potential. That power will help me protect the ones I love, protect the future I plan to start.

I rub my stomach one more time as I gaze into the dark abyss of the ocean. Yes, that power will be the key to keeping my family safe.

Chapter 8 – Lucy

Demand

March 10, 3061 8:11 AM

In lab. Started morning early. Went to holding cells. Tranquilized captive. Brought him to research room to start. Have specimen on table. Finished extraction process one hour ago, then proceeded with termination. Subject is deceased. Sedated before execution. Did not want to deal with screams, roars, possible physical altercation. Animal large, might have taken out battle drones. Sedation makes matters less complicated. Gathering other vitals for research.

Process messy. Medical drones help harvest. Are precise and efficient, however, still not clean. Lab area extremely dirty. Like butcher shop. Fluids overflowing. Organs. Muscles. Bones. Nerves. Tools. Compcubes. Measuring instruments. All items strewn about. Not attractive site, not organized.

Current after-process difficult. Earlier process easy. Genetic code already obtained. Have tools for sample taking. Drones help make life easier.

After sample retrieval, drones store in cryo-chamber. Use later during hybrids' creation. Will decode structure, reassemble with other species. Like puzzle, but task has complications. Difficult to recode genetic structure from scratch. Changer ran into problems, forced to do birthing solution. Not option here. Must do work on own. Will take time, but will be done. For now, must collect data from specimens before continuing task.

Genetic code needed for building. Organ harvesting needed to study development of brain function, growth, implant testing, etcetera. Also vital to have tissue and bone structure for testing. Personal preference has always been to keep what can. Do not like wasting good materials during creation process.

Two Van Faye supplier. Collected from her on time. Crime boss from Shogun. Unofficial title "Elephant Queen of Crime." Flamboyant. Extravagant. Only answers to credits. Dangerous. Controls criminal underworld at whim. Has many convicts under employ. Boss of bosses.

Despite greed, is reliable partner. Gets job done. Provides product on time. Is discreet. No questions asked. Follows instructions clearly. Ruthless. Such characteristics desirable in business.

Current subject is lion species. Large animal, had drones carry him. Fur ragged, hygiene unsavory. Teeth gnawed down. Has several bruises and cuts, possibly received from Van Faye. Only fifty years old, but looks beyond that. Estimated to have died in a few years from body abuse. No matter, not concerned with cosmetic damage.

Similar to other specimens obtained from Van Faye. Most subjects are in less than desirable states of health. Come from shambled pasts. Example, lion had prior life as drone engineer. Intelligence average. Lost job. Developed drug problem. Bought from Van Faye. Got sucked into Van Faye's gambling casinos. Credits disappeared. Owed to Van Faye. Became target on Van Faye's hit list.

Hit list means candidate for collection. No close family, low members of society. Will not be missed. Would have been killed by Van Faye anyway. I pay for candidates. Works for both parties. Collect and dispose body for Van Faye, Van Faye makes decent credits off transaction. Debt of candidates covered by payment. Only request is captive is alive. Van Faye agrees to this.

Not concerned with unfavorable qualities of candidates. Species viewed as losers by society. Most addicts, some gamblers, some petty criminals. Case no different in creation of first of kind. Changer's hybrids birthed from prostitutes. Bodies wrecked by disease. Many poor mothers. Several lacked intelligence.

However, results ended successfully. Example myself. Iris Lawton, Bastion also excellent product. Athletic, healthy, intelligent, precognitive. Only need specimens as basis. Enhanced traits come from nurture and implants. Future hybrids will be smart, strong, perfect. With control in creation, desired qualities will be realized.

Business of trading animals is self-sustaining. Supply and demand. Always need for demand, always available supply. Types like Van Faye make living off model. Only ones to suffer are others, not selves.

Changer had similar model, except paid prostitutes. Cannot follow same model. Subjects knew too much. Required cooperation from too many. Self only requires cooperation of Van Faye. Specimens collected unwilling to be a subject. Unfortunate, but can be overlooked. Do not care about rights. System is efficient. Discreet. Sacrifices can, must be made.

Extermination necessary for two reasons. First, as discussed, organs and tissues needed in research. Second, loose ends tied up. Secrecy important. Cannot let subjects live. Possible they will expose us, hybrids in general. Must remain undercover. Cannot risk Alliance infiltrating facilities, destroy all work. Eventually world will know of plans, but now is not time.

Cannot avoid destiny that work guarantees. To remain in stale state of life denies opportunities. Must take advantage of gifts.

Done what can with current specimen. Genetic samples intact, organs and tissues collected. Most excited about extracted brain. Interested to test new mental implants. May be improvement over current ones.

Clothes messy. Too much blood on coat. Stench foul. Floor stained red. Tired, hungry, need time to rest. Will have drones clean up. Wish there was more delicate way to conduct research. Anxious when planning phase over.

Now must dispose. Instruct drones to transport subject to industrial vaporizer. Nothing vital left to collect. Only pieces of corpse remain. Vaporization necessary.

Walk back to holding area. Most animals drugged or unconscious. Only have few specimens left to harvest from. Unacceptable. Still do not have enough data for certain breeds. Tigers, lions, gorillas samples obtained. Need cats, dogs, cheetahs, rhinos for next phase. Must send communication to Van Faye. May take few days for Van Faye to produce specimen.

Activate compcube.

"Start communication," I say. "Send to Van Faye. Subject, cat specimen."

Compcube records words.

"Body, need cat specimen. Urgent delivery. Will pay 1.5 times normal payment. Available to pick up. End communication, send."

Expecting to hear back soon. In meantime, will shower and eat. Expect reply when finished. Van Faye very prompt. Gets back within hour. Looking forward to response. Excited to see when next shipment available. Want to add to collection, to obtain more specimens to gather from.

Chapter 9 - Two Van Faye

Supply

March 10, 3061 9:02 AM

My eyes open when I awake from a long night's rest. The fine cashmere blanket wrapped around my body falls to my cushioned bed as I get up and stretch. Yesterday was a crazy night, but that's business as usual. After all, the casinos aren't going to run themselves, and I'm always happy to collect from the high rollers. Then I followed it up with an inspection of my brothels. Have to make sure the pimps aren't skimming from me. Lastly, it was off to the labs to see what the cooks had for the masses. I even tested out a few non-addictive narcotics to make sure it was grade-A stuff. I wouldn't be caught dead as a junkie, but I do like to indulge once in a while. A few hours of partying and I hit the hay, waking up nice and relaxed for another day of business. That's my routine. The life of a Van Faye is never dull.

Grand is one word to describe my family's dynasty. Every one of us has lived large and I'm no exception. My penthouse is on top of the largest, tallest building in Shogun. It's enormous enough to not only hold myself, but a mass of people. I regularly throw extravagant celebrations from up here. I have a personal chef ready to cater to my needs, bar stocked with premium drinks, high-priced furnishings, and of course a small armory in case I need to handle guests that get too comfortable. I also employ at least ten underlings on this floor alone, on duty, with rotating shifts.

I have my morning music on to get me into the swing of things. Sound fills the room, a smooth balance of low-key notes and steady rhythm. It's from a human musician, and I'll give them their credit. They are good at the arts.

The temperature is cool and the room is a tad dark. I could use some natural sunlight to enliven my wake-up routine. Luckily for me, the walls are made of translucent synthetics, high-quality stuff. I can change any spot from opaque to clear with a single voice command.

"All walls clear," I say. Just like that, they become see-through. The only parts that aren't are covered by mirrors and artwork.

Sunlight immediately shines in, and it feels nice. I have a beautiful view from the top, and I can see the city of Shogun in all its splendor. Some say there's not much to look at during the day because the holo signs and laser advertisements don't shine brightly unless you're in a dark corner of the city. Others talk about how the sunlight exposes the grime and filth that makes up this town. Still, every time I look out at my view, I can't help but be amazed at how big and bustling the place is.

In the air, above some of the skyscrapers, hovercars of various sizes whiz by, passing through clouds. One weaves left and right through the air, traveling next to a flock of gulls. Pit stops, floating rehovering stations, and bars are dispersed in the sky in case travelers have to a break in mid-air. We don't have as many levitating buildings as some of the Alliance cities, but the need for them is rising, and in twenty years, I wouldn't be surprised if our city was as state of the art as the rest of the world.

The view is so entrancing that I want to see all the fine details. I grab my magnifying specs with my trunk to get a better look. On the streets far below are many animals starting their day, like me. Some walk busily to their destination, others saunter hazily, probably in a drug-induced stupor, while others recover from their hangovers. I'm sure some of them owe me money. These animals hustle around like ants, aimlessly, while I observe them, a high queen atop my invincible throne.

I am the sole heiress to the Van Faye family business. We are the elephant gods of crime in one of the world's most prosperous, and dangerous, cities. The buildings rise high, the traffic bustles. Flocks of different animals litter the streets, hoping to get some easy money or a quick fix. This city has police, has officials to create a guise of order. Really, though, it's lawless, a place where we reign freely.

But it wasn't always like this. Before it became a sprawl of decadence and corruption, it was simply a small rural fishing community on the southern tip of Japan. Even during the early twenty-sixth century, when human technology was at its peak, the city, known as Sata, remained relatively unplugged. The citizens relied on their natural gifts and were prideful of this fact. They enjoyed their calm lifestyle. The landscape was known to be beautiful. Trees and plant life flourished and a walk along the beach could take away your breath. It was a haven hidden beneath the technological backdrop of modern Japanese society. One could lose themselves there.

Then the Event happened, and this land, this serene paradise, was decimated. A blinding flash of light filled the sky, and in its wake roared a tidal wave of fire. The mere force of the bomb leveled cities, and Sata, along with most of Southern Japan and Eastern China, crumbled in an instant.

The Event killed most plant life, animals, and, of course, humans who were its inhabitants. What wasn't obliterated in the explosion died a slow death from the fallout. The skies rained ash and the water turned green. Plants either mutated or decayed. The soil was highly radioactive and the air was filled with toxins. It was known as No Man's Land.

After the Event, the rebellion ceased. Humans and animals started negotiations to distribute pieces of land to the represented species. However, both sides were in agreement that they wanted nothing to do with No Man's Land. It was a wasteland, uninhabitable and ravaged by pollution. Nothing could be grown there, and the leaders didn't want their citizens to live on top of the desolate badlands. Thus, it remained empty, unsanctioned, and ungoverned.

Many predicted that it would stay this way forever, but many underestimated the power of greed. To those seeking a profit, a lawless land free of charge is the perfect place to start a kingdom. There's nothing to regulate or hold you back. It was a free market where any commodity could be sold. While other areas of the world made things such as gambling or prostitution illegal, the lack of establishment in No Man's Land made many things possible. It was a dream scenario for those looking to profit off of masses that were hungry for excess.

Naturally, this attracted the most powerful, treacherous creatures. They wanted to claim the newly uncharted lands as their own. And these suitors were always big shots from the criminal underworld. It was territory where the kings of crime could make their own rules. They would be coming in droves, hoping to change their statuses from small time hustlers and block bosses to legitimate owners of a crime paradise.

However, the only gangsters who had the banking to back their investment were ones that had history. I'm talking about human crime families. The other animals had only been intelligent a hundred years or so, and they'd been living underground. The Event allowed their freedom, but none had established societies yet. Only humans had that. Dogs, wolves, crocs, even my kind, the elephants, were still small potatoes compared to the naked apes. Thus, humans were the only ones who had the crime culture in their blood.

The human mobsters quickly stormed into No Man's Land to resurrect the area for their purposes. They built over the ruins with gaudy buildings and artificial landscapes. Facilities sprouted up like flowers. Utilities and energy sources were installed to power their new structures. Shipments for goods and food came in by the thousands—no, millions. Teleporters, transit systems, the works, developed almost overnight. Some even brought in agricultural experts to help regrow and produce legitimate, sustainable items. In the course of a few years, the collective sum of criminal organizations completed their mecca. They had constructed functional cities that could prosper. They did what the government didn't want to do. The country looked clean, but it was smoke and mirrors, an illusion that covered the corruption they planned to unleash.

All of this was done out in the open as the watchful eye of a newly formed Alliance kept tabs on the transactions. That's all they could do, watch. With so many other issues to deal with, this small, flourishing metropolis was the least of their worries. Many Alliance members were hoping it was simply a fad, a society with no stability, and that perhaps the families would eventually cannibalize each others' businesses.

Years had passed, and the underworld was no longer underground. It had blossomed into a real empire. The name of area changed from No Man's Land to Fan Zui Bin, as locals had christened it. It's based off an old language called Chinese and means the "Crime Shore," a fitting name for the lands that encompass the Pacific. Citizens of the FZB had access to things they never dreamed of in the land of the laws. New drugs, new ways to please themselves, new ways to throw their money and their lives away.

Those seeking a thrill flocked to the promise land. The fresh arrivals were mostly animals. The bosses weren't welcoming to them at first. Humans wanted Fan Zui Bin to be the last bastion of untouched human civilization. At that point, the Alliance already brokered the lands off to the different animal species. Fan Zui Bin was not part of these negotiations, and the crime lords were happy. They didn't want to mingle with animal scum.

Yet money talks and naïve animal species were easy targets for making creds. The ruling humans took advantage of the green citizens. The humans preyed on the immigrants, hooking them in with their promises and goods and supplying their addiction while they shook their pockets until they were empty. They underpriced and sold, then doubled the cost. Animals threw credits at the bosses like charity. Classes started to brew. The syndicates that were on top were humans. The humans lived in decadence while the animals lived in shambles.

Not all was well for the families, though. When you have big egos with little scruples, trouble is bound to happen. The families owned cities independent from Alliance rule, but not from each other. Cities within Fan Zui Bin expanded, and suddenly, the territory wasn't big enough to hold every would-be tyrant of the underworld. A turf war quickly developed. Every big gangster was at each other's throats. Mob lieutenants would kill generals, generals would assassinate capos, and henchmen would mow down lieutenants. Round and round it went like a murderous cycle.

It was like the old days, long before the Event, when humans were killing humans. The war was never ending, raging on for decades. No one was winning, no one was losing. The conflict was in a state of eternal gridlock. And all the while, the animals that lived underneath them were growing in numbers and getting restless. They were tired of being stuck in the middle of the humans' war for power. Thus, they banded together, much like they did during the Ark Rebellion, to seize Fan Zui Bin for themselves.

It was easy enough. The crime lords were blindsided by the assault and their numbers were depleted thanks to the gang war. The masses they stepped on overthrew them as all-out battles raged within their urban jungle. It became a survival-of-the-fittest competition to see who would end up at the top. Every animal wanted a piece of the pie. Much like the groups they were trying to topple, these animals formed their own gangs. What one couldn't do on his own, one could do in a mass. It was an all-out mob Armageddon.

That was the most dangerous time. You couldn't walk down the street without worrying about getting caught in the crossfire. The Alliance enjoyed this. What they predicted was true—the citizens were devouring each other. They predicted in a few years, Fan Zui Bin would collapse on itself and they could sweep up the remains and settle in the remnants that the old bosses had built.

As time moved on, victors emerged in each of the major cities of Fan Zui Bin. The more powerful gangs gained momentum on their battlegrounds. The old human gangsters had been pushed out. Animal equality happened. It was a triumphant moment for the lower class of Fan Zui Bin.

With this, leaders came. They helped settle down Fan Zui Bin, relying on the tactics the humans had used. The new animal crime families encouraged peace and enticed their recently gained citizens with the same temptations the humans offered. In the end, it worked. The structure was the same as before, with cities being ruled by mob groups, except this time, none were human.

My family, the Van Faye family, took over Shogun, the busy metropolis on the southern tip of Old Japan. It was where Sata used to be. My ancestors toppled the human regime at the time, the Amagis, just as others had done in their cities, and weeded out any rivals vying for the top spot. Reaching for the top was never difficult. The Van Fayes were, and still are, ruthless, cold, and clever. We won because we had the population on our side. Our family business is smuggling. If you want it, we'll get it, and when you give others a good enough thing, they'll do anything for you, including fight by your side.

We have ruled Shogun for hundreds of years unchallenged, and things don't look like they're going to change. There have been a few uprisings here and there by small-time thugs and wannabe street rulers, but my family has always squashed them like bugs. The citizens are on our side. We are the people's family, giving them what they want whether they need it or not. Who are we to say no when demand is high and supply is plenty? Profit has always been our interest and nothing more.

Before they were rulers of Shogun, my ancestors started with nothing. Like all the other animals, they lived like peasants under the human rule. But when the gang wars started, they protected those too weak to defend themselves. Elephants are big, intimidating creatures. Humans left us alone. The other citizens took notice and word started to spread about the noble Van Faye family.

That's when my ancestors struck while the iron was hot. They supplied the residents with goods at a cheaper price. I'm not talking about food and clothes either. I mean real goods, drugs and sex, the stuff that made different species flock to Fan Zui Bin in the first place. We also smuggled in weapons for ourselves and our followers. Eventually, the unrepresented masses were at our beckoning. The untouchables became devoted to the Van Fayes. They championed them as their new, unofficial leaders.

Once the Amagis found out, they tried to crush my ancestors. They sent in their men to storm the ghettos of Shogun. But their forces were weakened from their war with the other bosses and my ancestors' army was rising and hungry. Armed with determination, they easily overpowered the Amagi's men and killed every last one of the family. In the end, the Van Fayes were the rulers of Shogun.

Flash forward a few hundred years to the year 3030, and you reach the day when I was born. When I was birthed, the residents of Shogun celebrated. The princess of crime had arrived, ready to usher in the next chapter of the Van Faye legacy. My parents had me and no one else.

I learned the ways of my family quickly, and by the time I was a teenager, I was running my own operations under my parents' watchful eyes. I learned how to extort animals. I oversaw shipments and made sure distribution ran smoothly. I sent my lackeys on runs to collect overdue payments. Yes, I was on my way to becoming the future leader of Shogun.

Then suddenly, tragedy struck. My parents were assassinated. A planted bomb on our teleporter took their lives. I was devastated. They taught me everything and loved me to the fullest. I wouldn't even be close to where I am without their guidance and support. Our motto has always been family first, and there weren't two more perfect examples than my mother and father.

The perpetrator was one of our own underlings, a rhino by the name of Memphis Reimer, who grew tired serving my family. I made an example of his death. I put him on display in chains for all of the public eye to see. Then, I ordered my lieutenants to sever one of his limbs slowly but keep him alive. Then the next day, they would cut another one off, and another, until, by the end of the week, there was nothing left to chop but his head. His torture sent a grisly message to those who tried to usurp me. My legend grew. I graduated from princess to the Elephant Queen of Crime.

That was long ago. I've been queen for some time, and I love it. I hold true power. We have a mayor, somewhat of a government, but those are masks that we put on to appease the Alliance. Everyone knows Shogun is Van Faye territory. I supply this city with anything they desire, and coincidently, as I open my inbox this morning, the first message that pops up relates to my work.

"Body, need cat specimen. Urgent delivery. Will pay 1.5 times normal payment. Available to pick up."

Signed *The Collector*. Ah, yes, my newest, high-paying client. When I say I'll supply a paying customer anything, I mean it.

I first received a request a little over a year ago from the entity known as The Collector. It was a short message inquiring if I could give the creature any animals that I planned to dispose of. At first, I assumed the creature meant bodies, and I assured The Collector that I had plenty of corpses of animals who failed to pay me on time. But then The Collector clarified that the creature wanted them alive.

This wasn't that big of an issue for me, but I insisted to be paid a high amount. When The Collector responded with an offer, I was very pleased. I asked for the specifications and made arrangements for a time and place where I could deliver.

The Collector requested a lion first, being very specific about the species I provided. It had to be a lion and nothing else. I searched my books and found one such feline. He was a wandering drifter named Ducco Futang, a former member of the Lion's Army who went AWOL during the Lion-Gorilla War. Eventually, this lion became an addict, first wallowing in his pain around Vegas until he made it to Shogun. He'd stayed here since and owed one of my drug bosses a few thousand creds. This Ducco character was homeless and usually hung out in the slums, begging for credits from those who passed by. Occasionally, he would get aggressive with bystanders and caused headaches for my underlings once in a while. I didn't really care though. He was a nobody. However, once I found out he was six months late with his payments, that's when I cared. Such actions always mean death.

Ducco's body had been ravaged by drugs. His lungs were failing, he was out of shape, and his heart was slightly enlarged. Nonetheless The Collector didn't specify what kind of condition the product had to be in, so I figured Ducco passed the test.

I sent a few of my goons after him. They tracked him down, beat him with a few energy batons, and within the hour, his unconscious, bruised, and bloody body was presented in front of me. They put on a sleep band after they knocked him out. His mind was gone. We put him in a box and were ready for delivery.

The Collector and I met on a rooftop at our scheduled time. I was there first with a few of my bodyguards, just in case this was some kind of ruse. A few minutes later, a masked figure appeared before me. I couldn't determine what species The Collector was, but the creature was bipedal, which made me conclude it was human. It wore a large, black cloak that sported a hood. Underneath the cloak was a dark, tough-looking armor that hugged The Collector's body from head to toe. It was shiny and had a few electronics on it, but overall, it was minimalist in design. The Collector also had on bracers that looked dense and combat boots. The most distinguishable feature, though, was the creature's mask. There were no eyeholes, nor an opening for a mouth. It was pretty blank, black and smooth, like everything else on its body. However, there was a vine-shaped design on it, etched in white, that stood out. It swirled around and slithered its way on the empty canvas of black, which made the mask entrancing, mesmerizing.

The Collected approached me.

"Do you have the product?" it asked. I still couldn't figure out if it was male or female because of the muffler it used. The voice that came from The Collector was monotone and indistinct.

"Right here," I said. "Gentlemen."

My guards presented the box to the being and opened it. The Collector peered in and scanned the lion.

"Do you mind if I do some inspections?" The Collector asked.

"Not at all. Be my guest," I said.

The Collector paced around the lion, examining it like a used hovercar. It kneeled down and grabbed one of its legs and inspected Ducco's fur. Then, The Collector opened one of the lion's eyelids and stared directly into the comatose creature's pupils. Finally, a bioscanner popped out from The Collector's front chest-plate, and the being used it to finish up the investigation.

"Everything satisfactory?" I asked the cloaked being.

The Collector turned off the bioscanner and set it aside.

"The readings check out," it said. "This specimen is good enough."

"Excellent," I said.

"Your credits have been deposited. This transaction is complete."

"Hold on one second. I'll need to access my accounts to confirm."

I looked at my guard as he waited for communication. A few moments later, he nodded his head to verify.

"Creds are good," he said.

"Wonderful!" I exclaimed. "It has been a treat doing business with you. If you need another animal, let me know and I'll be happy to accommodate."

"Thank you," The Collector said. "I look forward doing business with you as well."

And that's how things went with The Collector. Since that first meeting, I've been providing the creature with a slew of deadbeats. I never ask what will result of these dealings. I'm simply here to give. The Collector has always paid on time and has never caused any trouble. The creature is a perfect client—business with little risk.

That brings me back to the request. A cat specimen? Better run the books to see what's available. After some searching on my compcube, I come across the perfect candidate, a cat gambler who's behind in payments for three months. He seems to owe me a lot of money and has only come up with excuses every time my thugs collect.

Adachi Konoe is the cat's name. He'll do. I'll let The Collector know that the being can pick up the package in a few days. I never like to disappoint a customer.

Chapter 10 - Bastion

Protégé

March 11, 3061 10:57 AM

Today I woke up with a strange feeling. It was a mixture of sadness and curiosity. I normally have an ambivalent mood when I wake up these days, but on this particular morning, I felt troubled. At first, I couldn't pinpoint what it was. I just felt slightly depressed. I didn't have a bad dream, and yesterday was a normal day like all the others. No, I was simply off. Since it wasn't anything big, I simply shrugged it off and continued my routine.

I got dressed, took a shower, and made my breakfast, a delicious meal of chicken eggs on toast. The classics never go out of style. I also poured myself some orange juice and turned on my streams to see what was going on in the rest of the world. There was a report about missing animals in Shogun, but I didn't really pay too much attention to it. I was starving and focused on devouring my meal.

After breakfast, I exercised for a bit. Today's routine was strength, legs, back, and core. It was quite a workout, serene and therapeutic. I was without Ivy. Though lonely, I had a clear mind. It's been a while since it's been like that. The years have been wearisome, and the situation I find myself in is something I wouldn't have predicted. Moments where I find some ounces of peace are rare.

Thinking about Ivy, about Iris, about the last decade while working out made me realize exactly why I was feeling so down. A few days ago, when we trained, something was off with Ivy. It wasn't her behavior. She always has her angry face on whenever she's around me. I can picture it now, her scowl with narrow eyes. And it's quite common for her to respond to my instructions with sarcasm. It's been like that ever since our relationship fell through the cracks. No, that wasn't what was bothering me.

It was how she left. She asked me if I was proud of her and had this sad way of asking it. Not since she was a young child could I recall when she actually cared about my opinion. What did she do that prompted such serious questions?

Whenever we train, it's normally business as usual. We do our exercises and that's it. I try to make some small talk here and there, but she normally evades my attempts to converse. She dislikes me. I know it. I've known it ever since she was a little girl. It's a combination of her mother's influence and some past events that have fractured our relationship. There are days when I wish I could go back, to mend things and prevent us from falling apart. But all I can do is realize that the past is in the past and nothing more.

It's been this way ever since Lucy left our lives. Ivy was a little girl when I banished Lucy from this place, and it greatly traumatized her. She was too young to understand why I labeled Aunt Lucy as "bad." Ivy thought I was the evil one, the creature who ripped her away from her favorite teacher. She didn't understand that I made Lucy go away for her own protection.

There are many issues I had with Lucy that didn't involve Ivy, but their bond troubled me greatly. I knew

Lucy was evil, a mad genius, the kind that wanted to change the world and not in a good way. I didn't want Lucy to influence my daughter. If it were up to me, Lucy and Ivy would have had as little interaction as possible. However, Iris thought differently. She was friends with Lucy, so I allowed Lucy to spend time with Ivy in order to appease the one I loved. I have regretted that choice since.

I made Lucy Ivy's teacher since she was best suited to do so. Nevertheless, my expectations were low. Lucy has a brilliant mind, but genius doesn't always translate into good teaching. I was fully anticipating that Lucy's lectures would be filled with fractured sentences and wide-eyed confusion from Ivy.

But I was floored. Lucy was actually an excellent teacher. How could this be? Ever since I knew her, I had a hard time understanding her. Even to this day, it's like that. Ivy, on the other hand, understood her perfectly. She was fully immersed into her lessons and mesmerized by Lucy's brain. She was my daughter's intellectual mentor. Ivy would come home from her lessons and describe in detail what she and Lucy did. She always praised her teacher. I could tell a part of her wanted to be like Lucy.

Lucy and Ivy met together every other day for sessions. Iris taught Ivy language because Lucy's skills were, to be kind, lacking. Lucy went over everything else with Ivy. They studied math, science, and history. Lucy would assign my daughter some homework and go through an agenda. She was a strict teacher, disciplining Ivy whenever she goofed off or got something wrong, but she was also fair. Ivy always understood the reason for Lucy's harshness, and she was only six.

Lucy communicated differently to children than adults. She spoke to Ivy in a considerate manner. She had this softness that wasn't present in my exchanges with her. I greatly underestimated Lucy's capability to handle the youngster. Lucy was full of surprises.

Lucy also took quite a liking to Ivy. Before, the closest thing she had to a bond was with Lionel, and even that was a stretch. I was shocked how far Lucy's emotions had developed. Her interactions with Iris must have helped. I mean, during Lucy's entire life, she didn't know anyone she could call a friend. Here she was connecting with Iris and Ivy. Perhaps the innocence of youth is able to win over the strangest of hearts. Iris was the mother, and she taught Ivy life lessons. I was the father and taught Ivy how to control her muscles and strengthen her body. Lucy was the intellect. She taught Ivy how to expand her mind.

I suppose deep down inside, a part of me was jealous that Lucy shared a connection with my daughter that I didn't have. Even though I raised Ivy, we never had the close relationship I wanted. She didn't treat me with the disdain she does today, but she didn't love me like she loved Iris or Lucy. Ivy didn't view me as her father, it was more like I was an acquaintance.

I didn't get the hugs that Iris got from our daughter. Ivy didn't seek my attention or compliments, but her face glowed every time she received a high remark from Iris or Lucy. She cared about their opinions, but I was an afterthought. She went to Iris and Lucy for guidance, but never once did she ask me for help. It pained me. There were days when I wondered if Ivy even loved me. I don't know, maybe I wasn't cut out to be a dad.

Still, we were closer back then than we are today. I tried my hardest to get involved. If Ivy wasn't going to treat me like a dad, then heaven help me, I would make her. I tried to spend as much time as I could with her. I spoiled her rotten, catering to her every need. Iris warned me not to do so, that it wasn't the way to get close to Ivy. I ignored her. Some might say I smothered her, but I really had no option. In hindsight, perhaps Iris was right. A father shouldn't be a friend.

I didn't care. Our relationship improved. I thought we started to have a real bond. But I was a fool. I should've known I couldn't compete. I started noticing Lucy's subtle influences on her. Ivy developed hints of that odd speech pattern unique to Lucy. You know, the mumbled words and disjointed sentences.

Ivy also started to adopt Lucy's trademark lack of empathy. One time, the two of us took a walk in the wilderness. A small lizard crossed our paths. I watched it slither toward us slowly, curiously. I was about to pick it up when suddenly Ivy jammed a stick into its abdomen. I was startled, shocked, at what she did.

"Why did you do that?" I exclaimed.

She looked at me, not a hint of emotion on her face.

"I wanted to see what was inside," she said. She then picked up the lizard, still stuck to the end of her stick, and observed every detail of its impaled carcass. The state she was in wasn't childlike curiosity. No, it was scientific observation—cold, calm, and unemotional. I could see her innocence fading away and grew fearful of the monster she would become.

And then Ivy came home with the gift that caused so much controversy. It was after one of her sessions with Lucy. I was the only one around at the time, and she rushed over as excitement filled her face.

"Dad, I have something really cool to show you," she said, giddy as can be. "Do you want to see it?"

"Sure," I said happily.

"Okay, but you can't tell Aunt Lucy. I took it from her, and she doesn't know."

I was charmed by her enthusiasm and was interested in what she was going to present. She pulled out a living rat from her pack, and I reacted with a mixture of shock and confusion. What was she doing with this thing? Why did she want to show it to me? Was it something she caught in the jungle?

"Um, I'm confused, sweetheart," I said. "Why are you showing this to me?"

With both hands grasping the creature, she calmly raised the rat toward my face.

"Look closer," she said.

I observed the rat carefully, and to my surprise, the rat's eye wasn't organic. From a first glance, it looked like the real thing, but then I saw tiny flashes of electricity glimmering from its pupil. Something had been done to this creature, and I knew what it was. Implants.

But I didn't care about that too much. Lucy installed all three of us with implants. No, what bothered me was the rat's tongue looked like a snake's. It was a hybrid, something that shouldn't exist.

"What... what is this?" I said with a raised voice.

"It's a new animal," Ivy responded sheepishly. She sensed my sudden concern. "Isn't it cool?"

I was horrified and scared. How could Lucy expose my daughter to this world? I wanted her to be free from species creation so she could be rid of all the baggage that came with it. Lucy, someone my daughter idolized, was introducing her to something illegal, outlawed. She'd be in danger. There's no telling what the future would bring, but I knew it wouldn't be anything good.

I didn't know what Lucy was planning. Even now I don't. The only kind of plans she has are grand ones, and her increased interest in Ivy made me wonder what Lucy had in store for my daughter. It was when Ivy came home with her creation I realized why Lucy wanted to be so involved with her. Lucy wasn't only teaching her, she was training her in the arts of biomechanical installation and genetic manipulation. And there was only one real reason why she would do such a thing. She was looking for someone to pass her knowledge to. She was looking for a protégé.

I had to squash it. Lucy was feeding Ivy dangerous information. I didn't want my daughter to be the next Lucy, to be some freak on a mission. I wanted her to be safe, attract as little attention from our pursuers. She wasn't going to go down Lucy's path.

Besides, Ivy wasn't the only reason I wanted Lucy out. The hybrid experiment that Ivy presented got my attention. It made me wonder what else Lucy was up to. It became clear she was back on her quest, her vision to continue Lionel's legacy and create her own. That would bring nothing but trouble.

I thought that was it. I thought the experiment Ivy brought home would be enough to push Lucy out. But then another development, a very unexpected one, came, one that didn't only put Ivy's life in jeopardy, but her future. Ivy had a dark secret. I was horrified to learn this revelation, and I was even more shocked when I discovered Lucy had known about it before I did. With this discovery, Lucy's plans would only escalate, and it was a certainty my daughter would be involved. It wasn't going to happen, not on my watch, so I decided it was time for Lucy to go.

With an energy blaster in hand, I delivered the message to Lucy. I was prepared for a stormy confrontation, but she didn't offer resistance and was actually very calm when she got the news. I suppose she was expecting it. Some of her things were already packed. I think this place limited her. She knew I would uphold my rules by force if I had to. The last thing she wanted was a standoff.

Ivy cried and cried and cried when it happened. She begged and screamed for her to stay. She didn't understand my reasons.

Iris, on the other hand, didn't say one word. She was a neutral party but wanted to do whatever it took to prevent this family from falling apart. She was sad about what played out but was resistant to protest. The last thing she wanted was for Ivy to be torn apart by a family conflict. Iris put on a tough face, but inside, her heart was broken. She had to watch Lucy leave. She shed a few tears to show the immense grief she held inside.

After Lucy was gone, Ivy hated me. It's been this way for a long time, and it doesn't look like it's getting any better. Iris tried to be peacemaker to keep the family together, but a few years later, she turned on me as well. I was kicked out of our home.

When I think about it, her hate surpasses Ivy's. She didn't talk about it much, but I knew she couldn't bear to see Lucy go. There would be days where I could tell she yearned for Lucy's company. They used to go on walks and Iris cooked meals for her. She lost her friend, and it rattled her mind. At first, she pretended she was okay with my reasoning. But she could only pretend for so long. Eventually, it got to her and she took it out on me.

It's more apparent to me now that Iris has always had a soft spot for Lucy. When Lucy was polluting Ivy's mind, Iris showed little concern. I assumed she would have been enraged, but I couldn't have been more wrong. It was like she thought Ivy's behavior was acceptable. Strange indeed. I guess the bonds of friendship can overpower the opinions of a husband.

My morning routine is finished, and I sit in my humble abode, reflecting on it. But that brings me back to what irked me this morning, what Ivy said.

"Are you proud of me?"

The words bounce in my head, and I think hard about what it means. Then something else hits my brain.

"There's been a disappearance of various animals in the crime city of Shogun."

That… that was from this morning's news. But no, it couldn't be, could it?

"Replay today's report," I say to my visual stream. "Target on Shogun report regarding disappearing animals."

The streambox processes and up pops a holo-video of the report.

"In recent news, there's been a disappearance of various animals in the crime city of Shogun. Though homicide rates are high in the heavily populated city, authorities have been noticing a rise in cold cases of missing animals. Creatures are vanishing off the streets, and officials have no idea the cause of their disappearance. Many have suspected that local crime bosses are responsible, but no conclusion has been found. Residents are worried that the rise in these bizarre instances is a sign that crime rates and violence are getting out of hand in the city. There are rumors about the possible suspect. Witnesses claim seeing a cloaked, bipedal creature stalking areas of Shogun, though these rumors have nothing to substantiate them. Alliance leaders have yet to step in, as they remain strong on their no-involvement policy in Fan Zui Bin. However, a representative from the Alliance has commented that they will conduct an investigation, but details remain classified."

The feed ends. Immediately, I go on my compcube and run a search on messages I have received in the past month.

"Where is it... where is it?" I mumble to myself as I rush through the results.

Not so long ago, Lucy had messaged me out of the blue. I hadn't talked to her for years, but the message inquired how Ivy was doing. I remembered there was something about Shogun in it.

"Found it!" I exclaim. "Replay message."

A holo-image of Lucy pops up and the recording plays.

"Bastion, greetings. Sending communication regarding Ivy. Would like her help on mission in Shogun. Understand not fond of idea. However, important that I contact her. Working on project, need help greatly. Life or death situation."

That was it, just a short message. The way she presented herself was calm and casual, like she was asking for a small favor. I suppose she's like that. She appears semi-autistic at times and it wouldn't surprise me if she didn't understand the gravity of her question. But still, I don't know what she was thinking. Had she forgotten everything she's done to me? The idea that she would even try to reach out to me was absurd. I never responded to her message. I'm not sure what kind of reply she was looking for. I thought she had truly lost her mind.

And her request had to do with Shogun. The crime city, the cesspool of the world. And it was possibly in public. I wasn't going to let Ivy go anywhere. There are so many things wrong with the message. I'm sure she knew the answer I would give.

There couldn't be a connection between Lucy and Shogun. I mean, what are the odds? These kinds of cases happen all the time. How could Lucy even be involved in them? The authorities are incompetent in Shogun, and the residents are low-class idiots. Of course they would blame it on some kind of bipedal boogieman. I'm sure it's some crime boss or something. And I'm sure it has nothing to do with Lucy.

Yes, it's nothing to worry about...

...But you never know. Lucy's message bothered me at the time, and this report reinforces my fears. I couldn't figure out why Lucy sent it, I still can't. What could be so important, so grand, that Lucy would be desperate enough to reach me? What was she planning? Was it really life or death? Lionel had those grandiose visions, Lucy's the same way. Is she trying to get me back in action, to be her muscle? But she knows I hate her. Why'd she even go through me? Why not contact Iris or Ivy directly?

Maybe all this paranoia is true. Maybe Lucy does have something monstrous in store for this world. Maybe Shogun is involved. And perhaps she needs all our help, even mine, even Iris's, even...

That's when I realize it, why Ivy was acting so strangely. Lucy probably contacted Ivy directly. The only reason Ivy would ask me if I made her proud was if she were harboring some kind of guilt. If Lucy is doing something in Shogun, there's no doubt it would be bad. Missing animals and kidnappings? That's a play of no conscience for Lucy. But not for someone as young as Ivy. And if she really is involved, I'm sure that guilt is crushing her, so much that she would even run to me for solace.

Has my daughter done something horrible? That damn ape-girl better not have sullied my daughter's hands with her filthy influence!

But all this is speculation. I won't know for sure unless I investigate. There are so many questions running through my mind, and they won't be answered if I sit here doing nothing. If I confront my daughter, if it's true that Lucy has her involved in something horrible, Lucy will pay. I may be older, and I may have been isolated on this island the whole time, but I can still carry out a mission or two. I will kill Lucy.

I'm done hiding. I head out of my dwelling to go to my daughter. I need to fight for my family. Speaking of which, one particular question burns my brain. Where's Iris in all of this?

Chapter 11 – Iris Lawton

Beach

August 15, 3050 2:01 PM

It's a hot summer afternoon, the perfect opportunity to spend a day on the beach. Ivy and I are heading there, trudging through the thick jungle coverings that stand in our way. There's no direct path to the beach. We have to do a small amount of trekking to get there. Bastion decided to stay behind, and Lucy isn't really an outdoors person. That's okay. I prefer to have some mommy-daughter time.

Ivy is a curious child. She asks so many questions for a four-year-old. She often comes running to me, holding a plant or rock that she hasn't seen before, and demands to know what it is. I warn her that she shouldn't collect things she's unfamiliar with. This island is filled with exotic vegetation and some of it could be dangerous. Lucy has done her best to classify the plant life around here, but there's still a lot left to be discovered. The last thing I need is for Ivy to break out with some kind of rash.

But naturally, her excitement makes her forget my warnings. She's like a sponge, ready to soak in knowledge, except for my lessons. She explores and discovers, satisfying her thirst for information. And when she doesn't know something, it bothers her. Her attention shifts until she can find an answer. I suppose the old human saying about cats and curiosity rings true.

Sometimes, I worry her precociousness will bring trouble. Despite all this, she is my daughter and I wouldn't have it any other way.

There are moments where I wish she would calm down, this being one of them. She is a handful at times. If I take my eye off her for a few seconds, she might be gone. Lucy has confirmed there isn't any wildlife in the area that's dangerous, but that's not enough to assure me Ivy will be safe. What if she falls down a hill? What if there's some poisonous spider Lucy hasn't discovered? Lionel Changer may have built backup facilities on this island, but that doesn't guarantee that we know everything about it. There are still areas on this island that I haven't reached, and I've been here for seven years.

I will not let my daughter be in harm's way because of the unknown. I watch over her like a mother hen, and I'd do whatever it takes to make sure she will grow up to be an adult. That's what mothers do.

Lucy has helped. I trust her with my daughter. In fact, soon, she'll be Ivy's teacher. There are lessons that I simply cannot give Ivy. Lucy has a wealth of information, and Ivy has demonstrated she is a very intelligent little girl. I want my daughter to blossom to her potential, perhaps become a genius like Aunt Lucy. And I'm confident that Lucy will be able to instruct her. She is my friend, my confidant, and has aided me greatly. She will not fail.

Bastion is skeptical about Lucy's teaching ability. But then again, Bastion can't see the truth.

Lucy also helps me with keeping tabs on Ivy's health. Ivy is the first pure hybrid created from birth, from two hybrid parents. Thus, she is the first of her kind, like how Lucy, Bastion, and I are the first of our kind. I was worried she might be born with a deformity or undiscovered illness. Anything is possible with a new species. Look at Zorro. He was the first hybrid and he aged rapidly. My daughter will not suffer the same fate.

Luckily, Lucy hasn't discovered anything that is a cause for concern. She analyzes Ivy on a monthly basis, doing a full body scan so we can discover any problems early. Ivy is as healthy as any child, maybe even healthier thanks to some of the implants Lucy put in her. Bastion wasn't too fond of the idea, but these implants aren't enhancers. They're essential for her living. Immunization boosters, reflex speeders, just to name a few. They increase her rate of survival. I'm not going to take any risks when it comes to my child's life. That's non-negotiable. Lucy has developed quite an array of implants, and we all have them in us in one form or another. That includes Bastion, so it'd be hypocritical if he denies his own daughter these privileges.

Lucy also discovered something about Ivy during her examinations: she doesn't have precognitive powers. There might be a potential, but there's no evidence to back up this claim. I'm sure Ivy will develop something. She's already very athletic, so perhaps she's inherited Bastion's genes instead of mine. Bastion and Lucy may not have precognitive powers like me, but they do both have their own unique skills. Lucy has intelligence, Bastion has physical prowess. Sometimes I think my brothers and sisters also had the potential for such abilities, but they weren't raised in HORUS, thus there was no way to nurture it. Their hidden powers had no chance to blossom.

Nevertheless, even though what Bastion and Lucy can do is impressive, I'm the only one with the gift of precognition. Lionel Changer's theory was wrong. My gifts aren't being carried to the next generation. That was

Lionel Changer's goal, wasn't it? To breed an army of mentally powered hybrids to squash the other species and reclaim Earth for humans using his genetically modified soldiers? Yeah, seems a little convoluted to me too, but the guy was kind of crazy. Smart, yes—insane, definitely. I guess I shouldn't talk down on him too much. Without him, I would've never existed.

He was right about one thing though. My powers have continued to increase thanks to the implants he prototyped and Lucy perfected. I've had some more work done as Lucy has upgraded the equipment. She's also made the process less... traumatizing. It's now a simple injection to the arm, and the nanotech goes directly to the target. That's the high-level overview. Lucy doesn't really get into the details. I wouldn't have understood anyway. It's hard to comprehend Lucy when she's speaking in technical terms.

The first few years, my range of precognition was only a week. Anything beyond it was hazy, random, without an element of control. Now the length is longer, going to about a month. That's a big difference. Hell, a few minutes are a big difference. Any increase gives me those extra valuable seconds to react, to anticipate what is coming. Knowing what can come a month before it happens has proven extremely useful.

It's not only the range of my precognition that has advanced, but also my ability to look into alternate futures. Before, I could look into my visions and only get a handful of what-may-bes. Now, that number has expanded exponentially. It's in the hundreds. So many different branches of time to look at, yet only one single path I can choose. It's impressive, but I still have a long way to go. However, if I keep on going, the sky's the limit. I may have the power to know every possible existence, every single outcome that can branch off from the actions of the collective world. It could be infinite. I would know what it'd be like to be God. I'm not sure if I'm equipped to wield such gifts. It's not my way. But I must accept my fate. I wonder what else may come in the long run. Too bad my power isn't almighty yet, because if it were, I wouldn't have to wonder at all.

That's way too big for me though. My priority is to use these powers to keep my family safe. I'm constantly on what I call "the scan," looking into my visions, to anticipate any unwanted visitors. So far, we haven't had any, and that's a good thing. But if I ever see the Alliance coming, I will scout all my visions and find a path where their arrival is prevented. I would then study that path and figure out what actions need to happen in order for it to come true. It's like watching game film. I close my eyes, find a desired outcome, and then replay it over and over, making sure every step, every circumstance is fulfilled in order to get there. One wrong move could lead me to a different path, an unwanted one. I remain careful and detail oriented to make sure this doesn't happen.

Lucy will continue to supply me the equipment I require to control and enhance my abilities. She has gone far past what Lionel Changer envisioned in terms of her implant crafting skills. I'm amazed at some of the things she can do. It is without a doubt that her intelligence far surpasses any creature on this planet, human, chimp, or otherwise. Truly her brain is a gift unique to her.

She wants to continue her hybrid research. I know what her goals are, to create the perfect species by mixing creatures. And I understand them. Bastion, Lucy, my daughter, and I are being hunted down. The Alliance, the animals of this world, fear us because we are different.

But what if we weren't? What if we were all the same?
Then there'd be nothing to fear because no one would be
different. The only creatures left around would be us, the
hybrid, the halfkind. It makes sense. In fact, it's the only
thing that makes sense. What doesn't make sense is all
the bloodshed I've endured in my life, simply because
I'm not one of them.

I support Lucy in her goals. I'm proud of what I am.
I look in the mirror and see a beauty, not a monster. If
Lucy is doing something to advance the development of
my species, then I think all of us should root for her. We
shouldn't have to hide on an island, we should be
honorable members of society.

Bastion doesn't agree. He isn't fond of the idea of
Lucy continuing her research. He's okay with the
implants, but genetic manipulation, future hybrids,
remain off the table. I can tell Lucy disagrees with his
rules, but she follows them anyway. I follow them too.
The truth is both of us are a little afraid of him. We know
what he is capable of, what means he will take to track us
down. If we leave, he'll find us. I mean, he was able to
track me down in the middle of the Wolf's Den
wilderness when Fenrir had done everything he could to
make sure we were off the grid. Bastion is that good. If
he puts his mind to it and has enough preparation, he
becomes a force to be reckoned with.

He trains us in the art of combat, but even with this, I
cannot overpower the master. I feel like a prisoner at
times. This is different than when I lived in Primm. It's
true that my mother bound my siblings and me with strict
rules, but she was my mother. I followed them because I
loved her. I'm not sure if it's the same with Bastion. I
follow his rules because I'm afraid of what he'll do.

It's a strange relationship that he and I have. One-sided is the best way to describe it. I don't love him. I don't hate him. I simply don't share the affection he has for me. It sounds horrible, considering he is the father of my child, but the love simply isn't there. How do I explain it? I don't have that feeling of giddiness when I see him. I don't worry when he goes on expeditions and returns late at night. I don't care about what he has to say even though I appear to pay attention. I simply act courteous to him as I would any other being, but it's by custom, not by desire. When I look at him, I don't see a partner. I just see someone who I used to have a child.

When Ivy was born, I tried hard to convince myself that he had a place in my heart. When I reciprocated his gestures, I saw the glee upon his face, and it made me happy that I could bring joy to someone else. Yet that got old, and found myself masking my indifference to him. We never meshed. I can't make myself love someone. I'm not sure if, at this point, he detects my apathy or not. I hide it pretty well. He still treats me like I'm the one, and judging by the way he acts, he probably has no idea what I really think.

Things have become more complicated since Ivy's birth. I put on this false pretense of a happy marriage for her sake. The world is already a complicated place for such a creature. If Ivy grew up in a broken home, it would add to her list of troubles. I grew up in a place where the bonds of family were torn apart. I will not submit my daughter through that. Everything I do—the fake smiles, the pretend laughter—I do it for Ivy. She needs to be raised by parents who not only love her, but each other. So I put on the best face I can to get her through the days. At the very best, I try to view Bastion as a roommate, a domestic partner, and nothing more.

Though some days, I can't fight it. I want to run away. I want to take Ivy and flee in the middle of the night, meet up with Lucy, and leave this island forever. I want to come into contact with the world. I can't stand this feeling of being underground. The constant loneliness, the regret and fear that I will never live a normal life, that I will never experience the wonders of this world. I want to vanquish this feeling of paranoia, that we're just rats hiding from our predators, hoping not to be found, hoping that the Alliance hasn't gotten hold of our location. I want to be out of Bastion's grasp. In spite of that, I must suppress these feelings. I have too much to lose.

Besides, it's impossible to stay away from Bastion. He's obsessed with me. He calls it love, and I'm sure to him it is. But it's a thin line that separates the two.

Every night, if I go out for a walk, he demands that I return at a certain time, like a curfew. Me, a mother of one, an adult, following a curfew? Ridiculous. Some nights, he insists that he walks with me, but I am often able to coax him out of this. He doesn't trust Lucy, and when I visit her at her lab, he always wants to know what my purpose is for visiting her and what we discussed. If I don't, he gets hurt and thinks I'm plotting something with her. This couldn't be further from the truth.

These instances are just a small example of what it's like living under his domain. He creates rules and regulations for just about everything. I constantly have to check in with him, and any activity with Ivy must go through his approval. He's not strict about his rules, and I'm able to talk my way out of it many times because of his devotion to me. Still, it becomes a tiring exercise to persuade him to ease up.

A constant thought that runs through my mind is why I even follow these rules. Who made him king of this island? Nevertheless, I don't challenge him because I don't want to cause a ruckus. Besides, he does it with good intentions. I know everything he orders is for the safety of this family. He makes them out of pure-hearted concern, not because he's on a power trip. He loves Ivy, and that's a good thing, and I know he would do anything for her, for me. That's why he puts his laws in place, for the safety of his family, to make sure the future we have is bright. Things with Bastion aren't black and white, they're complicated.

I stay here because it's easier than the alternative. I don't want to run anymore. I've been on the run from the Alliance already, and if I leave, I'll be on the run from him. I'm tired of running. As sad as it is, I'd rather submit to my fears than have to spend another ounce of energy fighting my pursuers, whether it's the Alliance or Bastion.

Besides, he does anything I ask, bows to my needs. I can't complain too much. Maybe in the long run, I'll open my eyes. Maybe his obsession is a good thing. It protects me from the threats out there, and I feel safe on this island. Perhaps one day I'll give Bastion a chance and I'll realize that denying his love has been a mistake.

Who am I kidding? I know these are just things I tell myself to get me through the day. I could never love Bastion. It's not the overprotectiveness that prevents that, nor is it his opposition to Lucy. If I truly loved him, I could overlook all those things. No, there's only one real reason that makes me reject his affections, something I think about all the time.

He's no Fenrir, and it's a damn shame.

"Over there!" Ivy yells as she runs ahead of me.

I use my hands to clear out the brush in front, and before me is a beautiful beach. The water sparkles and the sand glistens small rays of light. The smell of seawater hits my nose, refreshing my mind like a summer morning.

"We're here!" Ivy yells with glee.

I look at her and smile.

"Yes, we are," I say.

Chapter 12 – Ivy Lawton

Cliffs

March 11, 3061 2:42 PM

Another beautiful day in paradise, not a cloud in the sky. It's a sweltering afternoon, hotter than the past few days. The air is humid, but a gentle breeze blows against my back. The sunrays glisten on my arms. I feel cool and snug at the same time, and I find myself basking in the weather.

I stand on the edge of the coast, high above ocean level, on a place we simply refer to as "the cliffs." It's barren, as there isn't any plant life near where I stand. However, behind me is a wall of trees and bushes. In the late afternoon, the vegetation creates a nice shade, and at times, I'll sneak off here to rest in the heat.

The cliffs are relaxing, the perfect setting to let your troubles float away. There's a fantastic view of the ocean, and the height lets you see miles and miles of water. It's so blue. This water is as pure as it comes. This island is a mystery. It hasn't been touched. Thus, there's little pollution to taint what is pure. The sun illuminates the azure that flows, a giant pool of sapphire goodness. The sky absorbs this color, and it's a beautiful thing. I truly value that view of the ocean.

At the bottom, the waves crash against the rocks. They set a hypnotic rhythm that helps me dive into further tranquility. I take in the salt-water smell. It tingles my nose, and I sniffle a bit. But it's a pleasant feeling, a refreshing one. This place brings back so many memories, and good ones at that. And surprisingly, they don't involve my mother, they involved my father.

I remember when I was a young girl Bastion would take me here to watch the sunset. Some days he'd bring some food and we'd have a small picnic as we watched the sun go down. Other days, he'd read me stories as I drifted into an afternoon nap. The sounds of the ocean calmed me back then and still do today. He cherished these moments. This is his favorite place on the island because of that.

I was always a curious child and would look past the horizon from this cliff and wonder what waited for me beyond the sea. I wanted to know what else this world offered. Would it be adventure? Would it be freedom? When would I be there? I was innocent and had no concept of the prejudices of the world. I just wanted to go to a place where I wasn't trapped, where I could live my life, where I wasn't my father's prisoner.

As I got older, this sentiment grew. But so did my knowledge of society. I understood the dangers that loomed for creatures like my family. But I didn't and still don't care. I'd rather be free and persecuted than not be free at all.

If only if it were so.

I hear some rustling behind me, and from the shrubbery I see a figure emerge.

"Hello, Ivy," my father says.

"What do you want, dad?" I ask him.

"I need to talk to you about something."

I received a message from him earlier this morning. He said it was urgent and that we needed to talk. It had to be in person. As much as I hate meeting with him, urgent is urgent, so I confirmed and we agreed to meet here at the cliffs.

"Well, out with it," I say indifferently.

"The other day, when we worked out, you asked me if I was proud of you," he says.

Crap, I knew that was going to bite me.

"It was nothing," I say dismissively.

"Well, the answer is yes, of course I'm proud of you," he says. "But I was worried. You never ask me those questions."

"Like I said, it was nothing."

My facial expression hardens, my voice rises. My father looks a little astonished, but he presses on.

"Look Ivy," he says. "I know things haven't been smooth between us for a long, long time. But I'm glad you still let me be a part of your life. I enjoy every minute I spend with you, even if you may not reciprocate those feelings. I know you care about me. The fact that you're willing to meet me here today proves that. It's a lot more than what your mother would have done."

I'm slightly touched by his words. For once, my dad is being earnest about his feelings rather than holding them inside. But I continue to put on my tough front. A few sentences don't push aside years of anger.

"Where are you going with this?" I ask him harshly.

"Well, I thought about what you said, or more importantly why you said it," he says. "And then I realized that recently, someone tried to get in contact with me. She was asking me about you. I shot her down, but I realized if she was back in your life, she would no doubt cause the concern that I saw on your face that day. I connected the two together and realized maybe she was on your mind."

"Who are you talking about?"

"Lucy."

My eyes widen a bit and I shake my head in disbelief at my father's words.

"Why would you bring her up?" I yell at him.

"Well, because I couldn't think of anyone else who would put you on tilt," he responds.

"Shut up! Don't act like you know me."

I see the fury flush across his face. His eyes narrow and his breath becomes heavier.

"Hey!" he yells. "Don't talk to your father like that!"

"Don't you dare," I say. "You're no father to me."

"That's because you and your mother won't let me! I tried to get close, to keep us together, but the two of you have pushed me away so far that I don't even know who my daughter is."

"Whose fault is that? You tore this family apart the day you kicked Aunt Lucy out, the day you set all these rules. From the moment I was born, I've been a prisoner on this island, and mother is no different. You are horrible!"

His rage swiftly turns into sadness. My words have pierced through him like a dagger to his heart. He quickly changes the subject.

"I'm not here to talk to you about this," he says, trying his best to hide his broken psyche. "I'm here to ask you if Lucy has contacted you recently."

I look at him straight in the eyes, trying to gauge his intent.

"No," I say abruptly. "But I wish she had."

Again, he's stunned by my response.

"Why would you say that?" he asks.

"Why do you think?" I say. "Are you that blind?"

"Ivy, I know you loved your Aunt Lucy, but when will you realize what she is? What she intended to do?"

"I know what Aunt Lucy is. She's a mentor, a friend, the hybrid that opened my eyes to the knowledge that's out there."

My father starts shaking his head.

"Oh, Ivy, you're wrong," he says. "Lucy is a horrible creature who has maniacal schemes to continue her genetic experiments, experiments that are outlawed. She's a criminal. We've already been hunted down once. If the Alliance found out where she was, we'd be hunted again. She puts you in danger. Don't you realize that?"

"You know nothing!" I yell. "I know what Lucy's plans are. Do you think I'm stupid? Mom told me all about it. And you know what it makes me think?"

"What?"

"You hate what you are, what we are!"

His jaw drops. He's stupefied at my claim.

"How could you make such accusations?" he asks me.

"Because it's the obvious answer," she says. "Aunt Lucy is the only shot our species has to continue to exist. She's planning to create more hybrids so we won't become extinct. Me, you, mom, and my aunt are the only ones left. Without her, we will remain that way. Why would you deny her the chance to help our species survive?"

He remains silent. The only thing he can do is look at the ground in disgrace.

"It's because you hate what you are," I say bleakly. "You don't want any of that because all you see in the mirror is the result of experimentation instead of the future of evolution. You have no pride in what you are. All you have is shame."

"That's absurd," he says softly.

"It's true. That's why you keep me and mom on this island. You don't want the world to know what we are."

"No, that's far from the truth. I don't want the world to know what we are because they'll kill you."

"That's your answer to everything. If you really were proud, you wouldn't cower in fear. You'd fight for freedom. You would do something about it. I may not have talked to Aunt Lucy in a long time, but I know what she's doing is exactly that. She fights to keep our species alive."

"You don't know Lucy like I do."

"You don't know anyone anymore."

The more words I lay into him, the more his heart breaks.

"It's true. I've been alone for a long time," he says. "But I'm trying, Ivy, can't you see? I am. And what you say is wrong. I am not ashamed of what I am. And I am definitely not ashamed of you. When I say I'm proud, I mean it. Why don't you believe me? What must I do to prove you wrong?"

He spills his soul to me, but I'm still not convinced. My father says a lot of things, but I know what I know.

"Let us go already," I say. "Don't show *me* that you're proud. Show the world."

"That just can't happen," he says. "You don't know the world like I do."

I scoff at his reply. Despite what he says, nothing has changed.

"Well, I guess you know everything, then," I say. "This conversation is over."

I start to walk away, but as I pass him, he grasps my arm.

"Are you going to tell your mother what we talked about?" he asks.

Disgust instantly shows on my face.

"I'll tell her what I want to tell her," I say. "But I doubt she'll want to talk about your inquiries on Lucy."

"I'm telling you, Ivy, Lucy is bad news. Stay away from her. Don't listen to what your mother has said."

I glare at him.

"How dare you!" I yell. "I'll listen to mom long before I'll listen to you. Just stay away from us!"

The memories I have with Aunt Lucy and my father start rushing through my head. I become drenched with emotion as the images bombard me. Happy moments with Aunt Lucy in her lab, fun moments with my father at this very cliff. I feel so conflicted. Tears roll from my eyes.

I can't take this. I bat away his hand away and run into the jungle, away from the cliffs, away from my father.

"Ivy, wait!" I can hear him yell as I continue my sprint. "Don't run. I didn't mean to upset you. Let's talk it out."

It's too late. We couldn't sort our differences back then, and we can't sort them out now. The time for talking has passed.

Chapter 13 – Adachi Konoe

Shogun

March 13, 3061 5:01 PM

Neon lights and city sounds, just the way I like it. Shogun is the place to be if you're on top. Hell, Shogun is the place to be when you're on the bottom, as long as you have a way to get out of there. You need outs.

And I always have outs. Outplay, outrun, outsmart. A lot of the animals I know don't think much of me. If you talk to my parents, you'll see what I mean. They think I'm a lowlife, a cat that wasted all the things they gave me. I didn't squander anything. I used it to do the things I wanted to do. They want me to live a boring life, the kind they have. Go in, work in the field in the morning, eat lunch, work some more, come home and go to bed. The next day it's the same. Over and over, round and round, like a hamster on a wheel. That ain't for me. I'm going to be a somebody, living the life of a high roller and never looking back.

Even my friends underestimate me. They don't think I have what it takes to make it to the top. They're my pals, but they probably think I'm a loser. They see me fail and expect it to happen. Everyone runs into bad luck once in a while, everyone gets kicked to the ground. But what makes you a winner in this world is how to get out of it. I'm always thinking ahead, always got something up my sleeve. Most people only plan out their vacations. I plan out my future.

My friends say that makes no sense, but they're not ambitious like me. What they lack is confidence, something I have in abundance. I'm not arrogant, I just know what I want. They don't. They're happy with their schedules, stuck to their routine. I always tell them they can't start the next chapter of their lives if they keep rereading the last one.

Those are a few of my quotes, hopefully to inspire them. I'm an inspirational kind of cat, y'know?

I wasn't always like this though. I used to be an average schmuck like a lot of the citizens of Shogun. Hell, there was a time when I didn't even live in this city. I grew up in a decent family in Selina, a small town here in Fan Zui Bin. I was born Adachi-Davian Konoe. I'm not sure why my parents gave me two names, so I dropped the silly Davian part. My colleagues just call me Adachi. That's a good name. I heard they were a family of samurais, human warriors who used swords and took what they wanted. It fits my personality.

Selina isn't like Shogun. It's a small rural town that lacks the luxuries of a place like this. No parties, no drugs, no gambling. Sure, it's quiet and isn't as dangerous, but where's the fun in that? You can't grow in a place like Selina. Look at my dad. He's what they call a "pest technician" for the fields in Selina. That's the official title, but we all know he's simply a glorified rat catcher. That's the kind of ceiling you're looking at if you live in a town like that. Here in Shogun, the sky is the limit.

I had to get out of that shitty village, so I did what I could to claw my way here. First, I had to speak human. It's the national language in the big cities of Fan Zui Bin. It was that way when the human crime bosses ruled the country, and it stayed that way after. It's kind of ironic that humans are lower class in Fan Zui Bin, but their language prevails. My parents only spoke cat because they had no use to speak human. I went on the infospace and learned. They knew what I was up to and disapproved, but they don't respect higher ambitions.

After a few years, I finally mastered the language and had the creds to move out. I got my things and settled into this tiny loft in the city of my dreams. This metropolis was built by animals that were willing to do anything it takes to get a piece of the pie. I was going to get mine no matter what.

It's not easy though. I've been here two years, and I'm still at the grind. My goal is to make it in the entertainment business in Shogun, to be a producer. Shogun has a lot to offer in terms of the nightlife, and a performer would have a hard time getting a gig without a solid producer backing them up. That's where I would come in. I'd use my connections and transform them from sideshow to main attraction.

Getting clients isn't easy though, but I have this day job as a janitor in a gambling hall ran by the Van Faye group. I clean the high rollers' spilled drinks on the main floor, and those high rollers are often stars in Shogun. If I could just get a connection with one of those guys, I know I'd be on my way to dream street. I always try to give them my info and state my agenda. Sometimes, the pit bosses tell me to scram, to leave their customers alone, but I'm not afraid of them. In a few years, they'll be working for me. Karma is a bitch.

Working in the casino is also great because I get to spend my off hours there. The liquor is always pouring, and the games are always busy. Sometimes me and my fellas go on these benders and bet down my credits like we're made of the stuff. I lose big, but I win big too. I also need the creds to build the foundation of my empire. You can't make money without spending it first.

I'm in a bit of debt now because of my bad streak. I'm not worried. Everyone starts at the bottom in their lives. I know guys who lived in Shogun for years, like me, with nothing in their pockets. They started at places even worse than me, spent more time in the gutter than I ever will. Yet here they are today, owning their mini-empires, buildings shining under the hot Shogun sun. I don't plan to wait forever. I just need a lucky break, and soon I'll be shooting for the stars.

Even with my current pickle, I wouldn't trade these past two years for anything in the world. I've lived more in this short amount of time than I ever did in Selina. I could die tomorrow and I'd be happy. Some say living for the moment is for fools. I say if you don't, then you're the fool.

Others wonder how I live this crazy life when I'm struggling to cut a paycheck. It's simple. All you need are connections. I know how to hustle, how to get what I want out of the dopes. I'm not talking about the little guys either. It's like shooting fish in a barrel getting what I want from them. No, a real hustler can pull from the top, the big guns. I have power players wrapped around my paw.

Hell, right now I owe a local boss some credits. Okay, not some, quite a substantial amount. It's a temporary loss, but you know these bosses. They always want this, always want that. And they spout their idle threats. A smart cat like me knows there's no bite to their bark. Every time one of those thugs comes collecting, I talk my way out of it. After a few stern words, they go on their way and that's that. I mean, what are they going to do, kill me for a few thousand creds? Please. They have better things to do.

And at this very moment, so do I.

I finished my shift at work, and now I'm on my way to meet some buddies at The Seventh Heaven, this new chimp-owned bar that opened up in the ritzy district of Shogun. It's getting dark out, so the neon lights are in full shine. I look above and see a digitally rendered spacecraft whiz by. The boom of its engine vibrates in my ears. It's the new holo advertisement for that space epic that's coming out next weekend, and it looks exactly like the real thing. It should be a good movie.

I'm currently in a district known as Old Square. There are strange symbols that decorate many of the buildings. I think they were glyphs the humans used to read, back in the old time when the animals were still dumb. What was the name of it? Oh yes, kanji is what the humans called it. No one uses it anymore. I'm not sure if there's even a human on Earth that understands it. It's old-timey stuff, outdated. The only reason we have it up is because it looks cool.

Then again, a lot of the architecture in Shogun is influenced by that period. It's of Japanese origin. The country may not be around anymore, but their design is present everywhere in Fan Zui Bin. The buildings are shaped like the buildings of their time, even if the material is modernized. There are statues of mythical Japanese creatures, with some of the syndicates using them as symbols. It's pretty cool actually. Even though their nation went down in flames, I have to admire their style.

The streets are also really crowded. They're wide to accommodate the different species. If it's too narrow, I'd worry about an elephant crushing me. They have rules to control the traffic. Smaller animals on the right, larger animals on the left. I haven't had any incidents since moving to the big city, and I don't plan to in the future. But I better hurry. I'm running a bit late. I pick up the tempo and dodge and weave through the mass of bodies. I guess having cat agility has its advantages.

As I make my way to The Seventh Heaven, the delicious smell of fried chicken skewers fills the air. I become distracted with the scent, and now a food stand has my full attention. I haven't eaten anything all day and my stomach is rumbling. I'm sure the guys won't mind if I'm late by a minute or two.

I walk toward the stand where there are a few animals waiting in line. I take my place and stand patiently. My mouth waters, but then a familiar voice yells at me from behind.

"Adachi!" the creature hollers. I turn around, only to see another cat sprint his way toward me. It's Silverman, one of my coworkers at the casino.

"Silverman, what are you doing here?" I ask.

"I've been looking everywhere for you pal!" he says, exasperated from his run. He continues to breathe in deeply. "I heard something before I left the gaming floor. It involves you."

"Really? And this couldn't wait for later? What did I do this time? Did I forget to lock up again?"

"No, it's not work related. The pit bosses, they were with these guys who were dressed really nice, looked really dangerous. I think they work directly for Two Van Faye. They were asking the bosses where you were, and I think it has to do with collecting. You owed them creds, didn't you? I remember you talking about it during one of our breaks. I think they came to shake you down."

Crap. I knew I owed the Van Faye family, but last time when they were looking for it, they sent some low-level thug, not professionals. I'm not sure if I can dodge my way out of this one.

"What did these two guys look like?" I ask Silverman.

"One was a frog, bullfrog I think," he says. "He's recolored, so he had blue skin. The other was a cheetah with some fakey sunglasses."

Chris and Tian. I actually know them, and they're not very bright. Maybe I can weasel my way out of this after all.

"The frog and the cheetah? Those two are goons," I say to Silverman. "Don't worry about me."

"Are you sure about that?" Silverman asks in a worried tone. "I mean they work for Two Van Faye. Even if they are on the bottom of the Van Faye family barrel, the fact that they work for her is still something I'd be scared of."

"The Van Faye family isn't all-knowing and super powerful. They're just like any other crime family. I doubt they're going to worry about small potatoes like me. So it's cool. I'm pretty sure I have nothing to worry about."

"Yeah, but there's also rumors that their organization is involved with the recent disappearances that have been occurring."

"Rumors shumors. You act like that kind of stuff never happens in Shogun. It happens every day. I don't know why the media is trying to sensationalize things, trying to blame it on some made up boogieman."

"Well, I'm just telling you, Adachi, be careful."

"Don't worry about me. You want a skewer?"

"No, I'm good."

"Okay, I'll see ya, then. Thanks for the warning, but they're probably just going to try to scare me and that's that. I'm not in any physical danger."

Silverman goes the opposite direction, and I order my skewer. I use my paws to grip the stick of meet and gnaw off chunks of chicken. It's hot and the simmered spices explode with flavor in my mouth. The chicken is juicy and tender. Simple moments like these are when I realize I wouldn't trade this life for anything else in the world.

After I'm done, I dispose of my stick in the trash incinerator and continue on my way to The Seventh Heaven. I think a little about Silverman's warning. I don't take the Van Faye family lightly, but if Silverman's right and it really is Chris and Tian, then I'm not scared. I've dealt with them a few times whenever my creds were low and I had a debt to pay. I'll find some way to outsmart them and be on my way.

"Adachi Konoe!" someone yells behind me, stopping me in my tracks. I turn around, and like magic, there stands a cheetah with a bullfrog on his back. The cheetah is slim, athletic looking, and wears a slick suit and fancy shoes on his four paws. He has on a stern face and hides his eyes behind his knockoff glasses. I'm not intimidated though. The shades are simply a façade. He's a nobody.

The frog on his back is a rough-looking little guy. He wears some gaudy-looking suit. I think he was going for a smooth style, but it just looks tacky. It doesn't match well with the blue skin job that he has.

"Chris and Tian," I say. "I heard you two were looking for me."

"What you hear is correct. You owe Two Van Faye money, and she's here to collect," Chris, the frog, says.

"Yeah, well, you know, I don't have it right now, but I'm good for it," I say.

"It's not like the other times. You've done this too often," Tian says. "This time she's collecting your head. She specifically named you and gave the order directly to us to locate you."

"So you got the direct message from the big boss?"

"Uh, well, not exactly, but that doesn't matter who told us what. What matters is Two Van Faye is looking for you."

I've never met Van Faye before. I've just dealt with her lackeys. I'm a bit shocked that such a powerful figure is looking for a small fry like me.

"Why me?" I ask.

"We don't have time for questions. We've already wasted too many minutes," Tian exclaims. "Cannons, arm!"

In a flash, two automated cannons burst out from their suits and point at me. The non-violent encounter I was expecting has shifted and I'm staring straight down the barrels of several guns. Crap, I guess I'll have to think of another way to con my way out of here.

Chapter 14 - Mark Allen

Flight

March 13, 3061 5:01 PM

"How are preparations going?" General Rox asks me. We're in the laboratory where all my equipment, tools, monitors, and streamlinks are set up. I'm tinkering around with the Alphas before the big show. This will be our command center when we send the Alphas on their mission.

"Good," I say. "Diagnostic tests have been positive. They follow instructions received by the communicators in their armor. We also have a manual override in case the verbal commands malfunction for some reason."

"Manual control?"

"Yes, their receivers will disable, and I'll use my compcube to control their movements, like a drone."

"Excellent. However, I was concerned that this task might be too large for you to handle on your own, so I called in another expert. I believe you are familiar with him."

In walks a chimpanzee who I indeed know well. He actually helped me with development of the Alphas, so he's very knowledgeable about the wolves' capabilities and the technology behind them. I met him a long time ago, right about when I got arrested at HORUS. In fact, he was one of my captors.

"Eli Winde!" I say with a friendly smile. I extend my hand to shake his. "I'm surprised you're out here."

"General Rox teleported me in," Eli responds, shaking my hand in return. "He said there's a very important and classified mission the Alphas are embarking on, a milestone. I couldn't say no."

"Also, since Eli was there firsthand when the wolves were apprehended and since he's had a large role in the creation of the Alphas, I figured he was the perfect animal to assist you this evening," General Rox says. "He was and still is an excellent technological expert, and I'm sure he will be happy to help you with his vast wealth of knowledge."

"It's been a while since I've last taken a look at the Alphas," Eli says. "I recall their weapon capabilities, but I believe you installed something new to them recently."

"Yes, boosters and anti-gravity devices," I say. "They are able to fly."

Eli looks impressed with the news.

"Could I see a demonstration?" he asks. "This lab has enough room for that."

"Sure," I say. "I actually prepared some demos before today, and flight is one of them. Begin flight mode demo."

The pair receives my calls and initiates the protocol. Plates on their armor slide to reveal boosters. Small anti-gravitation nodes protrude from different parts of their bodies. It's a mass of fluid movements, metal, and chrome shifting around like organic material. After a few seconds, the changing parts stop and the Alphas are ready.

Blackwolf starts first. It floats in the air as the rockets charge. A short moment later, the boosters fire, echoing a large blast throughout the lab. Blackwolf streams around the open space, whizzing and zigzagging about like a child's toy. The creature is moderately fast and maneuvers through the air with ease. The three of us and a few of the guards look up to watch the sky show, our eyes closely following the onyx-clad wolf.

"Flying dogs, who would've thought?" Eli says.

"They're not dogs," General Rox says in a scornful tone. "Don't confuse their kind with mine. Wolves are nothing like us."

Eli Winde and I look at each other as an awkward tension surrounds us. I bring up a new subject.

"Now it's Silverwolf's turn," I say. "Silverwolf, initiate demonstration."

Just like Blackwolf, Silverwolf goes through a similar starting sequence, switching to flight mode and powering its boosters. The wolf quickly gets into the air and zips around seamlessly, at a much faster speed than Blackwolf. In fact, as they both zoom through the air, Blackwolf seems like a snail in comparison to Silverwolf.

"What's with the speed difference?" General Rox asks me.

"Silverwolf was designed with stealth and speed in mind," I respond. "Blackwolf is more of a tank. Thus, Silverwolf has better boosters and agility, but is equipped with lower impact, precision weapons while Blackwolf has larger blasters and armor. As a tradeoff, Blackwolf is heavier and slower."

"Interesting strategy," General Rox says. "I guess we'll see how that plays out during the mission. I've seen enough. You can stop the demonstration now. I'd ask for a weapons test, but I've read the reports, and we don't have the time to go through a full offensive run. We need to start this mission tonight."

"Demonstration complete," I command to the Alphas. They turn off their boosters and glide their way to the ground. Once they land, they stand still and switch to standby mode.

"So what is the full agenda?" Eli asks.

"As you know, there have been a myriad of animals being plucked off the streets in Shogun," General Rox states. "I have reason to believe that these kidnappings are tied to the Van Faye family."

"Yes, I've read the small briefing," Eli says. "But why is this important? This is Fan Zui Bin we're talking about. Disappearances like these happen all the time. I wouldn't be surprised if Van Faye was involved in all of them. Even if she is, these kinds of crimes aren't worth investigating."

"Maybe," Rox continues, "but there's been some interesting information according to one of my contacts."

"Such as?" Eli asks.

"The involvement of a third party," Rox says.

General Rox sets a compcube down, and an image renders in the air. It is a cloaked figure, all black, lean and tall. It's bipedal, fully armored and masked. However, the image isn't very clear. The subject is kind of blurry and the lighting isn't very bright. The creature is also obscured by some buildings.

"This is the creature that is believed to be Van Faye's partner, but we're not one hundred percent sure," General Rox says. "Information has been murky, but there have been some leaks to the media regarding who this mysterious creature is. We have to find out who or what this third party is. My contact out in Shogun has some information regarding this investigation. It may help us understand the way Van Faye's operation works and what role this third party has in all of this. There's a lot of gaps, and we need to fill them in."

"So who is this contact you have in Shogun?" Eli asks.

"He actually works for Van Faye," Rox responds. "He's a cow by the name of Bo Harada. The cow's an underling, but not exactly a bottom feeder. He's a collection boss but has the means to get us this inside info. We'll send the Alphas to him first. I don't have an exact itinerary of what the investigation will entail, but Harada will be our starting point. After we convene with him, we'll look for clues until we have some more leads to follow. This investigation is varied, so it may wrap up in an evening or last several months. But it's a good test to see what the Alphas are capable of."

Eli stands back and puts his hand on his chin. He takes some time to think about Rox's assessment.

"Agreed," he says. "I'm eager to see the fruits of our labor."

"Excellent. Allen, prepare the Alphas to teleport to Shogun," Rox says. "I will contact Harada and let him know we will be meeting soon. We plan to start this mission within the next hours. We're moving fast on this one, as this third party we're dealing with is quite shifty. I hope you do well on this, Allen. We're looking forward to seeing what the Alphas are a capable of."

I'm a little nervous with Rox's declaration. I hope they do well too. My freedom is counting on it.

Chapter 15 – Adachi Konoe

Debt

March 16, 3061 5:27 PM

"Can't we work this out, fellas?" I ask nervously as the cheetah and frog have a cadre of weapons pointed at me. Chris and Tian are oafs, so I'm still hoping my mouth can get me out of this dilemma.

I'm quite surprised they escalated things so quickly. I've dealt with them before, and they're usually pretty slow to act. You'd think they were top bosses the way they're sticking their weapons at me. I suppose the bounty on my head is bigger than I anticipated if even the lowest thugs come blasting. Then again, this is an order straight from Two Van Faye. Who knew a debt of a few thousand creds could cause so much trouble that even the great Elephant Queen of Crime would be looking for me? I feel a little honored that I'm getting such attention.

"There's nothing to work out, cat," Tian, the cheetah, growls. "You owe Van Faye. She specifically sought for you, and it'd be wise if you come with us. Two Van Faye doesn't take rejection well."

"I can imagine," I mumble to myself. "But listen, guys, there are a lot of cats out here. Who's to say that I was so easy to locate?"

"What are you getting at?" Chris, the frog, replies.

"Well, let's just think about this," I say. "I'm a hard guy to find, elusive and indistinct. I'm not the pick of the litter. What if you two just say you tried your hardest, but you couldn't find me?"

Both of them look at me and laugh. Loudly. For almost a minute. After they regain their senses, they stare at me.

"Why would we do that?" Tian says, still recovering. "Van Faye would come down on us hard. We'd be dead and replaced in a matter of seconds. And I'm pretty sure you have nothing that we want."

Nuts, he has a point there. I don't really have a good answer for them. I'm broke as a joke. That's why I'm in this mess in the first place.

"Have some mercy," I say in desperation. "I mean, aren't you tired of being Van Faye's crumb-bums?"

"No, and it's still better than where you're standing," Chris says.

"Can't you just give a cat a break?" I ask.

"If this is the best you can do, then you really are that pathetic. There are no breaks in Fan Zui Bin, only losers," Tian replies.

Fuck these guys. My brow furrows and I give them an instinctive hiss. I ain't a loser. I've had hard times, down streaks, but I ain't no goddamn loser. They're the losers, a bunch of lackeys working for peanuts, handed out by that elephant bitch goddess. I don't answer to anyone. No one's the boss of me.

"You two are losers, asshats," I say defiantly.

This immediately gets their attention. Their weapons get closer. Didn't mean to escalate the situation. Whoops.

"What did you say?" Chris says angrily.

"Eh, nothing, nothing," I say.

"That's right, take back what you said," Tian goads. "While you're at it, why don't you bow down and grovel?"

"Fuck you," I say, looking up at him defiantly, straight in the eyes.

"You mouthy cat!" Tian says.

He raises up his right paw, claws fully exposed, and swipes at my body. I try to dodge it, but it's too fast, and a tear is heard, direct contact is made. I tumble over from the force and a sharp pain shoots across my torso like an electric shock. My body cringes and I look over to see a chunk of my clothes torn off with a dark red gash replacing it. Bits of fur float in the air. That asshole!

"Damnit!" I screech in pain. "What the hell is your problem?"

"You're coming with us!" Chris says, his eyes bulging. He hops off Tian's back and lets out a ribbit. "Come peacefully and you'll be fine. Don't and, well, Tian's paws will have more red on them."

The situation gets bleaker, and I'm grimacing from the pain. I can't take another blow, but if I go with them, I'm dead. I'm screwed. But then, in the corner of my eye, I see a large, pedestrian bear a few meters away. The lightbulb goes off in my head. She doesn't see me since we're in an alley, and I doubt she'd come to my rescue even if I begged for it, but I think I have a plan. I only have one shot.

"I can't believe Van Faye sent a bunch of after-products to get me. Couldn't even get an Ark Original to do the job," I mutter. I've just laid down the greatest insult of insults to these two, a verbal assault on their species.

I see the rage instantaneously flash across their faces.

"You idiot," Tian says. "Forget the peaceful option. You crossed the line, you disgusting little runt."

"I don't care. That's what you are. You and the frog, your whole kind, are nothing but the results of secondhand experimentations by the lions and pigs. You weren't created like the rest, by humans. No, you were created just for the purpose of being slaves to the creators."

Talking about the origins of intelligent frogs and cheetahs is taboo enough. Openly insulting it to their faces is on a whole new level. I hope this pisses them off enough to do something stupid.

I continue my little speech.

"And guess what? You are slaves to all of us. Secondhand experiments transformed to secondhand citizens. You think you're a boss because you work for Van Faye. That's all you'll ever do, work for someone. Not surprising for a frog and a cheetah, though. Maybe that's why the Alliance stopped the lions and pigs from continuing their work long ago. It's not the fear of more genetic experimentation. It's that they didn't want any more idiot species, like yours, ruining it for the others."

"Shut the fuck up!" Tian says. He raises his claws once again, but this time, I anticipate it. I quickly dash in the opposite direction toward the bear. The two react. They weren't expecting me to flee, and they bumble through their movements. But before they can even start their rush, I'm at the target.

I run by the bear, who stands there confused at the sudden mass of bodies coming her way. With my claws ready, I swipe her arm. She instantly rears up and roars in pain, clutching the scratches with her other paw. It's probably nothing more than a sting for her, but she looks pissed.

"What the hell, asshole?" she screams. She turns in my direction and snarls as I scurry away.

"Sorry!" I yell behind me.

Her reaction sets off the chain of events I was hoping for. She's angry, and her large body blocks the opening to the alley where I was being accosted. I was able to get past her, but Tian and Chris may be hard pressed to slide through. I'm already meters ahead of them, and I'm hoping this distraction will give me even more time.

It does, kind of. I look behind me to see that Chris and Tian have collided with the poor victim of my desperation. All three are on the ground, discombobulated from their respective tumbles. However, Chris and Tian both recover at a record pace while the bear remains on the ground. They jump to their feet and have me in their sights. Crap. Well, at least I was able to get away for a brief moment.

I turn back forward and continue my escape. Where I'm going, I don't exactly know, but I have to get away or I'm toast.

This is easier said than done. Only a few seconds have passed since I continued my sprint, and the two are on my tail. I can't quite make out where Chris is, but Tian is getting close, real close. Within a few more seconds, he'll catch up. What was I thinking trying to outrun a cheetah?

And of course, he has a few blasters attached to his vest. He lets out some energy shots and they careen my way. It's a hard thing looking forward while you're being shot at from behind. All I can do is make my movements erratic, going from a straight line to a zigzag, hoping I'm lucky and he misfires. Surprisingly, I'm successful. One shot errantly goes past my head, another hits a wall. I'm in an empty street, so there's no risk of innocent bystanders getting shot. Then again, this kind of stuff happens so often in the streets of Shogun that I doubt anyone's going to raise concern.

Tian continues to fire more shots, and I continue to outmaneuver them. I guess he has really bad aim. Despite that, he's only a leap or two away. I can hear him breathing. I have to act fast because it won't be the guns I'll be worried about, but those damn claws. He's faster than me—that's a fact—so I have to look for another path. I look up and see the same high-rise buildings and neon lights, the same as on every street in Shogun. They're tall, and as I look at them, I realize they're climbable. And I'm small, light, and agile. I think I found a way to get this cheetah off my trail.

I see a small ledge protruding from one of the buildings. It's not too high either, so I coil my hind legs and thrust them up. I float through the air and grasp my paws to the ledge. My front legs secure my position within an instant and I use them to hoist the rest of my body. I then jump once more to a higher ledge and pull myself up to safety.

It happens so fast that I forget to see where Tian is. He's below me, looking up in confusion and frustration. He knows I'm in a spot he can't get to. Tian is no doubt a dangerous climber as well, but the ledges are the only steps he has to reach my height, and he's far too big to utilize them. All he can do is try to jump up, but every attempt is futile. He can't reach me. I smile with glee.

"Tough break, jerkoff," I taunt him.

"Damn cat!" he bellows.

He aims his blasters up and rapidly fires his ammo. It's no use. The ledge provides great cover, and his shots don't come close to hitting me.

I use this time to look around. There are a few more ledges that I can get to. It's like climbing a tree, with the various structures being my branches. My eyes follow the trail until I envision an escape route that leads to the roof. I'd like to see Tian try and get to me once I'm up there.

"Give your boss my regards," I yell as he furiously tries to claw his way up the building. I turn my head back to the target and leap toward it.

In midair, I feel something sting me at the side of my belly. My body instinctively twists. The blow doesn't hurt. It feels like a light tapping, but it throws me off my trajectory, and I miss the ledge I was aiming for. Instead, my front paws hit the perpendicular wall, and I frantically shuffle my limbs, hoping to grasp something. In milliseconds I went from surefire escape to freefalling to the ground below. I'm desperate to clutch something. I have to be, or I'll be a stain on the pavement.

I'm unable to grab on, but my efforts slow my descent. My plummet loses speed, and by the time I have a small handle on the chaos, my body thuds into a pile of trash. For a few instants, I'm out. Nothing but darkness fills my eyes. But seconds later I wake up in a daze, tired and sore. It feels like a stiff object has smashed into my torso, and I slowly roll over in order to recover from the collision.

I take a look around at my surroundings. I'm in another one of the inconspicuous alleyways that litter this city, but this one is filled with garbage. There's a trash vaporizer nearby. I must have landed behind a restaurant or something. The area is also gated off with a solid metal fence so high even I couldn't jump over it.

Lucky for me, Tian can't either. He followed my descent from the heights and stands on the other side of the gate.

"Lucky cat!" he screams. "Damn garbage saved your life. And this crappy fence! Looks like I'll have to call reinforcements."

I'm grateful that I'm out of his reach. It gives me some time. While he jibbers something over his communicator, I start retracing the prior events. I was in midair when something knocked me off course. What was it?

That's when I see him, his blue body hoping his way down. I was so busy with Tian I didn't notice where the small bastard went. That mother fucking frog.

"Guess we're not so incompetent after all," Chris says. "You'll be eating your words."

I see he has some small, very small, guns attached to his suit as well. That was what must have smacked me in the air. They must be voice commanded or perhaps he presses the trigger button with his tongue. In either case, the caliber looks small. I doubt he'll mortally wound me with that.

"Your blaster looks a bit undersized," I say confidently.

"Don't be fooled. You don't need a big gun to pierce through a small brain," he says.

"Perhaps, but you need a big body to withstand a small blow."

"What?"

Swiftly, I swipe my paw at a rock on the floor and it flies toward Chris. It's not large, but neither is he, and he's too slow to dodge it. It smacks him straight in the head, and he's airborne. The frog lands with a thud and is out cold.

"Well, that was easy," I say to myself.

"What happened?" Tian asks. I can hear him through the fence. "I can't see through this wall. Chris are you still there?"

"I handled him," I yell back. "Can't say I'm impressed. So these were the reinforcements you were talking about?"

Right after I ask the question, a large thump is heard and I look over to the wall only to see that it's dented. What the hell? A few seconds later, another crash echoes through the wall. One final smash and the wall collapses in front of me while a cloud of dust fills the air. When it settles, a large behemoth of a creature stands in front of me, fully armored and all business. He's scary as hell, and I'm literally about to piss myself.

"Sai," I say to myself.

Everyone knows his name, but few dare say it. He is one of Two Van Faye's top enforcers, a huge rhino with rough, grey skin and an eternal scowl. His horn is massive, and I hear it's electrified to stun his opponents. His body is all muscle, hard as boulders and sculpted like marble.

I've never met the rhino face to face, but I've heard legends about his brutality. Van Faye sends him to collect the big guys, fellow bosses and dangerous thugs. He tears through bodyguards like paper, his melees often the subject of Shogun lore. I heard that one time there was a guy, a gorilla, who owed Van Faye millions. Knowing he was in danger, he hired like fifteen guys to keep him safe. Different animals too. Lions, dogs, wolves, crocs, the slew of them. Sai took down every one of those fools, and by the time he was finished, the room was a bloody mess. Then he gored the gorilla on the spot, electrocuting him with his horn. Crazy.

I don't get it. Why did Van Faye send him after me? I'm not a big shot. I'm just a casino janitor. And I only owe the Van Faye family a few thousand creds. Sure, sending two punks like Chris and Tian I can understand, but the legendary Sai? It doesn't add up. I'm a small fry.

"Please, guys, it's just a measly amount I owe. No need to send in the big boys," I say to Sai and Tian, pleading my case. "Beat me up, teach me a lesson, whatever, but it doesn't have to come down to him."

The other thing about the legendary Sai is that he doesn't talk. He does every job with nothing but a cold expression on his face. I should've known begging would do little to help my cause.

"Sorry, cat, this is how it's going to be. It's a call directly from Van Faye," Tian says. "You're her property now."

Sai gets closer to me, his head nearly at my body. I scoot back, but I'm cornered against a building. I hear the sparks fly from his horn.

"Please, no!" I scream one last time.

It's useless. Sai bucks his head, and his horn makes direct contact. The electricity surges through my body and I convulse. My vision distorts and colors blend into one until there's nothing but darkness. I feel my limbs and head shaking uncontrollably, and my hearing fades out. That's it. I'm out cold.

Chapter 16 – Two Van Faye

Payday

<u>March 16, 3061 6:10 PM</u>

I'm in my office at the penthouse of Van Faye Tower, looking over the books for the day. Seems business is running smoothly as usual, but it's a rather slow day. That's when I get a buzz from my communicator.

I answer and the holoscreen pops up in front of me. It's Tian Lau, a cheetah, and one of the incompetent bozos I sent to accompany Sai on his retrieval mission to get that Adachi character. He's also with his frog pal, Chris Ren.

"Um, Ms. Van Faye," he squeaks out. He looks terrified to talk to me.

"Yes, Tian, right?" I say. "What is it?"

"Um, we completed the assignment you gave us."

"You mean the assignment I gave Sai. You and the frog are his subordinates. Speaking of which, where is he?"

"Um, who, Sai or Chris?"

"My rhino, you idiot."

He seems to be petrified of my impatient demands. When I sent Sai to retrieve Mr. Konoe, I contacted the local bosses where Adachi worked. I needed some local thugs to assist my rhino of carnage, and the boss recommended me these two. I didn't need them for much, only to show Sai where this cat would be.

"Oh yes, Sai is with me. Chris got injured by Konoe when we were pursuing him," Tian answers.

"Figures, can't send a frog or a cheetah to do a real animal's job," I say.

Tian looks slighted by my remark but restrained enough to know his place. I was a bit skeptical when I found out that the two goons I hired were cheetahs and frogs, but I suppose they got the job done.

"He got a little knocked out, but he's fine," Tian says about his partner.

"I don't care about your friend," I say sternly. "Where's Sai?"

Tian directs his communicator to Sai and the rhino acknowledges me with a nod.

"Do you want him to say anything?" Tian asks me.

"No, he doesn't talk, even to me," I say. "That's why I hired you two cronies, to be his mouthpiece. So the assignment has been completed, eh? Let me take a look at the cat who'll be my payday."

"Okay, but do you want me to show you on the communicator or bring him up?"

"Wait, what? Where are you?"

"Um, downstairs, on the ground floor of Van Faye Tower."

I look at him in disbelief.

"You idiot, why didn't you just come up?" I admonish him.

"Uh, I didn't know I was allowed to," Tian says meekly.

"You're with Sai and you have my captive. Of course you can come up. Quit wasting my time and hurry your ass to the penthouse, now!"

My short temper frightens him even more. He gets off the communicator and within a few minutes, the frog, Sai, and the cheetah appear before me. Sai drags a sack by his foot, which I assume is the package.

"How did it go?" I ask Sai.

"It went smooth," Tian says. "Ran into a little bit of—"

"If I want you to speak, I will ask you," I say harshly. "Sai?"

He nods and gives me a stonewall look.

"Good," I say. I turn back to Tian and his partner. "Is your frog friend going to be okay?"

They look surprised by my question. The frog hops forward.

"I'm, um, fine, ma'am," he says. "Just a bruise."

"Okay then," I respond. "Sai, present the package to me, please."

Sai stomps forward and presses a button on the sack. It unfurls, and from it rolls a tabby-looking cat, breathing and completely knocked out. I approach it and use my trunk to feel his body. He seems healthy and I can tell he's not a drug user. I chose my cards well. This is an excellent specimen, better than the others. The Collector will no doubt pay me a healthy sum for this creature.

"Poor Adachi Konoe," I say. "Only owes me a few thousand creds, but that's enough to justify his abduction. Did anyone see you take him?"

I'm looking at Sai, but I expect one of the two to answer since my agent is mute. They don't pick up the hint.

"Gentlemen, I'm talking to you," I say to them. "You are supposed to be my rhino's mouthpiece after all."

They look at each other, wondering who is going to speak. Tian steps up to the plate.

"I don't think so," Tian says. "We chased him through empty streets."

"What about the bear?" Chris asks.

"Bear?" I say.

"Oh yes, we collided with a bear during our pursuit of Adachi," Tian says.

"Morons. Konoe shouldn't have even escaped in the first place."

They lower their heads in shame. I roll my eyes. I didn't want there to be a big fuss in the Shogun rumor mill. The law and media have already pointed their fingers at me in this whole missing animal issue, and the last thing I need is some loudmouth witness testifying. I'm not afraid of the cops, but this operation has been getting a bit out of hand, and I need to tie loose ends before bigger eyes notice.

"That's a shame that happened. Now that bear must die," I say coldly. "I'll send a couple of my goons to track her down. Not you two, but someone who can actually do the job. That bear's head is on your conscience."

The two look at each other, mortified by my comments.

"No witnesses allowed," I respond calmly.

"So what happens now?" Chris asks.

"We have the package. Now it's time to deliver."

I pick up my tablet with my trunk and set it on my pricey vintage oakwood table. I use my trunk to navigate through it.

"I'm going to send my business partner, The Collector, a message saying I have what it wants," I say. "Then he or she will come here, check out Konoe, take what is theirs, give me my credits, and leave. It's as simple as that."

The message is complete and I send it out.

"That's it?" Chris asks.

"That's it," I say. "You two idiots will stick around until the transaction is done."

A beep emits from my tablet.

"Looks like I already have a response," I say. "The Collector is usually very prompt at getting back to me."

I read it and then look at my subordinates.

"The time is set," I say. "The Collector will be here at eight. Go get something to eat, relax, play in my casino, whatever. Just be back here at that time. You know what will happen if you're late."

"Yes, ma'am," the two say in unison. They turn around and leave in a hurry. Sai follows them. That was a productive meeting. I wish making credits was always this easy.

Chapter 17 - General Rox

Search

<u>March 13, 3061 6:39 PM</u>

"Systems are operational. The Alphas have arrived in Shogun," Mark Allen says. "Visual and audio feed continues to go live."

Allen has a nice setup. He's seated in front of a command console and is diligently studying the Alphas' statuses. Screens, holoscreens, buttons, and keys are all within his reach. I've put him in charge of controlling the Alphas during their visit to Shogun. Winde is here for observation, and I'm here to give direction.

He has a headband-like device on his head that shines mini holographic displays in front of his eyes. There are also some devices on his wrists with lighted wires coming out of them. He's fully integrated into his system, literally plugged in for this mission. It's an amusing sight, and his mechanisms require a lot of attention, but I suppose that's what it takes to get the job done. I'm confident in Allen's ability to micromanage.

The only devices I'm concerned about are the two giant holoscreens that show us the Alphas' visual feed. One is for Blackwolf, the other is for Silverwolf. It's like I'm looking through their eyes, as the visual feed is mounted right on their foreheads. We see what they see. Both wolves are also installed with audio feeds so we can hear what they hear. The pair responds to Mark Allen's physical controls and verbal commands. Winde and I also have access to give verbal commands, but I use Allen as a middleman to communicate with the Alphas.

Currently, the two are roaming the streets of Shogun after exiting a teleporter. I'm glad the teleportation didn't damage any of their tech. Allen assured it wouldn't. They arrived just after the sun set. The night sky is now out, but through the visual link, it's hard to tell with all these lights, lasers, and neon flashing above the Alphas. That's the Fan Zui Bin way of decorating their beloved city, with tacky spectacle.

The street isn't too crowded, but there are a few pedestrians walking along—rhinos, elephants, tigers. Fan Zui Bin always seems to attract the most exotic species around. I suppose the decadence, drugs, and debauchery appeal to the lowest of lives. As my wolves walk by, I see the obnoxiousness and filth that litter Shogun and all of FZB. In one corner, I see a rowdy bear and tiger getting in a drunken altercation. In another, I see a gorilla soliciting herself. Disgusting.

As the wolves move along, the bystanders appear increasingly shocked, surprised, and curious at the armored canines among them. Mark Allen's creations are certainly not the norm and create quite the spectacle. Still, those who pass by don't interfere or cause trouble because of the large Alliance logo that adorns both wolves. Regular citizens, even those in Fan Zui Bin, know if it's official Alliance business, then it's best to keep your mouth shut and pretend nothing out of the ordinary is happening.

Besides, delays must be avoided. The Alphas are on a tight schedule. They are on their way to rendezvous with my informant, Bo Harada. He's arranged a private meeting in some quaint, cow-specialized restaurant called

Kusa Eki. Harada has assured us that the place will be empty, that our business will be conducted privately.

Harada is a small-time boss that wants a way out of Shogun. He's grown tired of his life as a cog in the criminal machine. Unfortunately, it's not easy to walk away. Being part of the crime world is like being a slave, you're never truly free. Any decisions you make are influenced by the creatures you work for. Abandonment is frowned upon. The big bosses in Fan Zui Bin don't want their employees spouting off their mouths, giving vital information to rivals or outside enforcement, and in Shogun, the Van Faye family keeps tabs on everyone, no matter how big or small. That's why he reached out to the Alliance's informant services. He hopes that the information he gives will be his ticket out of here.

Normally, such a low-ranking figure wouldn't have the pull to be a good spy, but Harada is different. The cow is charismatic, knows his way around various species, and is smarter than your average thug. He doesn't have people working for him, but he gets a lot of favors because he is such a charming cow. I'm surprised he doesn't use his social skills to move up in the ranks, but it's difficult, and that's probably why he reached out to me in the first place. Climbing up the crime ladder is tough.

Thus, I'm the official who can pardon and help him flee from this crime-filled cesspool. With my approval, he'll go into witness protection. Any records of his life as Bo Harada will be gone, and he'll be living in a place across the sea. The Alliance will make sure his safety is well guarded.

As part of the contract, he needs to supply me with something that will aid me in this investigation of missing animals. I've given him a few months to work on gathering evidence, and our scheduled meeting is this evening. What a grand coincidence that we'll be testing out the Alphas' capabilities as well.

The directions to Kusa Eki have been programmed into their objectives, and I see through their eyes that the two are almost there. In the distance is a dingy-looking shack with a barely visible neon sign that reads "Kusa Eki." It's at the end of an alley, which is surprisingly dark and empty, much different compared to the busy street behind the wolves. The restaurant doesn't seem welcoming to potential customers. There is garbage littered on the side of the streets and the building is situated between two high-rise buildings. There's only two small windows and through them are barely shining lights. I guess this is what Harada has in mind when I told him to be discreet in his location.

The wolves walk past the alley and stop in front of the building. It takes a few seconds, but the automatic door slides open. The inside of the joint is just as unpleasant as the outside. The restaurant appears unclean, dusty, and dim. There are food scraps left over on one table and some unclean cups on another. The floor has cracks and dents, the ceiling is sprinkled with cobwebs. I'm guessing this establishment is used solely for criminal meet-ups, because business is far from booming. The restaurant is empty.

There are two cow workers and they react in a shocked manner at the sight of the armored wolves in front of them. They scramble toward the Alphas' direction, approaching cautiously and fearfully at the out-of-the-ordinary sight. One of them steps forward to welcome my wolves.

"Can... can I help you?" one of the cows asks.

A holoscreen pops up in front of them, projected from Blackwolf's armor. It shines brightly in the air, displaying the direct feed from Arkady. The cows see me hooked up to a communicator.

"This is General Rox of the United Species Alliance," I say as the cows watch the screen. "I am here to conduct official business. I am meeting my partner, Bo Harada. These two wolves will be representing me on my behalf."

"Don't worry, he's with me," a voice says from a shadowy corner of the room. The Alphas shine a light in that direction and from their feed, I see Bo Harada emerge from the darkness.

"Harada," I say through the communicator.

"Rox. Ladies, you are excused."

The two cows saunter away slowly and retreat to a back room. Mark Allen controls the wolves to walk to Harada. He looks closely at the creations, eyeing every crevice on them with intense curiosity. He even raises a hoof and taps Silverwolf on the side. They remain still. Harada then turns to the holoscreen to address me.

"Interesting new toys you have here Rox," he says. "I know you told me you'd be sending some representatives, but I didn't expect them to be machines. What are these things, drones?"

"Not quite," I reply. "They're somewhat organic, somewhat mechanic. Somewhat a drone, somewhat a cyborg. It's hard to categorize exactly. All you need to know is that it doesn't concern you. It's classified."

"Fair enough. Well, tell your cronies to disarm and take a seat. I can't be too careful. I also have some fresh grass on the table."

"They don't eat."

"I wasn't asking them to."

Allen puts the Alphas into standby mode. Some internal gears turn and they sit down and remain neutral while Harada and I continue our discussion.

"Happy?" I ask.

"No, just more secure," Harada says. "We may all be criminals in Fan Zui Bin, but deception is a trait within every species."

"Poetic. Now if we're done with the musings, I'd like to go over any new information you have on our missing animals. The situation isn't cataclysmic yet, but there have been several rumors about who the perpetrator is and how they are doing it."

"I'm surprised the Alliance cares about such savages."

"We don't, but there are rumors that Van Faye and a mysterious third party are involved, and the Alliance never likes to be in the dark when such power players are present. Van Faye may be an immoral schemer, but she's practically the leader of the crime underworld not only in Shogun, but in many parts of Fan Zui Bin. The Alliance needs to have such characters in check. Unfortunately, we have yet to gather any concrete evidence."

"Well, then I suppose it's your lucky day, dog."

Harada kneels below the table, procures a handled compcube between his teeth, and places it on the table.

"Start program," he says.

A holoscreen flickers in the air and video plays. There appears to be a cat cornered in some garbage filled alley while confronting a frog. The frog has the cat cornered with energy blasters adorned on his suit, but the cat swipes a decent sized rock and it flies into the frog, knocking him out.

"What is this?" I ask Harada.

"The evidence you are so desperate to obtain," Harada says. "This cat will be considered missing in a few days. This is his abduction."

"How did you get this footage?"

"The buildings of Shogun have many eyes. Some of those eyes belong to me. Even Van Faye doesn't know the pawns I hold in my pocket. All I needed was a perched up spy to record this action."

"And you didn't intervene? You let this cat get abducted?"

"Yes. If I didn't, the evidence you seek would be gone."

"What evidence? This indicates nothing. For all I know, I could be watching a simple mugging."

"Just watch."

The video still plays and a large crash is heard. Suddenly, a rhino appears. But this isn't any ordinary rhino. It's a very distinct one with a noticeable wardrobe and an electrified horn that sticks out like a sore thumb.

"Sai," I say to myself.

"I knew you would recognize him," Harada replies to my astonishment.

"Of course. Everyone knows Van Faye's top enforcer."

Sai shocks the cat and the poor sap becomes unconscious. A cheetah then appears and helps Sai put the cat into a bag while their frog friend recovers. They then walk away and the video stream ends.

"So is that enough evidence for you?" Harada asks.

"Enough to at least confront Van Faye," I respond. "I'll need the Alphas to download the clip into their systems."

"Of course. How will they do that?"

"Just watch."

A cable comes out from Silverwolf's armor and latches itself onto the compcube. Within seconds, my sentinel locates the video clip and downloads it to their database. It then uploads on our end in Arkady and a holoscreen pops up, playing the image on Allen's control console.

"Got it," I say.

"Excellent," Harada says. "What do you plan to do?"

"Now that we know for sure Van Faye is up to something, I can send my Alphas to meet with her at Van Faye Tower."

"Like she'll let you and your freak show in."

"The Alphas are Alliance property. Even in the heart of Fan Zui Bin, the Alliance holds the keys. She'll let me in. And once my wolves are there, I will present her what you showed me to get the clearer picture."

"Whatever you do, don't tie this back to me."

"Don't worry, Harada. You're safe."

"And what about my deal?"

"Ah, yes, the pardon. You'll be given full amnesty as long as this evidence turns out to be useful. The Alliance will help you procure a new identity and cut ties in Fan Zui Bin. It'll be as if you never existed."

Harada breathes a sigh of relief.

"Thank you," he says.

"Strange, though, with all the influence you have around here, I thought you'd have never wanted to leave," I say.

"I can't play this game forever, and it's not worth the price. Being a boss in Fan Zui Bin doesn't lead to a long career."

"Well, I'm glad at least someone realizes it in this damned place."

Mark Allen cancels the Alphas' standby mode. He's back in control and has both Blackwolf and Silverwolf turn around toward the exit. Our journey continues on to Van Faye Tower.

But I'm curious about one thing.

"You wouldn't happen to have any footage of Van Faye's partner, would you?" I ask Harada.

"You mean the black armored menace?" Harada says. "No. That thing is like a ghost. All I hear are rumors. There's nothing to concrete."

I'm disappointed by his response.

"That's too bad. Perhaps we'll run into it as this investigation continues. Good-bye, Harada," I say. "I hope you find what you're looking for."

"I hope you do to," he says as he watches my creations walk out the door.

Chapter 18 - Fenrir Snow

Fugitive

April 5, 3042 9:06 AM

News has just broken out about what really happened during Operation Halfkinds. I'm done with this Brotherhood. So many years wasted, so much pain I've endured. No more am I theirs to use. I am my own wolf. I'm not a pawn, a rook, a knight, or a bishop. I'm not even a piece on the board. The game that is this military life is over, the board is destroyed, and I have a wonderful halfkind to thank for it.

I see Iris as a loyal friend. At first, I took care of her out of guilt rather than concern. Yet I have become more intrigued by her with each passing day. Every minute I spend with her, I yearn for more. She has become the bright spot in a life that was once dreary, filled with death and destruction and a false sense of duty. My mind is clear from the ghosts that haunt it. Iris is my exorcist.

And in my time of need, she is the only one I can rely on. Not my wolf brothers, not even my family, only her.

I knew I couldn't pull off this charade much longer. It was only a matter of time until the Alliance figured out I was lying. The United Species Alliance Science Division was always skeptical of my report, and I suppose they had done enough forensic investigation to figure out that it was only Isaac Lawton that was burned in that house fire, that Iris Lawton was very much alive. The meant that everything I wrote in my report was completely falsified. Thus, I was branded an Alliance traitor.

I heard that Don Leons had been demoted to the bottom of the barrel. He was the one that accepted my reports without questioning me. I feel the Alliance doesn't see him as a turncoat or conspirator like me, rather just some lazy buffoon. Still, he was punished for his incompetence. He's lucky a demotion is all he got. If the Alliance had labeled him a traitor, the punishment might have been death.

I, on the other hand, don't deal directly with the Alliance. Unlike Leons, who falls directly under Alliance jurisdiction, I am bound by the laws of the Brotherhood. However, since I was a Brotherhood representative to an Alliance mission, I still betrayed the trust of my Brotherhood colleagues. It's not like I care. But they certainly do, not so much that a member of the Snow family betrayed them, but rather that a member of the Snow family betrayed them while Alliance eyes were watching.

The Alliance and Brotherhood have a lot of tension. While other species are usually quick to help out this united front of animals, wolves have been known to be more resistant and difficult to work with. My failure gives the Alliance another reason to distrust the Brotherhood, and that won't sit well with them. They'll be after me, so I must go before they can lay down the law with an energy blaster. I'm tough, but I can only fight my way out of so many situations. The only option is to hide.

I don't even have the time to say good-bye to my brothers and sister, Fang. I've been estranged from them for a while. They love the Brotherhood and have sensed my disdain ever since I returned from Operation

Halfkinds. They probably think something happened to me. I know they've been suspicious of my behavior, and I'm not sure how surprised they'll be once they're informed of what I did. I can't associate myself with family members that would support such a brutal, harsh government. My siblings will never side with me, so I can't trust them or tell them where I'm going. It's the way of life here. Family isn't first, your duty is.

It is a certainty that they'll turn me in. The only thing I can do is disappear from their lives forever and hope the Brotherhood doesn't get them involved, or even worse, go after them. I'm not sure how they'll react when the news comes out, but I hope that they understand why I left.

Thus, I'm alone as I continue my journey to Iris's cabin. I've informed her of my arrival and she'll have a nice place set up for me. I've stayed overnight the past few months to ensure Iris would be safe so some of my personal belongings are already there. Everything else I've insta-itemed in. This is a prolonged stay. I don't know how long I will be here, but it feels permanent. I don't intend to leave Iris.

They know she's alive. I must protect her. I haven't felt this way for a long time, but now I am finally proud of myself. I have something worthwhile to fight for, someone I believe in.

I was weary of the kind of responsibility this halfkind would demand. About a year ago, I thought our situation would only be temporary. Yet things have changed so quickly and now I find myself thinking the opposite. Iris has charmed me with her ways, and I feel she is a true friend. I never would have thought something like this was possible after all the death and destruction I've experienced, but she gives me hope. An accomplice, a confidant. No one else can hold this claim.

I arrive at the cabin, and she is there to greet me with a smile.

"You look tired," she says.

"The long trek will do that to you," I say sarcastically. She laughs it off.

"C'mon, I have some food prepared for you."

I'm not sure what's going to happen from here. I'm a little scared. I guess I'll just hang here for a while. Maybe things will die down and I can return to my normal life, maybe not. It doesn't matter. I'm with a friend now, and despite the odd circumstances, things look bright.

Chapter 19 – Ivy Lawton

Daughters

March 13, 3061 6:47 PM

It's been a lazy kind of week. Other than the awkward confrontation I had with Bastion, I haven't done much. That was a couple days ago, and since then I've been lounging about at home, our little underground pod that hugs the ocean coast. I haven't done any training, haven't studied. Hell, I've barely stepped outside. It's just been the streams and me. Yeah, I know, it screams excitement.

I guess I've had a lot to think about. The conversation dad and I had was far from pleasant. Why'd he have to bring up Aunt Lucy? Because she contacted him? Because she asked him about me? Because he's worried that she's back in my life? It's none of his business. He's not really even a father to me anymore.

The only reason we don't leave is because we're afraid of him. Mom doesn't want to admit it. Hell, neither do I. We're afraid of him because he's so fanatically afraid for us. And it is this fanaticism that will cause him to go over the edge. He'll do anything to keep us within his grasp.

He seems weak and broken at times, but I know what he is physically capable of. Mom told me about how he kidnapped her a long time ago, how he was able to track her down to the middle of nowhere within the "ever dangerous to outsiders" territory of the Wolf's Den. Even as we train, he's still in peak physical shape. If he found a reason to, he'd go back to his determined self and follow us to the ends of the Earth.

I suppose in his mind, the only creature who would tempt us to leave is Aunt Lucy. It's like the real person he's afraid of is her. She's not dangerous, not to us. He thinks she'll bring trouble. Aunt Lucy is the last creature he should be worried about, trust me.

And what was his purpose anyway? Why does he care? Because he's a compassionate father? That he's concerned for my well-being? Psht, my ass. If anything, it's a control thing. He doesn't want her near me. He thinks she's a bad influence. He's dumb. I mean, she's probably one of the smartest creatures on this planet and was an excellent teacher. Why would he want to deny me the gifts of her knowledge? Doesn't he want me to be smart like her?

It's a personal thing. He hates Aunt Lucy and doesn't want her near me because he knows our bond. She's almost like my other mother, and I'm sure dad just wants to rub it in her face that she can't go near us. That's why he keeps us here, like prisoners. He says we're sheltered to hide from threats, but I think his biggest threat is Aunt Lucy.

This is why I hate him so much. He can't let go, and he never will. When I think about what I'll be doing in twenty years, I wonder if I'll still be stuck on this island. I hope not, but with my father around, there's no telling. I feel I have nowhere to run, and I wonder what kind of future will that be? I can only imagine what it's like for mom. She's spent the majority of her life being forced to stay somewhere by someone else. First it was her mom, and now it's Bastion. She's older now, and I know eventually she's going to act. She's going to do something that will set her free. And I'll be there right beside her.

She won't do it alone. I'll do what I can to get us out of here, away from him. Bastion, dad, can try all he wants to find out the truth, but I have my secrets hidden. I'll be damned if he finds out and puts a stop to it all.

But there's been so much to think about lately, and I need some time to focus on something else. Mom, dad, Lucy, all the drama, my future plans—it's overwhelming. I need some me time.

Luckily, our pad provides enough distraction for me to drown my thoughts. The streams and videos help me relax. I'm really into superheroes, about animals with special powers. Some of the abilities the writers imagine are so creative. Some can walk through walls, others can shoot lasers from their eyes. There are even stories about girls who open portals to other worlds. It's so interesting!

Of course it's fiction, but then again, anything is possible. My mom has powers, yet they aren't exactly superhuman. I mean, precognition isn't normal, but she can't fly, and she's not indestructible, but with the way technology is progressing, back to like how it was before the Event, anything is possible.

Other than the streams, this pad has everything I really need thanks to the good old insta-item. Food, drinks, electronics, the works. Mom mentioned that when she lived with her wolf friend, Fenrir Snow, it was a similar setup. Except now things are much more advanced. I mean, mom only had a dinky cabin in the woods. On this island, we have a whole backup facility that some scientist built, just for us. It's pretty sweet. The guy spared no expense when it came to creating this place.

All the pods were pretty advanced back in the day and have furnishings that were ahead of their time. Also, Aunt Lucy spent a great deal of effort upgrading things to make sure they were up to par. Now that she's gone, it's a bit less advanced than before, but still, it's holding up against time quite well.

Other than the insta-item, Aunt Lucy installed several state-of-the-art data and computing centers in each pod, ours included, for us to use in a variety of ways. I have entertainment, education, news, pretty much any information I want all at the touch of some holoscreens. It's the only way I can keep busy on this island. Everything is powered by generators, and I'm guessing this place is self-sustaining, enough to last a lifetime. We haven't encountered any problems at all. Lights, water, gas, everything works to a tee. I feel one day we'll have to figure out maintenance, but for the moment, I'm not worried.

There's also that fantastic view of the ocean from our looking glass window. Our lights compliment it quite well, and at night it's a sight to behold. The other pods are similar to our pods in layout and decoration. There's a lot of space because everything is built underground, yet there's a touch of class to it. The rooms were carved from the ground, giving the walls a cave-like feel, but it's smooth and you can tell it was built with a lot of care. I like the way our pod is structured. Lionel Changer, he had style.

And of course, mom has spent a great deal of time furnishing our home to her tastes. It's ever changing, but there's nothing an industrial insta-item won't fix. It's funny how my parents react to him. Bastion seems to love him, but mom says he was crazy. Aunt Lucy seems to speak fondly of him, but it seems it's a pure scientific admiration.

I never met the guy, but I just know we have his creds. It's pretty sweet. We probably never have worry about it again.

The setup we have here is fantastic, and I like living with mom. She's a great mother, and I'd do anything for her. She has my best interests in mind and truly cares for me, which is more than I can say for Bastion. Sometimes I feel my relationship with my father isn't really that of a father and daughter. He's just a trainer, that's all. It's almost like I was raised by a single mother.

There are days when I feel bad because I think this. He is my dad, after all, but those days seem to occur less the more time passes by. I can't forgive him for all he's done to us. I'm not sure if he was always like this or what prompted mom to have me with him. Maybe he was kinder in a past life, maybe he does care but doesn't know how to express it. In either case, the being he is now isn't one I can call my father.

Oh how the times have changed...

Suddenly, my thoughts break. The door opens from above, and I see someone coming down.

"Hi, mom," I say.

She's wearing a sunhat and has on a nice spring dress. It's rather hot here, and she looks a little exhausted. She must have been out in the heat all day because this is the first time I've seen her since yesterday morning.

"Evening, Ivy," she says with a curious look. "How are you doing this fine night?"

"I'm okay."

She walks toward the kitchen area, lugging a large bag on her shoulder. It appears to be heavy and full, but she has no problem hoisting it on the counter. Hell, she doesn't even break a sweat. It's like a bag of feathers to her. After all these years, she's still pretty strong. Aunt Lucy's implants will do that to you.

"What's in the bag?" I ask.

"Oh, some fruits and stuff I collected around the island," she responds. "Also, my garden is growing quite nicely, so I picked up some vegetables. I might cook something later this week. Speaking of which, have you eaten yet?"

"Yes," I say. "I just warmed up some leftovers."

"I see," she says. "That's good. I got hungry on the way here and ate some of my bounty, so I'm not that hungry either. What did you do today?"

"I stayed in."

She looks at me with a smirk.

"That's too bad," she says. "It's a nice day outside. You should've gotten some fresh air. It's not good to stay inside all the time, and from what I noticed, that's all you've been doing for the past few days."

I roll my eyes a little and smile back at her.

"I guess mother knows best," I say.

"Damn straight," she smiles back.

"By the way, where were you last night? I didn't see you this morning."

"Oh, I kind of lost track of time gathering. When I was halfway through with my errands, it was already getting dark out and I was on the other side of the island. I didn't want to have to journey all the way back in the dark, so I stayed in one of the pods nearby. It was one of Lucy's old research centers. There was a bed and furnishings, so I crashed there. Sorry if I worried you."

"I was worried, but only a little. I know you can take care of yourself."

Mom shrugs at my comment.

"Not like there's anything dangerous up there," she says nonchalantly. "It feels like I haven't seen you in a while. I don't even know what you've been doing in the past week. I think you trained with him at some point, right?"

"Yes," I answer tersely. She doesn't like talking about dad and usually asks these questions as a pleasantry.

"That's good. I hate him, but he's an excellent trainer."

Talking to mom about dad is kind of awkward considering the circumstances. She has her opinion of him and that's that. I may disagree with her, but I support my mom's choices. When the choice comes down to him or her, I'll choose her one hundred percent of the time. No doubt about it.

"Is that the only time you saw him this week?" she asks. I'm a bit surprised because the conversation would normally have ended at this point.

I think about our little confrontation on the cliffs and my dad's inquiry about Aunt Lucy. I decide not to tell mom about it because it'll only get her riled up. She might do something rash. It's totally out of her character, but it's gotten to that boiling point where even the smallest thing might cause her to go off.

"No, it was only training. That's all," I lie.

She doesn't respond right away. Instead, she eyes me like an interrogator. She must know something is up.

"I see," she says. "That's good, I wouldn't want you spending time with him if it's not necessary. Hopefully soon, you won't have to spend time with him at all."

To my surprise, that's all she says. She doesn't call me out on my bullshit even though we both know I'm not being completely truthful. I get off my seat, walk to her, and give her a heartfelt hug.

"Remember, mom, I love you and I'm with you all the way," I say.

She seems a little surprised with the sudden emotional outpour, but receives it warmly. We release our embrace and she looks at me with a mother's affirmation.

"I know you are, Ivy," she says. "I know."

"So did you want to do something this evening?" I ask. "We can stay in, make some snacks. I'm pretty much free."

"Actually, I'm going to do some more collecting, so I'll be out this evening as well," she says. I flash a brief but disappointed look. Immediately, I sense the guilt that shows on her face. "I'm sorry, Ivy."

I quickly change my demeanor to look happier.

"Don't worry," I say. "It's nothing. I mean, we have all the time in the world, and I know you enjoy your private time. I'm not a baby. I'll be fine."

"Well, you're always going to be my baby," she says. I give her a dogged look.

"Geez, mom, that's so corny," I say.

"Well, it's true!" she laughs. "Anyway, since I won't be around, what will you be doing, my dear?"

"I'm not completely sure yet," I say.

"Well, like I said, it's a nice day out. Should be a nice night too. Get some fresh air. Going outside might do you some good. It seems like you've had a lot on your mind lately."

I hesitate to answer.

"How'd you know?" I ask.

"A mother always knows," she says.

I look at her, wanting to tell her everything on my mind. What dad and I really talked about, the mention of

Lucy, the confusion and anger I feel, all of it. But I cannot. She's my mother, my best friend, and I love her, but sometimes there are some things you can't express no matter how badly you want to.

"Yeah, maybe I will go out," I say.

"That's my girl," she says. "Well, I better head out before it's too late. You sure you're going to be okay?"

"Yes, yes, no problem."

She gathers her gear and walks toward the elevator that leads to the surface. Before she steps on the platform, she stops in her tracks and turns around.

"Shoot, forgot my canister of water," she says. "Do you think you can pass it to me? It's on the counter."

"Sure," I say.

I look to the left and see it, a shiny metal bottle. I raise my hands, palms outstretched in the canister's direction, and concentrate. It rumbles a little, and as I focus harder, it starts to levitate a few inches from the counter. I apply even more of my mind, and it's now floating completely in the air, hovering its way to my mom. She reaches out her hands and grabs it.

"Thanks, Ivy," she says. "You're getting better at this."

"Yeah, but it's just coins and cups," I shrug. "Not like I can lift anything heavy. I thought having telekinesis would be more... glamorous."

"Practice, my dear, practice. You never know, maybe one day you'll lift mountains."

"Nice one. I guess I can dream."

We both chuckle as my mom starts going up on the elevator. Our conversation was brief, but it was enough to put my mind at ease for a few seconds. I spent the last two days conflicted over my thoughts, my feelings. That conversation with Bastion on the cliffs sparked it. I lounged about, wasting my time to look for a distraction. I found nothing, but I realize I was looking in the wrong place. My mom was the only distraction I needed.

"Bye, mom, be safe," I say as I see her off.

"You too, my princess," she says.

Chapter 20 – Iris Lawton

Banished

October 10, 3052 4:40 PM

It's late in the afternoon, the sun is about to go down, and Bastion is hot tempered. We're in Lucy's pod, smack in the middle of her lab. The mood is tense as Bastion starts his tirade against my friend. Lucy has an emotionless, almost condescending look on her face. I can't tell if she's scared or doesn't care about what he has to say, but I think it's the latter.

I've seen this argument play over several times in my visions, yet I cannot do anything to prevent it. It's fate.

I'm torn. This feud has been brewing for quite some time. Bastion has grown paranoid, distrusting Lucy's every action. I see his reasoning. He's afraid Lucy will endanger us all. Yet Lucy is a dear friend. We've been on this island for almost ten years, and Lucy and I are closer than ever. I knew about what she was doing before Bastion found out, and I kept it a secret. Perhaps that is my mistake, perhaps I should have notified him. He is the father to my child, after all, and he deserves to know these things.

To be honest though, I've grown weary of dealing with him. He loves me, this I know, but his love borderlines obsession. He has become fearful of everything, his reason always being for the sake of our safety. I should've seen the signs years ago. He holds us tightly, has become more protective than he should. We aren't allowed to go out unless he thinks it's safe. From what? It's only us on this island. And it's become such a hassle to meet up with Lucy. There are days when I get angry. Who is he to command me like a slave, to watch me like a prisoner?

It's my fault though. I give in to these demands. I have to. He is my daughter's father, and we need to raise her in a happy family. Sacrifices have to be made, not for him, but for her. She's only six, a young child. Her life is already complicated enough. Why make matters worse with a broken home?

And I'm also a little afraid of Bastion. When he's like this, in his protective mode, he only sees his answer. Any other way of doing things causes him to lash out, to belittle me, to make me feel that I don't know how dangerous this world is. I feel like I have no one to stand up for me, and I'm scared of invoking his wrath. He claims to keep me safe, but he is overzealous about it. Hell, when he heard about what Lucy's been up to, he came charging with a blaster in hand. Why? What purpose does a gun serve in a situation like this?

I am here, stuck between two foes. One is my confidant, the other is my partner. When we arrived on this island, I thought I wouldn't have defended either. But now I find myself endeared to these relationships.

"How could you do this?!" Bastion screams. "You exposed my daughter to this sullied world you're a part of. I saw what she brought home. Genetic experimentation? I don't want her to be like you. I don't want this family to be involved with any of that anymore. Time has passed. Lionel is dead. I respect him, always will, but priorities change, and my daughter will not have her life endangered because of the things you taught her. I want her to live a simple life, away from this mess!"

"Influenced nothing," Lucy responds. "Ivy shows interest in work. Will not deny her what she desires."

"It's not up to you. It's not up to her. It's up to me! I know what is good for her, and this isn't it."

Bastion throws in front of Lucy the rat-lizard hybrid, the one that my daughter presented to him a few days ago. It's dead now. Bastion was horrified when he saw what it was and ended its life with a simple twist of the head. Ivy bawled her eyes out, confused by the dark actions brought upon her proud achievement.

Lucy looks at the creature without reaction.

"Not approve of daughter's creation?" Lucy asks disdainfully.

"Approve? Are you serious? How dare you say those words," Bastions says. "You expose her to this and now you taunt me? I ought to shoot you right here."

"Bastion, don't!" I yell.

"Quiet, Iris! This is between me and the chimp," he retorts.

Lucy picks up the creature, observing the damage that Bastion has done to it. She eyes it carefully and then places it down gently on a nearby table.

"Curious that hybrid creation causes such anger," Lucy says. "Sense something else. Sense jealousy."

"Jealousy?" Bastion asks in a disgusted manner.

"Yes. Relationship between Ivy and self strong. Unlike yours. Fail to connect with daughter. Sees how daughter adores self, unlike you. Is jealous because of this. Wishes to be me."

The words pierce Bastion's fiery soul like a dagger. I can see him getting more enraged by the seconds.

"Shut up, Lucy!" he screams. "You know nothing about relationships!"

"True lacks level of emotional sophistication ," Lucy says. "But quite obvious observations are correct."

Lucy is right. Every evening when Ivy comes home and talks about her admiration for Lucy, I see the envy flash across Bastion's face. He did his best to hide it in front of his daughter, but it is painfully obvious that he doesn't understand what she sees in my dear friend. He didn't understand why he isn't the one that is admired. Ivy's ignorance to his feelings shatters his confidence. I suppose it's hard, being a father to a little girl who loves someone else more than him.

But he refuses to show weakness to Lucy. He'll never admit these feelings to her face.

"No, that's not the case at all," Bastion says. "I'm furious because I found something else about her, something that shocked me, something that I suspect you had a hand in. And if you did, so help me, I will shoot you in the heart."

"Referring to what?" Lucy asks.

"A few days ago, Ivy came home from one of your teaching sessions. She was energetic and excited, must've been a very engaging time. I prepared her afternoon snack, some sliced mangos grown from the island. And that's when I saw her do something incredible. Do you know what I saw?"

Bastion's voice is raised. I look at him and don't utter a word.

"She floated one of those mango slices in the air and into her hand. She didn't use any device or technology. She simply looked and pointed, and there it was, levitated in front of me. She did it with her mind."

Lucy remains stoic.

"Not surprising," she says. "Mother has powers. Always stated telekinesis not out of picture."

"So you knew, didn't you?!" he screams.

Lucy looks at him, at first weary to respond. But then her eyes narrow, and in an almost mocking tone, she dryly responds, "Yes."

Bastion is reaching his boiling point. He raises his arm and points his gun at Lucy. She remains apathetic and simply looks on. But I am not so passive.

"Bastion, no!" I yell.

"Like I said, stay out of this, Iris!" he retorts.

"But Bastion…"

He then turns in my direction and gazes at my eyes. He looks at my face, my mouth trembling, my eyes watery, ready to release a tear. My whole body is shivering, scared of what he might do. His face then becomes bewildered. He has successfully read what my mouth refuses to communicate.

"You knew, didn't you?" he says with anguish in his voice.

I am unable to speak and can only nod. His gun lowers and his body slumps down in a shell-shocked daze. Both of us are frozen by our emotions. However, Lucy is not.

"Should be proud," Lucy says. "Daughter has impressive power."

Bastion sharply raises his gun once more, this time aimed at Lucy's head. His hand shakes and his fist clenches. He looks livid and uses all his restraint to keep himself from firing the weapon.

"I don't even want you mentioning her in my presence," he says.

"Why?" Lucy asks inquisitively.

"Because I know you. Ivy is my daughter, but to you, she's a scientific curiosity, another part of your plan. You'll take her in, use her, exploit her, and dissect her in order to figure her out, like a damn experiment. She isn't your pet project to play with. She is my blood, and I swear you will leave her alone."

Lucy looks surprisingly sullen by the accusation. She looks at me, not Bastion, and her shoulders slump in disappointment.

"Why such conclusion?" she asks.

"Because I've seen it before, when you found out about her," Bastion says, pointing at me. "When Iris was first born, you and Lionel wanted to prod and poke her, to figure out what made her tick. She didn't have thoughts and feelings. All you two saw was her power. That's why Maya Lawton left, because you were planning to endanger her child. I'll be damned if that happens again."

"Long time ago," Lucy rebuts in a sad tone. "Have grown close to these hybrids. Wish to continue relationships with them. Time passes, emotions, feelings change."

"They don't. I'll always believe you'll be the same."

"You agree?"

Lucy addresses me and I'm put in the spotlight. I look at Bastion and then at Lucy. Both are hanging on my response. The seconds seem like an eternity and I hesitate to answer.

"I don't," I say to Lucy tearfully. "I like having you around."

Bastion looks at me spitefully. I've betrayed him.

"It doesn't matter what Iris thinks," he says. "I don't want you near any of us."

Lucy takes some time to look at her surroundings and think about the situation. After a few moments of silence, chin rubbing, and awkward stares, she responds, "Then will leave this island. Anticipated confrontation, made arrangements elsewhere. Planning to relocate later. This expedites plans."

Both of us, even Bastion, are a bit shocked at her response. My eyes start to flood with tears. I don't want my friend to go. We had a rocky start, but these ten years with her have been great. Bastion, on the other hand, is relieved with her answer. He smirks and sneers while I secretly want to tear off his head. But I do not speak.

"Good," Bastion says. "By the end of this week, I don't want to see your sorry face anywhere on this island."

Lucy simply scoffs at his remark, letting out a short sneer.

"Feeling mutual," she says directly to Bastion. She then turns her attention to me. "Apologize Iris. Nothing left on island for me. Will meet in a few days to say good-bye."

Before I can even reply, Bastion takes my hand and makes his way to the exit.

"Let's go, Iris," he says. "Let the chimp collect her things so we can be rid of her forever."

He drags me by the arm, heading for the exit, and I am too stunned at the sudden turn of events to resist. When we reach the surface, Bastion still has his hand grasped on my wrist. That's when I jerk it away.

"Why did you let this happen?" I scream at him.

"Me let this happen?" he says in a dumbfounded manner. "I'm trying to protect my family from that monster. You want to let her in. This is my fault?"

"She's not going to hurt us!"

"Yes, she is. I've known her longer than you. She schemes and plots, has visions of grandeur. She has no emotions. She only cares about her study and progress. We are simply pawns to her."

"No, you're wrong!"

"Am I? She keeps secrets about Ivy from us. The rat-lizard hybrid she had Ivy create, her telekinesis. She's sneaky, and I'm done with it."

"She's only like that with you because you're so close-minded."

Bastion is taken aback by my comment. He's offended that I give him such characterizations.

"Looks like she's gotten to you too," he says. "That's why both of you kept Ivy's telekinesis from me."

I'm a bit ashamed that I didn't tell Bastion. I should've, but he would have freaked out. He's certainly validating my suspicions right now.

"How could I not see that Ivy has these powers?" Bastion says to himself. "Are things between her and me already that distant? It only makes sense she has some kind of mental abilities. You are her mother, after all."

This time he looks disappointed, not only in the situation, but himself. His face becomes saddened and his ears lower.

"I can understand why Lucy kept it secret," he says. "But why you, Iris? We're in this together. Why'd you have to hide this revelation from me?"

"Because you don't need to know everything," I say as my voice trembles. "You're a control freak. You dictate my schedule, what I should do with Ivy, when I should meet with Lucy, when I can go out at night, everything! You never let up. You treat me, even Ivy, like we're your prisoners. If you knew about Ivy's powers, you'd go ballistic. And now Lucy's gone because of you! My only friend!"

"But Lucy is putting Ivy's life in danger. How could you call her a friend?"

"Because she is! We survived HORUS together! She fixed my hand. If it wasn't for her help, Ivy would have never been born. She's one of us. I'm wrong. She's not a friend, she's family. I don't turn my back on family."

Bastion doesn't back down.

"Well, she's not family to me," he says. "And I disagree. She's not one of us. Lucy has her own goals, her own ambitions that jeopardize all of us. Family doesn't do that to each other. A real family keeps each other safe. That's my job."

"But... but..."

"But what?"

"But I don't want your protection!" I blurt out. "You say your only purpose in life is to shield Ivy and me from our enemies, from Alliance soldiers. But in the process, you're suffocating me! I... I want to leave someday. I can't be confined to this island all my life. I need some freedom."

"You want to leave?"

Bastion looks heartbroken and confused by my statements. I've stabbed his heart with a dagger and turned the blade.

"Well... I..." It's hard for me to stay assertive. My concentration becomes frazzled and I'm at a loss for words. But that's when Bastion speaks for me.

"You can't leave," he says as the scorn shows on his face. "I won't let you."

"What?" I say, completely flabbergasted.

"You... you don't know what it's like out there, how dangerous the world is."

"Don't give me that. All my life I've heard that. From my mother and now from you. You can't tell me what's out there. I know firsthand. Don't lecture me like a child. I want to start over, live a new life."

Bastion's contempt grows stronger as my words continue to strike at his heart.

"Not if it's without me," he says. "You need me, Iris. You may not think it, you may believe you can handle the world on your own, but you can't. I have the skills, the power, to keep you from harm, whether you like it or not. You may disagree, but I'm doing the right thing."

I step closer to him, boldly looking at him face to face to show I'm not scared.

"What if I just leave in the middle of the night? What if I take Ivy with me?" I say.

"Then... then I'll find you and I'll bring you back," he threatens. "I've done it before. I tracked you all the way down to the middle of nowhere in the Wolf's Den. I'll do it again."

At first, I'm furious. I want to stay defiant and keep my ground. But then thoughts rush through my head and I realize he's serious. Bastion is one of the most skilled, stealthy beings I know. When he wants to do something, he'll do it. If I couldn't even hide from him when Fenrir did everything he could to make me non-existent, how could I hide from him now? He'll follow me wherever I go.

I slump down, defeated by the argument.

"You can't do this," I say softly. "I can't stay here forever."

"I don't want you to feel like you're a prisoner," Bastion says. "I love you. I loved you the minute I laid eyes on you. I would never do anything to hurt you. I'm more worried about the others who want to. Lucy, the Alliance, they're all dangerous. I'll do whatever I can to make sure they don't touch you."

"No."

My eyes become watery, and I morph into a crying mess. My head is hunched forward, and I sit on my knees as I let my emotions overtake me. How did things ever get to this point? I let the tensions of this island play out while I watched like a bystander. I should've taken hold of the situation, should've guided my own destiny instead of letting others do so. I should've been strong.

Bastion reaches down and offers me his hand.

"Don't cry, Iris," he says. "I'm here."

I look up and am tempted to take his offer. But no, this is when I start to take control. I swat it away and start running.

Behind me, I hear Bastion telling me to come back, but I ignore him. He won't tell me what to do anymore. My sorrow becomes anger, and I'm fueled with a motivation that I've never felt. It's time for things to change. It may take one year, it may take ten, but one day I will leave this place. One day I will discover a way to remove myself from the bonds that hold me down. One day I will be free.

That I promise the world.

Chapter 21 – Adachi Konoe

Awake

March 13, 3061 7:51 PM

I hear murmuring in the background. It's muffled, hard to make out. I'm unsure if it's real or my imagination. They sound faint, then loud, switching volume in an unsteady manner. At first, the words are mumbles, but soon things start making sense. I try to focus, but it's difficult. My mind isn't quite all there. It takes a lot of effort just to concentrate on the sound, the voices. As the seconds pass, my consciousness becomes clearer, and I'm able to listen in on the conversation.

"The Collector is coming soon," one voice says. It sounds feminine. "Make sure the package is ready."

"Yes… we'll check right now," another voice says.

Collector? Package? What does that mean? Come to think of it, where am I? I'm so dazed and confused. Everything is pitch black. Must be a side effect of my hazy consciousness. Wait a second, why was my consciousness hazy in the first place? And why does it feel like I can't move, like I'm trapped in something?

That's because I am! Something malleable yet constricting wraps around my body. I struggle furiously to be free, but the darkness persists. I'm stuck in whatever this is. It feels like a bag. I thrash in an effort to pry myself free, but it is all in vain. I'm still trapped without any idea of my location or how I got here. Panic overtakes me, and my emotions run wild.

"Help!" I scream as I continue my attempts to claw myself out. "Somebody, I think I was knocked out!"

The two bodies become aware of my pleas, and I hear their murmuring in response to my petition.

"I thought he was unconscious," the female-sounding one says sternly.

"He's supposed to be," another murmurs in a trembling tone.

"Well, he isn't, you ingrate. You fucked this up!"

"I'm... we're sorry."

"Don't sorry me! Sorry doesn't get the job done. The Collector's directions are very specific. The package is supposed to be unconscious when it comes time for collection, and The Collector will be here any minute. You better pray this doesn't cost me any creds, or so help me, I'll have Sai gore you in the throat."

"Um... um... I'm sorry Ms. Van Faye. Is there anything I can do to fix it?"

"Yeah, get the job done, now!"

Van Faye? *The* Van Faye? My memory kicks in and I start to remember everything that happened. Chris and Tian confronting me, the chase through the streets, the fall into the alley, and Sai... Shit, I was knocked out thanks to Sai's electrical horn. And I'm guessing I was thrown in some bag and dragged to be presented to Two Van Faye. Trapped in a sack like a pirate's bounty, like a lowlife. Pitiful.

But I'm not here for long. The bag opens and I'm blinded as the lights rush in. My eyes have no time to adjust, and all I can see are shadowy figures as I squint through the brightness. Things happen quickly.
Someone pulls me from the sack with their teeth. It's a light tug but strong enough to drag me out. As soon as I'm out of the bag, I feel something sticky graze all four

of my legs. I try to struggle to flee, but I'm too discombobulated to make a successful attempt. The sticky feeling changes to something warm yet hard, wrapping itself around all four legs. Before I can even attempt to escape again, the object constricts, and in an instant, I find myself bound by all four legs, helplessly lying on the floor while trying to recover from the confusion.

"So you're the breed that The Collector is so interested in," Van Faye says to me.

I don't respond to her comment right away. Instead, I look down at my paws to see what has gotten me in such a tight bind. Energy cuffs, great. I continue to squirm in the off chance that my efforts will release me. They do not. Exasperated and out of energy, I stop and take a look around the room. I see the cheetah and his punk ass frog buddy looking at me with stupid smirks on their faces. He must've pulled me out of the bag while the amphibian applied the cuffs. That sticky sensation must've been Chris's tongue. Gross.

I turn my head in the other direction to figure out where I am. It's fancy looking here and really huge. There's some swanky furniture scattered about and a beautiful desk the size of a whale. The room is well lit. I must be in a penthouse of some sort. I continue to scope, and that's when I see Sai, still scary as hell, observing my vulnerable position. He's unresponsive in his facial expressions. And then I look above and see the leader of this crew, practically the leader of Shogun, Two Van Faye.

I'm actually slightly star-struck. She's not as scary as the rumors led me to believe. She's garbed in gaudy jewelry that adorns her body, even her trunk and floppy ears, and is dressed in some nice, silk-looking clothes.

Her mannerisms exude confidence. There's no doubt in my mind this is indeed the legend herself. For many years, I've had aspirations of meeting the most powerful players in Shogun face to face, and now it seems my dreams are coming true.

Yet I become sober at the realization that this is no dream, this is a nightmare. Two Van Faye doesn't meet a schmo like me for no reason. There's always one, and I'm willing to wager that my reason for being here isn't good. I know my life is danger and I'm terrified because I can do nothing about it. Van Faye's presence means only one thing looms around the corner: death.

"Why did you take me?" I groggily ask her. She seems a bit surprised by my question.

"So you have enough bravery to talk to the Elephant Queen of Crime. I commend you for that," she says snidely. "Yes, why are you here? I don't think I need to answer that question. I believe you know the reason."

"Creds."

"Looks like I was right."

My attention moves away from her and back to my surroundings. My eyes fixate on the three thugs that took me. Each is armed to the core.

"But I only owe you a few thousand," I say. "That's like a grain of rice in your bank account. You sent three of your underlings for that? I've heard stories, and I know you've sent a lot less for a lot more."

"Perhaps, but let's just say you are more valuable in the eyes of someone else," Van Faye says.

"So the rumors are true, then. You're involved with the disappearing animals."

"Partially, but I have a business partner who is far more interested in you than I am."

"But why? I'm nothing, a nobody, a faceless cat among the masses."

"A nobody? You know you don't believe that. I did my research before I sent my goons after you. I know your background, what you're up to. And I think I have a good idea what kind of character you are."

She lowers her head, inching closer to me, and our eyes meet.

"You're right," she continues. "You are a nobody. You came from a nobody town, live in a nobody lot in Shogun, and work as a nobody janitor in one of my casinos. You build a reputation to mask what you are. It's nothing but a web of lies with you. You pretend you're a big shot, yet here you are, cowering in fear in front of a real boss. You wish you were me. I have many creatures in my employ just like you. They brag and congratulate themselves because they think they're gods simply since they fall under my line. But I loathe these types. Your kind, the scheming bottom feeders, are a dishonest, vermin group that have nothing to back up your bravado. Your kind weakens my fair city with your false advertising."

She uses her trunk to prod me.

"But at the same time, I like having your kind around because I'm the one who can crumble the tower of glass you've built with your arrogance," she says. "When I make fools like you cower in fear, it fills me with delight. It shows this city, this city of nobodies, that I have complete power only because I decide when to make the nobodies somebodies, because you, all of you, answer to me. Would you say this is a fair assessment?"

As much as I deny it, I'm exactly what she describes.

No, I can't let her beat me. I'm not some peon for Van Faye to play with. I'm important. I have big plans.

She doesn't know me. She doesn't know what the hell she's talking about. There's a difference between arrogance and confidence. Even as I lie tied up in a helpless situation, I know I'll find a way out of this because I'm a winner, not a loser. I owe the Van Faye family a debt, but I won't pay with my pride.

"Fuck you, you hag," I yell. "You don't own me. Just because I live in this shitty city doesn't make you my master."

She swiftly wraps her trunk around my neck and lifts me and chokes me violently. She thrusts her trunk forward, and my back slams against the wall, hard. She does it once more, and I'm almost knocked out. She then raises me high in the air and places me at her eye level.

"You're wrong again," she says. "I do own you, like I own everyone else in this city. And right now, you are my property to sell."

Suddenly a knock comes from the front door. Van Faye drops me to the ground and shifts her attention. She appears startled by the interruption. She looks at her cronies, who, other than Sai, look just as flabbergasted.

"I wasn't expecting a guest without security notifying me," Van Faye says. "Tian, go check it out."

The cheetah looks nervous. "Me?"

"Do I have to repeat myself?"

"Um, no. Sorry."

He walks to the door and presses a button to open it. I can't see who it is because Van Faye and her thugs obscure my view, but Van Faye knows.

"How did you get past my security?" she asks the unexpected guest.

"I have my ways," the entity says as it moves forward.

Its voice is steely, cold, and impersonal. It's not natural, and I'm willing to guess it's the work of a voice box. As the view clears and I get a better look at this "Collector" my suspicions are confirmed. The creature is bi-pedal, cloaked and hooded, wearing all black, except for the white, curved engravings on its mask. They look like wild vines on a wall. The creature isn't too tall, its frame slender yet sturdy.

The being doesn't look like much. The creature lacks the imposing physicality of Sai or Van Faye. But the aura it gives off is quite intimidating. I've only had a small glimpse of the being, and I'm already petrified. I see nothing in this creature, simply darkness and armor, and as much as I try to find it, I see no soul behind the mask The Collector wears.

"So this is the subject you rounded up for me?" The Collector asks.

"Yes," Van Faye says cautiously.

"And why is he awake?"

"Blame my grunts over there."

The Collector turns its head toward Tian and Chris, and they look like they're about to shit their pants.

"I would have preferred that you follow instruction, Van Faye," The Collector says. "But this specimen will do."

"Wait a minute, specimen?" I ask in terror. "What do you mean? Who are you? What do you want from me?"

"These questions don't concern you. All you need to know is that you'll be leaving Shogun. You're coming with me?"

"What?"

And not a millisecond after I ask the question, I see The Collector draw a gun and fire. I feel a prick hit my neck and all of a sudden, I feel out of touch, woozy. My eyes start to shut, and my mind drifts. I fight to stay awake, but I cannot. The last thing I think of before I fall asleep is how further under my rock-bottom life has gone.

Chapter 22 - Two Van Faye

Agreement

<u>March 13, 3061 8:04 PM</u>

"The specimen is knocked out once more," The Collector says. "I will pack him up and make my exit."

The Collector grabs Adachi with one hand by his shirt and carefully places him back in the bag that we dragged him in. The sack closes and The Collector hoists it over its shoulder while facing me.

"As always, thank you for the punctual delivery. But next time, I'd like you to ensure that the specimen won't be conscious," The Collector says. "I get very irritated when things aren't according to plan."

I'm rather shocked. No one would dare talk to me that way, especially in my own home. This creature has a lot of cojones to throw around such words.

"I must know," I ask curiously, changing the subject, "what do you do with all these animals?"

"Do you ask the thugs you sell your illegal weapons to what they do with their wares?" The Collector's synthesized, robotic voice says.

"No."

"Then you don't need to know what I do with my purchases."

"Fair enough."

"Why did you ask? Is there a problem? I certainly hope not. I want my supply to keep coming."

"And it will continue. I'm simply wondering, that's all. Making my clients happy is what I'm all about. I take full pride in quality, especially when they're paying top creds for the merchandise. Speaking of which, my payment..."

"It's already been deposited. Check your accounts if you don't believe me."

I give Sai the signal and he's already verifying it on his compcube. After a few seconds of navigating, he nods his head in confirmation. The credits are there, and I've become richer. I smile in glee.

"I appreciate your prompt payment," I say. "As always, doing business with you is a pleasure. Will you be needing anything else?"

"I may require another specimen of the same type soon, a cat, male, healthy... and unconscious," The Collector says. "There's no deadline on the time of procurement, but be ready to produce. I'll pay extra because of the suddenness of this request. Keep on the lookout for this and contact me when you are able to provide."

"I will. They don't exactly grow on trees, but if there's any creature of interest, I'll send communication. Anyway, now that business is done, I trust that you know how to exit."

"Indeed I do."

The Collector marches to the front of my penthouse and goes through the double doors. They slide open and the creature steps through. Once the doors close, I make a nudging motion toward the exit to Tian. He scurries over and looks through.

"The hallway's empty," he says. "Don't see a sign of anyone."

"Vanished into thin air, like all the other times," I say to myself. "How is that possible?"

Suddenly, the communicator light flashes on the wall. It's security calling from the ground floor.

"What now?" I say to myself.

I use my trunk to confirm the link, and a holoscreen projects from the eastern wall. It's Vin Sanada, another rhino who works the entrance to the towers. He's much more talkative than Sai and is a decent guard.

"This is Van Faye. What is it, Vin?" I ask.

"Um, you have, um… some visitors," he says in a frazzled manner. He's usually very curt and this sudden instance of unprofessionalism surprises me.

"What is it?"

"Just take a look for yourself."

He faces his communicator toward my guests. In front of my screen stand two armor-plated monstrosities. Everything is covered, their faces, bodies, even limbs. The two remain cold, remorseless, like statues. They don't talk or move a muscle. They appear to be dogs, or wolves. I can't really tell the difference underneath all the gadgets and plating. Flutters of light gleam from their bodies, and brightest of all are the diamond-shaped glows coming from where their eyes are supposed to be.

"What in the world are these things?" I say to myself.

A holoscreen then projects from the wolf with black armor, and on it is a surly looking dog with a pressed uniform.

"What you see before you are two new classified military projects," the dog says. I've never met this canine before, but I recognize him from the news. It's not often you're talking to a high-ranking official of the Alliance's armed forces branch.

"Ah, so you are the legendary General Rox," I say.

"And you must be Two Van Faye," he responds. "Our reputations precede us."

"Indeed. So what do you want?"

"Let's start with an invitation to your penthouse. I have some questions about some of your operations. Just a meeting, that's all."

"And if I refuse?"

"My prototypes will force their way up. They're quite offensively capable, so I don't think you want to test me."

Damn Alliance scum. They throw their weight around like bullies on a playground. Fan Zui Bin has spent decades, even centuries, trying to isolate ourselves from them, but from time to time, when they visit us, they expect us to bow down to them like the rest of this planet.

Yet, even I don't have the power to stand up to the mighty Alliance. I'll just have to stay on my toes.

"Certainly. Your, um, soldiers, are more than welcome to join me in the penthouse," I say. "Vin, let them up."

My communicator closes and my crew anxiously awaits their arrival. The front door rings, and Tian opens it. In walk the two geared abominations looking as callous as they did from my communicator. A holoscreen once again appears in the air and from it General Rox's mug emerges.

"Interesting creatures you have here, General," I say as I try to gauge what these beings are.

"Yes, newest technology out there. You've heard of biotics?" he asks.

"Yeah, implant stuff. Nanotechnology that you use to give you strength, heal from injury, stuff like that," I say. "I heard they're really advancing the stuff in the medical field. This, however, seems like a new application."

"Yes. The Alliance has already approved biotic use for medical purposes. I'm trying to convince them to invest in military purposes as well. Hopefully these prototypes will demonstrate my cause."

"I've been reading about the progress the Alliance has made. The technological advances they've come up with so far in the implant field are quite impressive, unlike anything before. What caused the boom?"

"Oh, we harvested data from an illegal operation a while back, but that's classified. What do you think of my weapons?"

I peer at one of them closely, eye to eye. It doesn't even flinch.

"These look like wolves," I say. "But they're not robots?"

"Nope, they're alive, so to speak," Rox says.

"I can't imagine the Brotherhood of Wolves being happy with the Alliance messing around with their kind."

"You forget that the Brotherhood is a member of the Alliance."

"So they approve?"

"They don't know. We have jurisdiction over them. We have jurisdiction over everyone. The Brotherhood doesn't need to know about these things, and we don't need to tell them."

General Rox speaks with swagger. He believes that he is the authority over every domain. He scoffed at my warning of the Brotherhood. That's how the Alliance works. They are the world police, and they assume they have the right to do what they want. But I disagree.

"My project is a marriage of flesh and technology," General Rox says. "It is the first step to creating the perfect soldier."

"Flesh and technology? So these are cyborgs, then?" I ask.

"Beyond that. These two were practically reanimated from the dead. They're our test subjects. We don't want to create robots. We want to create soldiers, creatures with souls inside them."

I flash a smirk.

"They look pretty soulless to me," I say.

"They're just prototypes, test runs," the general says. "Once this phase is over, my models will be dismantled and put in storage. Then, with approval, I hope to apply such advancements to my own troops."

"With approval. So it's not certain yet? We'll see if your vision comes to fruition."

"Why wouldn't it?"

"I'm not sure if the Alliance would want to endorse a project built on a foundation of illegal activity and risk political backlash from a main player like the Brotherhood of Wolves. I'm skeptical how long your plans will last."

"Well, we'll see what the Alliance decides. I needed something to test on, and I couldn't very well abduct innocent animals off the streets. Unlike you."

"Excuse me?"

"You see, there have been rumors flying around, not only in Fan Zui Bin, but the rest of the world, regarding the suspicious disappearances here. Normally, I wouldn't care about Fan Zui Bin scum going missing from the streets, but the media has grown interested."

"Ah, you mean those puff pieces on the news? It's yellow journalism used to incite panic. Rumors are rumors. If you think I have anything to do with it, you're wrong."

"Perhaps, but I have some footage of your associates that you might find noteworthy."

Another holoscreen pops up from the silver colored wolf. It's a recording, shot from the top of a building, looking down at an alleyway. It's a little hard to make out, but as the video progresses and the projection focuses, I see who it is. Adachi Konoe. And also in the frame are Sai, Chris, and Tian. Shit. This is the abduction they did earlier today. This is evidence.

"Who recorded this for you?" I ask.

"I don't betray my sources," the general responds. "Besides, you shouldn't blame him, her, or me. Blame your thugs for their sloppy work."

I turn my attention to Tian and Chris and glare at them with fury.

"You dumb shits," I say. "How could you two be so careless?"

They look like they're about to piss themselves.

"We... we're sorry, Ms. Van Faye," the frog says.

"Yes... how can we make it up to you?" Tian trembles.

"Well, for starters, you two can prove your worth right now," I say.

I nudge my head and sway my trunk at the armored wolves' direction. That's their signal. Chris and Tian understand and immediately arm the blasters on their bodies to fire. The guns click to ready position, but before they can even say the word "fire," the wolves react.

The two monsters go from prone to assault positions. Cannons burst out from their armor and two booms are heard. Blue spheres of energy hurdle at my lackeys' positions. One makes contact with Chris, and I see his small frog body fly into the air until he hits the wall and there's nothing but a bloody splat in his place. The other shot smashes Tian's face and disintegrates it cleanly off his neck. His headless body wobbles a bit before it limps over like a stiff piece of furniture. Just like that, they're dead. It is done in such a precise manner that I'm left stunned. General Rox's creations are objective and accurate when carrying out their orders. After the action is done, they simply go back to their neutral positions while the general wryly smiles from his holoscreen.

"Impressive, aren't they?" the general asks. "I'd invite the legendary Sai to try something similar, but it won't end well for either of you. Can we have that civil discussion now?"

"I have no choice," I grudgingly say.

"Kidnapping goes beyond simple supply and demand. These are serious charges, and with the evidence I have, you might be in hot water. Answer my questions, and we'll see how much trouble you're in."

"As you wish. What do you want to know?"

"Where are the missing animals?"

"I don't know, and I don't care."

"How could you not know? You took them."

"Which doesn't mean I kept them. You see, I'm not a hoarder. I'm a seller. I provide a client anything they want, whether it be drugs, a good time, hell, even some lowly creatures to play with."

"So you traffic these animals you abduct?"

"I suppose. But I only have one client I supply to, one that pays very handsomely, one that I cannot refuse."

"And who is this client?"

"A cloaked figure that's always garbed in black armor, The Collector."

Rox gives me an odd look. He looks perplexed, almost skeptical of my revelation.

"I didn't create the name," I say.

"And what does this, um, Collector, do with these animals?" the general asks.

"Beats me. Conversation is usually pretty stiff. All I do is receive the request and fulfill the order. The Collector arrives, makes the payment, and gets the goods. That's as far as it goes. If you want to speak with the creature, you'll have to do it yourself."

"I see. Then I'll need you to set up a meeting right away so my prototypes can apprehend this Collector."

"And why should I do that? Business is good. It's not profitable for me to turn in one of my best clients."

"This isn't a deal. This is an order from the Alliance."

The wolves draw out their cannons once more, but I am unfazed.

"You can't come pointing your guns at the boss of Shogun!" I yell. "I will not subject myself to such demands. You may think I'm a small fry compared to your mighty Alliance, but you're playing in a different arena. You are in Shogun, you are in Fan Zui Bin, and here, my kind, the bosses, rule. I have the organizational power to stand my ground. If you want to start a war over one client, then do so, but I will not bow down to threats. I am a fair elephant, and I'm willing to negotiate."

The general narrows his eyes and tries to figure if I'm bluffing. I'm not.

"Fine, let's talk," he says. "What do you want?"

"As I said previously, The Collector pays well," I say. "I'd like to keep that coming. And, after this is done, I don't want to be prosecuted by any Alliance assholes for my crimes. Those are my terms."

The general doesn't look too pleased with what I've laid out. He mulls over his decision for some time but finally responds.

"Agreed. Those are the terms and nothing more," the general says. His answer makes me giddy. A Van Faye always gets it their way.

"Good," I say as I try to hide my excitement. "Our meeting has been recorded, so we'll use that as the proof in case you play Alliance games with me."

"I won't. So now that's done with, when can you set a meeting with The Collector? I'll want to get this over with as soon as possible."

"The Collector has requested another specimen, if possible. I'll just tell the creature that I have an additional package ready to pick up. Since your associates are already here to arrest, how about later tonight? Like in an hour?"

"You think The Collector will come on such short notice?"

"I guarantee it. The creature is very punctual, and last time we spoke, it seemed like it wanted another specimen as soon as possible."

"Excellent. My Alphas will be ready to ambush this being. This better not be a setup. You don't want to double cross me when the wolfpack is in your presence."

"Don't worry, you hold your end of the bargain, and I'll hold mine."

"Very well. I'll work with my team to lay the groundwork to this trap."

"Excellent. If you'll excuse me, I need to talk to my underling."

I walk away from the general's holoscreen and toward Sai. He has remained mute the entire time.

"This has turned out to be an interesting sequence of events," I whisper. "I've escaped Alliance persecution and am getting paid for it. I'm quite happy with this con. But I'm a little weary. Stay sharp when The Collector comes and the showdown happens. I have a feeling it'll be quite a spectacle."

Sai looks at me and nods his head. He never says anything, and he never has to.

Chapter 23 – Bastion

Snoop

March 13, 3061 8:31 PM

I don't like to wait and hope that the truth will reveal itself. I look for it myself, especially when my daughter is involved. If Ivy isn't going to show me what she's hiding, I'll discover it firsthand.

I'm not fond of sneaking around, not anymore, but it's what I'm good at. And I know Ivy is keeping a secret from me. Her odd behavior and defensive reaction when I approached her about Lucy are indications. I saw nothing but fear, shame, and anxiety all over her face. What have you done, my dear? Is it something dreadful? Is it something painful? And why can't you tell me?

It has to do with that chimp. Lucy's always scheming, always concocting some kind of plan. She reached out to me about Ivy. That ape wants something from my daughter, and Ivy is young and naïve enough to comply. I hope it's nothing, but with Lucy, it never is.

That's why I'm here on a breezy March evening. In front of me is the entrance to Iris's underground compound, my first home. It is where Iris, Ivy, and I lived together as a happy family. I had some good memories here, but that was years ago. I haven't been here since Iris banned me.

It's strange being an intruder in a place that I used to call home. I think about the past and wonder about the mistakes I've made, how I treated her, how I treated my daughter. Perhaps they're right. Perhaps I am too protective. But every ruling I've made, every choice that I've selected has always been for them. Can't they see that?

I realize dwelling on the question is useless. The damage is done, things change, and for better or worse, I can only live in the present. Even as I ponder my doubts, here I am making those same decisions this very second. I'm about to break into their home in order to find out the truth, in order to protect the family that has pushed me away. As with before, it's not about what they want it's about what they need.

I've brought some gear with me to help me with this task. It's nothing too high-tech and I have no weapons, just a scanner so I can see if anyone is home. I set the device on the ground and activate it. The machine beeps and rumbles as it starts up. Then a light emits from it, sending signals to scan the surface below. It takes about a minute for the thing to complete, but when it does, a rendered, holographic blueprint shines in the air.

It's a three-dimensional model of my old home. I already know the structure of the building like the back of my hand, but the ground scanner also checks to see if there are any living beings in the dwelling. The reading indicates there aren't. It's completely empty. That's what I want. Things would get messy if I bumped into Iris or Ivy during my snooping. Iris would disembowel me.

I wonder where they are. I guess I'm lucky no one is home, but I find it strange that the place is vacant at this late hour. It's not as surprising that Iris is gone, as I know she likes to explore this island, but Ivy should be home. She's young and often engulfed in her dramas and technology. What could she be doing at this time?

Perhaps I don't know my daughter as well as I think. Maybe she's getting too old for that stuff. I don't have many real conversations with her anymore. I only hope she's doing something safe and that my fears aren't true.

No, I can't think of that. I can only focus on the task at hand. With Iris and Ivy gone, infiltrating the place should be a snap. Iris might have changed some security features on her pod, but I'm still me. Besides, they're pretty lax. I mean, the only other inhabitant on this island is myself.

Within no time, I use my gear and the entrance snaps open. I board the platform and am lowered below.

Once I reach the ground level of the compound, I start my search. The pod is very spacious with few walls other than for the rooms. The kitchen, living room, and dining area are all connected. It's clean, a lot cleaner than when I lived here. The kitchen is clear, no plates or snacks messily strewn on the counters. The couch and entertainment area is neatly compartmentalized as if it hasn't been used in ages. When I lived here, this chamber had a homely quality about it, but now, it feels sleekly modern. It also appears less inviting.

I suppose it's just one of the many changes made to Iris's dwelling after my departure. When I was with her, I made most of the decisions, but now I see what life is like under her regime. It's curious because Ivy follows the rules as well. I never knew my daughter as an organized person, but from what this place reflects, under Iris's tutelage, Ivy is living quite a different lifestyle.

This compound has taken a new identity. I lived here for more than ten years, yet it doesn't feel like home. I look at the kitchen and think about the times I had with my love. We cooked together and she always seemed so happy. Was that fake? Was she really crying tears of sorrow underneath her smiles? Or maybe she never smiled the way I remember it. It could have been a mirage, a concoction of my imagination that I created to shelter myself from the truth that was always there. I don't know, and suddenly I become saddened that my memories betray me. I cherished them, yet I come to the realization that they were actually projections of what didn't exist.

But I mustn't get distracted. I broke in for a reason. My search for evidence comes up fruitless in the living areas. Of course it would. If Ivy is planning something under her mother's nose, she wouldn't be doing it in front of her. Any proof would be locked squarely away. Her room is where I'll find all the goods.

I walk past the kitchen and past Iris's bedroom to Ivy's. The door slides open and I step into a room that's as clean as the others. Once again, I'm surprised to see everything so neatly put together.

I scan her quarters and see nothing suspicious. I walk toward her desk and bed and rummage. I do it carefully, methodically, taking my time to make sure every corner of her room is inspected. I never leave any stone unturned during an investigation, and I am particularly mindful during this search. Still, even with a higher level of thoroughness, I find nothing disconcerting among Ivy's possessions.

But I haven't checked her compcube. If she's hiding something, it'll be there.

I turn it on and discover it's password protected. No problem. I grab a piece of equipment from my bag, attach it to her compcube, and in seconds I've gained access. I dive right into her files, furiously moving screens and interfaces, bracing myself in case I find anything that'll prove my fears true. To my relief, there's nothing. No files, no pictures, nothing odd or strange. But I haven't checked her messages yet. I open her inbox. It's mostly empty, save for one message. It has no subject and the sender is anonymous.

"Better safe than sorry," I say. I open it up and read the contents.

Ivy Lawton. Sending progress. Schedule on track. Expect no delays. Prepare to leave soon.

There's no signature. It's an odd message, and as I read it again, I get the feeling that I know the author. It's the way it's written that's familiar. The sentences are stunted, fragmented. I know someone who talks in that manner.

"Lucy," I say.

I am speechless and saddened. I blink wildly at the holoscreen, unable to come to grips with the truth. The ugly truth is clear. My daughter is in league with that evil chimp woman. I don't want to believe it, but I must.

The message is short and unclear. To what schedule is Lucy referring? It must involve some scheme that she's mapped out, perhaps a set of instructions for Ivy to follow. It's only a guess, but that appears to be the most obvious answer.

The greater question is what could they possibly be planning? One assumption is that Lucy is continuing her quest to make Ivy her protégé. That always was the goal when Ivy was younger. Lucy enjoyed teaching, Ivy enjoyed learning. With my daughter's mind ripe and young, the time to pass Lucy's knowledge is now.

I also speculate that Lucy has a vested interest in Ivy's telekinesis. Certainly that was what she and Lionel Changer hoped to accomplish back at HORUS, to use Iris so she could be mother to a generation of mentally powered hybrids. Ivy's gifts are the fruits of their research and labor. She represents a piece to the entire puzzle.

Lucy's message also tells her to "prepare to leave soon." There's only one place to leave, this island. Ivy is planning to escape. I start to panic. What if she's already done it? She's not at home, after all. But then I calm my senses and realize that her belongings are still here. She hasn't gone yet, but if I don't do something, she'll disappear soon. And then I'll have to start my own plans to locate her and bring her back.

Does Iris know about this, that Lucy is telling our daughter to run away? Certainly not. Ivy has probably been hiding this plot from her mother, living life normally while secretly exchanging messages with Lucy. From what I see in their home, things look as right as rain, no signs of trouble whatsoever. Ivy is good at keeping secrets. She did it so well against me. With my daughter maintaining her guise, Iris may have no idea.

I have to tell Iris. She's made it very clear she doesn't want to speak with me, but damnit, this is our daughter's life! There's no time to argue over our petty differences when so much is on the line. Once I explain the situation to her, I know we can work it out.

I need Iris with me. Ivy listens to her mother. Perhaps Iris can talk some sense into her confused mind. And I hope I can too. Ivy may hate me, but I love her. She is my kin, my blood, and I will have to save her whether she likes it or not.

Chapter 24 – Two Van Faye

Penthouse

March 13, 3061 9:12 PM

I'm a tad nervous over what's about to take place. I am betraying one of my most reliable and straightforward clients. If all my associates were as dependable as The Collector, I'd be ten times richer. I've never had a problem with the cloaked wonder and was looking forward to years of business with the creature.

Yet the Alliance has offered me a deal I cannot refuse. They are practically offering me amnesty for my help. The Alliance may not have jurisdiction over Fan Zui Bin, but time is passing and things are changing. It'll only be a matter of years before they try to push their might on us crime lords, so it's better to negotiate now than later. I won't be their enemy, but rather their business partner. It's the smart move to make if I'm thinking about the grander picture.

But I have this weird feeling, like I've made the wrong move. Confidence is something I normally have in abundance. It isn't a bad thing. In fact, it's a quality I take pride in. You need to be arrogant to survive in this world. If you don't, you become a weakling, easily swallowed among the masses.

The reason my feelings are off is because I don't know much about The Collector. I'm about to turn my back on this partner, and I'm unsure what the repercussions might be. The Collector actually instills fear in me. That's right, you heard it—the great Two Van Faye is afraid of someone.

It's not as outlandish as it seems. The Collector sends chills through my body. Business is good with the creature, but I am always on high alert when I deal with The Collector face to face. It's the whole getup, the black armor and cloak. The outfit gives the creature a supernatural element. The Collector's voice also is heavily synthesized, like a robot. It's impersonal, ghost-like. And then there's the mask. It's dark and glossed but also the only thing that gives the creature character. That vine pattern etched in shimmering white is fanciful and wild, which goes against the plain and dark exterior of the suit.

The Collector's body language tells the story. The bipedal creature's movements are smooth and fluid yet also strong and straight, like a human in the military. To me, it says only business is on the mind and nothing else. When The Collector arrives, it's often unannounced. I usually get the call from security downstairs informing me of guest arrivals, yet I rarely ever get one when The Collector comes. The being has found a way to evade my personnel, a feat not easily accomplished. How The Collector is able to move so fluidly on my grounds is beyond me. Despite the security breaches, The Collector never brings trouble. As I said before, it's all business.

This client is unlike anything I've ever encountered, a truly unique individual among the thugs and power hungry tyrants I often deal with. The Collector could be a simple human with no power whatsoever, but I get the feeling that's not the case. And that's what makes me so frightened of this coup.

My communicator pops open and there is General Rox on the holoscreen. The dog looks as eager as ever.

"How are you feeling, Van Faye?" Rox asks.

"Nervous," I respond bluntly.

"That's odd. I never heard the Elephant Queen of Crime to be the anxious type."

"Well, you haven't met The Collector yet. You'll see why I'm nervous."

"Whatever. My Alphas and your rhino will be able to handle it. Are they in position?"

I look at Sai, who calmly stands near the front door where The Collector normally enters, preparing himself for what lies ahead.

"Yes," I say. "And the wolves are hiding one floor below. Just make sure if trouble happens, they don't burst through the ground. This place isn't cheap to maintain. I better get reimbursed for any damage."

"That will be the least of your concerns," he says. "But don't worry, you will. I have confirmed with my technician that my Alphas are in their places. Remember the plan. It's a simple ambush. Once The Collector arrives, you will do what you can to stall the creature so it lowers its guard. Then, when we feel the time is right, Sai and my wolves will attack and apprehend the subject. Our goal is to capture alive. There are a lot of questions I want answered."

"As do I."

"Remember to keep your penthouse linked up. We have the feeds set up, and I want to monitor what's going on during the entire exchange. You've confirmed that the target will be arriving shortly, correct?"

"Yes. I informed The Collector that I had the specimen it requested earlier this evening, another cat similar to Adachi Konoe. Within seconds, I got a message back stating that the creature would be available to teleport back out to Shogun to, ahem, collect the prize.

I even got to charge double my rate. The scheduled time to meet is around nine, so the individual should be arriving any minute now."

"Excellent. And no suspicions were raised?"

"Not that I can tell. It's the usual routine for both parties."

"Very well. This check-in is over. I'll be monitoring the situation as it progresses. Let's hope we can capture this scum. Rox out."

The holoscreen closes and I'm left in my penthouse, waiting for the guest of honor. It's the calm before the storm. With only Sai in my room, I stand there in an eerie silence on pins and needles.

And then a knock comes from my front door. It's the usual entrance—no warning, no call from security, just the simple knock at the appointed time, like clockwork. The Collector has arrived.

Sai opens the door and in walks The Collector, just like a few hours ago. General Rox's wolves were hiding in the vicinity of the entrance, and I'm a tad worried The Collector noticed them. But it appears it hasn't because the cloaked menace walks directly to me. The being doesn't linger around. Instead, it goes straight to the point.

"Looks like I made the right choice in business partners. I didn't expect another captive so soon," The Collector says. "I'm extremely pleased with this outcome."

"As long as the customer is satisfied and willing to pay," I say.

I force out an arrogant chuckle, but I'm not sure how convincing it is. The moment I stop, an awkward silence fills the air. I stare at The Collector, unsure if the creature is staring back at me. We both stand frozen while Sai observes. Dozens of seconds pass and still a peep hasn't been made.

"Well, you know I'm not stingy," The Collector says, breaking the tension.

"Agreed," I answer tersely.

Another long silence interrupts the conversation.

"So can I see the specimen, the cat I asked for?" The Collector asks.

I didn't anticipate a cut to the chase so quickly. I'm stuck for an answer and try to think of a way to stall. Perhaps I'll pretend that Sai must retrieve it. That'll be the perfect way to signal the start of the ambush.

"Of course, but Sai will have to fetch it," I say. "You see, it's not in this—"

"You don't have it, do you?" The Collector says.

My eyes widen, head tilts, and I'm caught completely off guard. How did this creature know of the ruse? Were my tells that obvious? Did I overact or underact my position? Doubts fill my head. Being caught on my bluff is a feeling I'm not used to. I'm the one that puts fools on edge, not the other way around.

"Excuse me? What are you talking about?" I ask.

"Let's not put on this charade any longer," The Collector says. "I know there's no specimen for me to collect. In fact, I know about the whole hoax. The Alliance cut you a deal and you planned to betray me. Sai and some Alliance warriors are ready to start the ambush once you give the go. That sums up the purpose of this meeting, correct?"

I stand there stunned by The Collector's revelation.

"How did you know?" I ask.

"I have my sources," The Collector responds.

Shock invades my senses. We anticipate each other's actions. I'm no longer wrapped by fear or anxiousness. I accept that the inevitable has arrived, and I feel an odd easiness before the chaos unfolds. Calm before the storm indeed.

"It appears you have it all figured out," I say as I regain my trademark haughtiness. "Shall we begin this?"

"Let's," The Collector responds unflinchingly.

"Sai, Rox, it starts now!"

My priority is to find safety, so I dash behind one of the desks large enough to cover my body and then peer my head out so I have a front row seat to the action. Sai has not initiated The Collector yet. Instead, he circles his opponent to measure what he's up against. Oddly enough, The Collector simply stands there. The entity hasn't moved a muscle and doesn't even acknowledge Sai.

My rhino is unshaken by The Collector's confidence. He's focused. I can tell by the sparks flying from his electrified horn. It's his turn to strike. He rears back a little, getting ready for the charge. His nostrils flare and his breathing becomes sinisterly heavy.

One, two, three, off he goes, my battle tank, out to defend his master. Ever loyal is my Sai—stoic, fierce, a killer. My killer.

But then I blink and The Collector no longer stands in front of Sai. My rhino puts on his brakes and stops his stampede. He looks up at my fifteen-foot ceiling, and my eyes follow his. The Collector stands above us, upside-down, walking on the top, defying gravity. I am in awe of what I see. I know anti-gravity tech exists, but The Collector sprang up to the top so quickly it was like a reflex, an extension of the body. It was something natural, something I've never seen.

The creature tilts its head to us, and I swear it's looking at me. But its focus quickly shifts back to the enemy, back to Sai. The Collector gallops across my ceiling, running like it's on a track. Its legs churn, and it sprints like lightning, just as fast as it was when it jumped to the top. The agility, speed, and power outmatch any of the cronies I've hired, and it does this all while in reverse gravity. Amazing.

Within milliseconds, The Collector stands over the head of Sai and looks down on its target. Immediately it releases its hold on the ceiling and gracefully falls down toward Sai. It tumbles in the air, doing a full summersault, and lands perfectly on my rhino's back, straddling him like a human on a horse. Sai bucks wildly, trying to shake off the bipedal foe. But The Collector sticks to him like glue, riding out the motions as if riding out the waves of a storm.

During the frenzy, The Collector sticks both arms straight out, perpendicular to its torso, and appears to focus. It's strange, the palms are open, but they're only directed at the air. No weapons or hand cannons, just nothingness. I'm unsure what The Collector is doing and gawk at the creature.

But then I look around to see things floating in the air. They're small items—electropens, collectables, a few knives, nothing of magnitude—but they levitate off the ground and stay suspended. There are also a lot of them, about one hundred trinkets. Once again, I'm unsure if this is the work of high tech arms. There's no weapon that could control so many objects either. Even Sai stops his bucking to gaze at the oddities around him. Both of us space out like stupefied idiots.

That's when The Collector strikes. With a closing of the fist, the items jettison toward the middle. I notice as they fly closer to the center, they're not aimed at The Collector. They're aimed at Sai.

Oh no. Move out, my rhino protector. Can't you see you're trapped?

Unfortunately, there's not enough time. Each little object goes flying into him, enveloping him in a mass of junk, piercing the exposed areas of his body that aren't covered by armor. They rip his skin open and plunge into his hardened flesh with ease. It's like watching a knife dive into butter.

The blood leaks from the wounds, trickling down his enormous body. Some make their way into the cracks of his armor, other streams drip above it, painting his equipment red. Slowly but surely, he looks like a crimson mess. But he doesn't wince throughout the impaling. He simply stands there, taking each object like a fierce warrior. Blow by blow the strikes hit him, and blow by blow he remains strong. I am proud.

However, the mind can only do so much. By the time the last item, an antique dagger, flies into him, his legs become wobbly. The blood loss is too much, and he tries in vain to stay standing. In a last-ditch effort, he twitches his ears. It appears like a nervous tick, but he's actually arming the turrets hidden beneath his armor.

The guns pop out like lightning and have their sights on The Collector. It's Sai's last resort to capture this hostile. But just like before, the enemy opens its palms toward the guns and they magically twist in different directions, blasting the walls instead of the target. The cloaked menace then swiftly aims its hands at the fresh bullet holes and its arms violently shake. In fact, The Collector's whole body does, even its head.

I hear a rumble and as I look around, I realize the wall cracks from the misfire are getting longer and wider. It starts off slow, with small pieces of synthetic rubble falling to the ground. But then, in a flash, the cracks begin to expand and violently tear until their size has increased tenfold. With one final movement of the arms, The Collector pulls them forward, and in unison, two huge chunks of wall are ripped apart from opposite sides.

The slabs float in the air, heavy pieces that even a gorilla couldn't lift. They surround Sai while The Collector controls them. I peer my head out farther to get a closer look, awed by the feat of power on display, and turn my vision straight to the black armored aggressor. Surprisingly, the creature looks back to acknowledge me.

I'm sorry, Sai.

The Collector's arms close and the creature clasps its hands together. The pieces of wall come close in with great force with Sai's head stuck in the middle. It gets crushed in a split second, creating a sandwich where the gooey center is nothing but mushed blood and brains. Pieces of debris, muscle, and skull go flying in multiple directions. The Collector then releases its hold on the wall pieces and they fall harmlessly to the ground while Sai's decapitated body stands in the background. The Collector jumps off, and Sai's body stands for a few moments before it lifelessly slumps to the floor.

Before I can even do anything, General Rox's wolves come bursting through the door. They waste no time and start blasting at The Collector. But The Collector is smart and quickly ducks behind Sai's corpse, using it for cover from the onslaught of energy shots. Sai's armor and bricklike physique are enough to stop the wave of fire.

The Alphas approach The Collector cautiously while still engaging their mark. General Rox has seen the enemy's capabilities from what happened to Sai and knows he is trying to apprehend a dangerous target. I'm at a vantage point where I can view both parties. The Collector wastes no time going on the offensive. It raises its arm and sticks its palm outward, just like before, this time pointing it to my workstation. It's what I use for my compcube and docs and is quite large, fit for the size of an elephant.

It's no problem for The Collector, though, and with a raising of its hand, the creature lifts it up with its mind and hurls it toward the Alphas. My station towers over the comparably smaller wolves. It hurdles toward them and the silver one, Silverwolf, gets out of the way, but Blackwolf isn't as fast and gets smacked in the process. The station and Blackwolf go careening into a wall, and my possession gets smashed into hundreds of pieces. Blackwolf is down for the count, but the attack is not fatal.

Silverwolf lands from its leap and continues its assault. This time, it charges full speed toward The Collector. The creature is still hiding behind Sai, but as Silverwolf draws closer, The Collector leaps from concealment and jumps above the mechanized wolf. Two glowing wires shoot from its wrist and coil around the wolf's neck. Ahh, finally some tech I recognize. Can't go wrong with energy whips. They ensnare the wolf's throat like a noose while The Collector lands from its jump.

Silverwolf struggles mightily to free itself from The Collector's hold, but The Collector doesn't hesitate. The cloaked entity swings its arms, and the energy whips thrash in a circle, launching Silverwolf into the air. The Collector then jerks its arms again and releases its hold. The airborne wolf's body jerks in the opposite direction, and its momentum makes it fly right through my outer wall. General Rox better hope this canine can fly because it's a long way down outside.

The Collector has defeated both foes and now turns its attention to me. Shit, I'm dead. If Sai and the Alliance wolf freaks couldn't take down this creature, what chance do I have? I'm big and strong like all elephants, but I'm not a fighter. The Collector gets closer and closer, and I start quivering, counting the seconds I have to live. So this is how it ends for the Elephant Queen of Crime, huh?

Or not. Blackwolf emerges from the pile of broken bits of workstation. Like a mindless drone, it reengages its mission and a large cannon arises from its armor. It's powerful enough to destroy a hovercar.

Blackwolf sets, aims, and fires. The cannon booms an enormous ball of light and fire, and it screams straight at The Collector. But, as I've seen all evening, the being raises its hand and the blast alters its course, going straight toward my ceiling. A large explosion echoes, and my room becomes dusty. When it clears, I look up and see a huge hole that leads straight outside, up to my roof. Looks like I'm going to need to be reimbursed after all.

A rumbling noise is then heard from the new hole in my outer wall, and I turn my head to see Silverwolf intact, hovering in the air by a propulsion system.

A slew of flying wolf jokes run through my head. The Collector is now trapped between two armored freaks. I have to hand it to General Rox. These two canines have taken a lot of punishment. Perhaps when this is over, I can inquire the good general about making some of my own soldiers this durable.

In midair, Silverwolf fires a cavalcade of ammunition, but The Collector avoids it. The creature sure is agile. That's when Silverwolf switches it up and arms two grenades instead. Great, another high-powered, high-damage weapon. Can't the Alphas be a little more delicate?

Silverwolf projects the explosives, and they travel at The Collector. However, The Collector sticks its hand out and catches both of them with its mind. For a fraction of a second, the grenades stay stationary in front of The Collector's palms, but then The Collector opens them a little wider, and one grenade flies back to Silverwolf while the other shoots to Blackwolf.

Silverwolf, is able to dodge it for the most part, but the grenade still explodes near its vicinity, and the wolf goes flying into one of my walls, creating a large crack to the interior. It falls stiffly after the blow and makes a large thump as it hits the floor. Now it's Silverwolf who looks temporarily out of commission.

Blackwolf, on the other hand, isn't so lucky. The grenade detonates at pointblank range and explodes right in front of its face. The canine rockets to an opposing wall at much higher force than Silverwolf. When it makes contact, a storm of rubble and debris bursts from the impact.

When things clear up, I see Blackwolf on the floor, a smoking mess. The beast has suffered heavy damage. Its armor isn't polished, but faded and dented. A few sparks fly from various fractures. Even its glowing, diamond eye blinks on and off. It struggles to get back up, legs shaking and gears crackling. But it still appears to be battle ready as a cannon pops up from its shoulder.

The Collector isn't finished though, and it quickly propels energy whips from its wrist to restrain the dazed wolf. They wrap around the wolf's leg, pinning it to the floor. The whips then latch onto the ground while The Collector lashes out more, again attaching them to Blackwolf's other legs. Within seconds, Blackwolf has all four limbs held securely. Struggling all it wants, the wolf has no option for escape.

This time, The Collector lacks any haste and takes its time, approaching the enemy slowly and methodically. It stands above the wolf, looks down, and then kneels to observe it face to face. The Collector then stands back up and, in a sight I'm all too familiar with at this point, spreads its right palm open, right at the wolf's face.

Unlike the other times, The Collector actually has to focus at this task. Its hand shakes a bit, and it struggles to apply the same force it did on my workstation and walls. The hand vibrates more violently and the creature appears to be concentrating harder. But then it swiftly pulls its arm back and the wolf's mask rips from its face. The faceplate must have been grafted directly to the skin and attached to the rest of the body armor, which explains why it was so difficult for The Collector to pry off. But still, The Collector got the job done. The creature lets go of its hold on the mask and it falls harmlessly to the ground.

I now see the wolf's exposed face. There's no fur on it, just flesh that's been scarred and torn apart by fire. Skin that was charred, broiled, and burnt a long time ago. The wounds never healed. Its pupils are completely white and its snout is only half there. I don't even bother looking for ears. I don't know where General Rox got these so-called donors, but they've been put through hell.

I can't tell what The Collector is thinking, and I can't see its facial reaction, but it looks at the wolf for a few seconds, pondering some thoughts that I will never know. Then The Collector raises its hand toward a metal rod that was once part of my wall, levitates it, and sends it flying right into Blackwolf's exposed face. The rod crushes it upon contact, and the wolf is left impaled by the piece of wreckage. With the pole sticking out of its face, its head slumps to its left and the wolf lies there dead.

The Collector once again kneels down, inspecting its kill, and places a device on the creature. I can't really see what it is. The Collector is too far away. But as soon as The Collector stands, a flash of light wraps the wolf's body, blinding me. I close my eyes and when they open again, Blackwolf is gone.

"Was that a teleporter?" I say to myself. I've heard rumors of self-teleportation devices that were available on the black market, but they were only rumors. I'm a trafficker of underground goods, and if I haven't heard of it, it must not exist. But what I just saw tells me otherwise.

Silverwolf is still out, so that only leaves The Collector and me. It appears my death was simply delayed. Now is the time of reckoning.

Unlike before, I realize now that I must stay defiant. I will not cower in fear. Moments ago, I was afraid to die, begging for it not to end. That's no way for a queen to go out. Even in death, I have a reputation to keep. I will die strong, with power and grace, just as I have lived my life.

I rise from my concealment and The Collector takes notice. The being walks to me calmly and slowly, and I approach it in the same manner. We meet in the middle of the room. I look down and it looks up and we stand face to face, wondering what will happen next.

"So it seems this is how things end," I say. "I never thought it'd be one of my own clients that would do me in. Are you going to kill me now?"

"No," The Collector says.

To my surprise, the creature has relented. I try to hide the confusion on my face, but it's hard. I am generally perplexed.

"Why is that?" I say in an almost angry manner. "You have your chance. Do it."

"The time for you to die is not now," The Collector says. "But mark my words, one day I will be back, and one day it will be."

Its speech comes out coldly and sternly. I'm a bit terrified, but I remain composed and continue to stare down my opponent. But then our confrontation is interrupted by an errant energy blast. Silverwolf is back online and he resumes his attack. The Collector turns its head to its adversary and quickly turns back to me.

"See you soon," The Collector says.

The Creature then sprints away and toward the gap that was created by the earlier cannon fire. It springs forward, then up through the opening and onto the roof. Silverwolf follows its trail out of my penthouse.

The chase is still on, but it's over for me, and I'm left uncharacteristically unnerved by what I've just seen. This Collector may be the single most powerful being I've ever met.

Chapter 25 – General Rox

Rooftops

March 13, 3061 9:32 PM

Amazing. That's the only word I can use to describe the events of the last twenty minutes. I've seen a lot in my military career. Super jacked gorillas pumped up on enhanced steroids, artificially enhanced cheetahs that can run up to speeds of one hundred thirty miles an hour, even enlarged cat brains thanks to genetic tampering. And I've seen a lot of weapons due to my expertise in military technology. Gravity guns, cannons that turn metal into dust, even stuff that gives you minor telekinetic capabilities. Yes, I've witnessed every way you can kill and every way you can be killed.

However, The Collector, the black demon of mystery, trumps everything. The creature fought so fluidly and gracefully yet wielded heaps of power. It blew me away. It manhandled two elite fighting units and Two Van Faye's bodyguard without any trouble while all Mark Allen and I could do was watch helplessly from our Arkady facility in Russia. During the fight, both of us frantically tried to command Blackwolf and Silverwolf to take out the foe, but all of our strategies and programs proved futile. The Collector outmaneuvered and outfought both of them, and it was supposed to be our ambush!

Blackwolf has been taken offline. I guess it's considered "dead." Now Silverwolf is the only one left to get the job done. Mark Allen and I observe his visual feed as he pursues The Collector. The wolf has already followed the target onto Van Faye's roof. He's currently programmed to automation mode, meaning he's following his objective to capture while making decisions on his own. We do have some input in his approach and strategy though.

"The artificial intelligence you put in the Alphas has been less than stellar," I say to Mark Allen. I give my feedback to the prisoner and he makes sure Silverwolf obeys. "The two made a lot of tactical mistakes during the battle at the penthouse. They play too much offense, not enough defense. Program some less aggressive strategies into Silverwolf's system."

Allen fiddles around with the controls on his station.

"Done," he says. "You'll also be able to manually override tactics whenever you wish. Just voice your orders."

"Understood," I reply.

It was quite interesting observing the action in the penthouse, and watching this chase is no different. I see through the eyes of these mechanical soldiers. When Blackwolf and Silverwolf fired their weapons, I could almost feel the recoil. When Silverwolf rocketed to the roof, I felt the adrenaline rush. This is what I envision for the future. My abilities as a general will be much improved now that I can see and order my troops firsthand. Their fight will be mine.

Silverwolf lands on the roof, and on the other side is The Collector. The creature is simply standing there, observing Silverwolf, expecting its arrival. It does not attack nor ready itself in a defensive position. It simply looks on at my chrome-plated creation.

"Program Silverwolf to halt its attack, but stay on alert mode," I tell Allen. "I want to ask The Collector some questions."

"Understood," Mark Allen responds. "Linking you up to communications mode. It'll take a second."

Allen inputs my commands.

"You're live," he says.

"My name is General Rox," I say to the feed. "I am head of research and development of military tech for the United Species Alliance. I won't bore you with formalities, so let's get straight to the chase. We've been monitoring the missing animal situation in Shogun for quite some time now, and it appears you are the culprit behind the cases. My question to you is what is your motive?"

The Collector doesn't respond. The creature doesn't even move. No hints of reaction. It stands there motionless like a decommissioned drone. I have to wonder if there's even a soul behind the darkened armor.

"Silent, eh?" I continue. "I wasn't expecting an answer anyway. But I'll still ask my questions. You've done things that I've never seen any animal do. It was quite clear during the earlier battle that you are no ordinary creature. Where did you acquire the tech to do such things? Did you get it from the black market?"

Still nothing. I'm hoping that one of my questions garners a response, even if it's not a verbal one. I've done a lot of interrogations in my career, and any body language is good body language when getting a read.

"Did you steal it from a development firm?" I ask.

Once again, The Collector remains frozen.

"Or maybe you had a hand in its creation," I say.

This time, The Collector tilts its head slightly. That's the most I've been able to pry out of the creature and is a clear tell.

"Ahh, so perhaps it is that," I say. "What group are you working for?"

The creature gets back on track shutting down my questions. At this point, I grow impatient. This is going nowhere.

"So you don't want to talk," I say. "I understand. I'm in no position to demand anything. But once Silverwolf is done with you, I will be. You may have taken out Blackwolf and Van Faye's hench-rhino, but now that I've gotten a taste of your capabilities, this second battle will not be so easy. Silverwolf will capture you and we will question you. So good luck my, black-armored friend."

I turn back to Mark Allen.

"Disconnect me," I say. He does so. "Have Silverwolf engage."

Allen inputs my commands and Silverwolf arms himself. Six energy cannons open from holes in its armor and aim. The Collector gets in a fighting position, but instead of holding ground, the creature unexpectedly flees. It turns around and jumps off Van Faye's roof to the ground below. Silverwolf reacts quickly, sprints to the edge, and jumps off in hot pursuit of the enemy.

Silverwolf crashes to the lower rooftops at incredible speed. I can hear the winds rattle off his mechanical body during his decent. They are strong and they are powerful. Van Faye's building towers over most of Shogun, so it's an almost one thousand foot drop for both parties. Silverwolf powers its boosters to help guide him through the air.

On the other hand, The Collector plummets without any flight capability whatsoever. It simply dives through the air like a bomber, outpacing my wolf. The creature must have a plan. Thus far, The Collector has been calculating and precise. I highly doubt such reckless actions would be made without purpose.

And of course, I'm right. The cloak on its back flaps open, and The Collector proceeds to glide safely through the air using the momentum it gathered during the fall. It hovers over the roofs smoothly.

Silverwolf begins firing its energy shots, hoping to hit our adversary in this moment of vulnerability. The Collector maneuvers around and starts moving in a zigzag motion to avoid the hail of ammunition. Fire after fire, The Collector swoops, jutting left and then right and then left again, evading the blue streams of light. Its evasive movements are impressive. Silverwolf is an accurate shot according to our simulations, so it's not easy dodging his gunfire.

Fortunately for us, Silverwolf is able to clip the cloak. The creature goes in a tailspin, violently twisting in the winds as it tries to straighten its course. But it's not too far from a rooftop, and in a last-ditch effort, it abandons its glide and tumbles to the top of the building. The Collector summersaults as it makes contact and actually has a graceful landing. As it completes its roll forward, the being quickly gets to its feet and continues to run. Silverwolf thrusts to The Collector's location, landing bluntly on the rooftop, and continues its chase.

The Collector is heading to the edge of the building, running to another roof. Silverwolf sprints behind, following its path. But The Collector suddenly halts, and just when I think it's going to jump off this building to land on another, it turns around and opens its palms to a nearby generator that's bolted to the roof. As before, the generator rumbles. The base starts to crack and crumble, weakening with every second. The Collector then forcefully lifts its arms and with a giant screech, the generator goes with them. It floats in front of us, hovering silently in the air.

I know what comes next. Silverwolf only has a split second to respond before that thing comes crashing its way. That's when I remember the words I told Mark Allen earlier: focus on defense.

"Start up the level ten bioshields!" I exclaim.

The audio override initiates and Silverwolf's shields go up right before the generator makes contact. The machine collides with the force field of energy, pushing Silverwolf slightly. But at the same time, the generator bounces off and deflects harmlessly to the side. My wolf has remained undamaged by the massive attack.

The Collector appears a little confused, standing there silently for a couple of seconds. But then it starts the attack once more. It points its palms at a ladder from a parallel building and rips it from the wall it's securely fastened to. Then The Collector swings its arms in a punching motion, and the ladder goes with it, flying toward Silverwolf. It slams against the shield, but once more, the attack does nothing but push Silverwolf a few inches. My creation stands strong.

The enemy is persistent, though. It points its palms to a piece of the roof, tearing a large chunk into the air, and lobs it again at Silverwolf, and again, the bioshield blocks the attack. Yet, just as quickly as the creature's attack has failed, The Collector telekinetically grapples onto another object, this time a metal rod, and launches it like a javelin. But the bioshield blocks it head on.

Bits and pieces of the surrounding buildings get picked off by The Collector, each chunk finding its way to Silverwolf, each chunk ricocheting undamagingly away. Silverwolf absorbs all the hits, and the bioshield ensures its safety. The Collector seems to be drained by the work and slows down its attack. Hurling objects with the mind must be a very tiring process.

The classic rope-a-dope strategy has worked. This is Silverwolf's chance to attack.

"Have Silverwolf fire the plasma rockets now!" I yell at Mark Allen.

Allen enters some commands, and the rockets arm and fire. Thick clouds of smoke propel from their tails. But before they hit, The Collector presses some buttons on its wrist, and a large ball of light expands from it. Within milliseconds, the glow spreads, eventually covering its whole body.

It's a brightness that is all too familiar.

"Is that a teleporter?" I say to myself.

The rocket makes contact and explodes a large blue blaze of smoke. The cloud illuminates the darkened roof, shooting out flares and light. A wave of sound echoes throughout the night sky. Piping hot plasma splashes from the hit, corroding the impact zone and its surroundings. Bits of fire burn around the area.

"Direct hit!" Allen exclaims.

I'm a bit more skeptical.

"Have Silverwolf investigate the zone," I say to Allen. "I want make sure The Collector is finished."

Silverwolf approaches the area and investigates the blast zone. The flames have settled down and only traces of blue plasma are scattered about. The smoldering roof is charred black. Parts of debris are dispersed about. The damage that has been done is pretty clear, but I don't see a body anywhere.

"There's nothing. The fried corpse of The Collector should be here, but there's not even a dismembered hand," I say to Mark Allen.

"Perhaps the creature was vaporized by the attack," Allen suggests.

"Possibly. Have Silverwolf run a particle scan."

Allen configures his devices and Silverwolf activates its scanner. I hear beeps and pings while the wolf does its work. The laser examines the rubble thoroughly, looking for any traces of an organism.

"Results are being computed," Mark Allen says.

"And?" I inquire.

"Nothing. Not a strand of DNA left. It's as if the creature disappeared."

"What if it did?"

Allen turns around and looks at me with a puzzled face.

"What do you mean?" he asks.

"The Collector was engulfed by some kind of light before the missiles made impact," I say. "Did it look familiar to you?"

"It kind of looked like teleportation light."

"I believe it was. The Collector has the ability to teleport anywhere, without the aid of a teleportation station. Such technology exists, but it's illegal. Also, something as quick working and advanced as that is a rare sight, even on the darkest black market listings. But I know where it could be found, and you do too."

Allen is still confused.

"Think about your time with your former employer," I say.

All of a sudden, it makes sense to him.

"HORUS. We had those at HORUS!" he says. "They were called personal porters, a custom design by Lionel Changer. They would allow a user to teleport anywhere in the world to a receiving teleportation station. A sending station wasn't needed. But I never got to use them. They were only for his inner circle."

"Yes, I've seen the designs in his files," I say. "But they were incomplete and our scientists never could engineer a prototype."

"So you think they're related?"

"Possibly. Perhaps The Collector got its hands on some of our classified files. But it's too early to speculate. I'll have to look into this further later. Right now, capturing The Collector is still the primary objective. After Blackwolf was destroyed, the Collector attached a device on it, and it too was brought into a similar light. Did you have any luck locating Blackwolf with its tracker?"

"No. The signal was lost. It's supposed to work. Blackwolf was destroyed, but its tracker was still intact. Yet I can't locate it. The wolf appears to have gone somewhere too far for the tracker to get a signal."

The answer couldn't be clearer.

"It was teleported," I say. "Probably with the same tech The Collector used."

"What do you think The Collector wants with Blackwolf?" Allen asks.

"Who knows? We won't have any answers until we extract it from the mind of The Collector."

Suddenly, my communicator rings.

"What now?" I say to myself.

The holoscreen pops open. It's Van Faye.

"General," she says.

"What do you want Elephant Queen?" I say in an annoyed tone.

"Just want to see how the rest of the battle went. Your abominations and The Collector gave me quite a show. I'm curious to know how it ended."

"Not good. The Collector got away. Silverwolf is still on the search."

"That's too bad."

There's a small moment of silence in our conversation.

"So what do you really want?" I ask Van Faye.

"Well, now that your little hunt has destroyed my penthouse and killed one of my best soldiers, I want to make sure our agreement is still on," she says.

"Don't worry, it is. The Alliance will turn a blind eye to any activities you may carry out, as long as it happens on Fan Zui Bin soil. Our deal will last until your death."

Van Faye raises her trunk and smiles.

"Excellent. And my penthouse?" she asks.

"It'll be repaired," I say begrudgingly. "And you will be reimbursed for anything you've lost."

"Good. I suppose I'll need to look into hiring a new bodyguard."

"I suppose so. Are you done here?"

"Yes. As always, pleasure doing business."

I cut communications and the holoscreen closes. I turn my attention back to Mark Allen.

"For now, have Silverwolf continue the search for The Collector," I say. "This mission won't be over until our objective is done."

"Yes, sir," Mark Allen says.

He goes back to work and fiddles with his controls. However, he slowly peers side to side anxiously. I can tell he has a question.

"Spit it out, Allen," I say.

"What do you think of the Alphas?" he asks proudly.

"Well, Blackwolf is destroyed."

"Yes, I expected it. Even when the wolf was alive, it was the weaker of the two samples we acquired. Blackwolf wasn't an alpha. But what of Silverwolf?"

I shoot him a smile.

"I'm glad to say this. Silverwolf has performed admirably. We're facing an opponent with power I've never seen before, and your prototype is holding its own. Good work, Allen. Not bad for a HORUS flunky."

"Um, thank you, sir. So will this work in favor of a parole?"

"If you keep this up, you'll be leaving Arkady in no time."

"Thank you!"

"Don't get too excited, though. There's still a lot to do."

"Yes, sir."

Allen turns around and gets back to work. My prisoner is motivated. Good. Let's just hope Silverwolf can deliver. It's been a long night so far, and I think it's going to be much longer.

Chapter 26 - Adachi Konoe

Zoo

<u>March 13, 3061 11:31 PM</u>

I open my eyes, adjusting to the dark lighting. This is the second time this evening I've awakened in a place I don't recognize. I'm trapped in a small cell, barely larger than my own body. It's walled on three sides and has an opening in the front that's caged off by concentrated light. In the corner is some water, which is probably for drinking, and a bucket, which is probably for… stuff. From what I can see outside, there are other cells similar to mine stacked on top of each other. It's dank, depressing, and reminds me of a third-world prison.

The room is dim and flatly colored. The floors appear dirty and grey. The air is chilly, like a breezy night in Shogun. But unlike Shogun, it's impersonal and cold, like a morgue. That's the kind of vibe that I get in this first impression. I can't describe exactly why, but this place reminds me of death.

I'm confused at first. I can't recollect how I got here or who brought me. It's been such a crazy night so far, and it appears it has only started.

I jog through my memories. I remember the chase through the slums of Shogun and outrunning those idiots Chris and Tian. I remember getting knocked out by the beast Sai. I remember waking up in Van Faye's penthouse, captured and helpless. I remember all these things clearly, and I remember…

A prick on my neck… a gun being fired… feeling woozy… and… the cloaked figure… that dark armor and faceless mask.

The Collector is the reason I'm here. That prick must have been a tranquilizer of some sort. I was knocked out cold before I even knew what happened. That's probably when I was dragged here and imprisoned in this cage, like a rat, like an animal at the zoo. I wonder how long I've been out.

Well, if this place is indeed a jail, there has to be other prisoners. The cells appear to be empty, but the darkness makes it difficult to tell if they really are. Only one way to find out.

"Anyone else here?" I yell.

There's no response. I realize I yelled it out in cat, and there may be other species around. I switch it up to human, as it's the most common language.

"Anyone there?" I say again in human.

Nothing. I sit there disappointed with the lack of response. I'm confused, alone, and scared.

"Guess no one wants to answer," I say to myself.

"They don't want to answer because there's no one to answer you," a voice says to me. The reply startles me and I get to my feet as I try to peer out from behind the bars. But they obstruct my view, and all I can see are the empty cages in front of me. It definitely didn't come from there.

"Who said that?" I shout back. "Where are you?"

"I'm over here," the voice says. It's coming from the right.

"You speak human. Are you one?"

"Nope. Sorry to disappoint, but I'm a tiger."

"A tiger that speaks human. How'd that come about?"

"You have to speak human if you want to live in Fan Zui Bin."

"Ah, a fellow resident. Nice to meet you. Name's Adachi Konoe from Shogun. What's yours?"

"Mack Kirijo."

Mack's voice is heavy and raspy. He sounds drained, and I imagine a grizzled looking tiger with crusty fur and tired eyes as the mouthpiece behind the voice.

"You don't sound so good," I say. "How long have you been here?"

"I'm not sure. A week maybe?" he says.

"I see. And you were captured? Kidnapped?"

"Yup."

"Why'd they take you?"

"Well, why did they take you?"

"I think it's a matter of debt. I owed Two Van Faye some credits."

"The elephant? Don't they call her the crime queen of Shogun or something stupid like that?"

"Yeah, something like that."

I hear a yawn coming from Mack. Sounds like he's stretching.

"Well, guess I'm here for the same reason as you, then," he says. "I owed a crime boss some credits and was ducking every opportunity to pay. A few days ago, I was on my way to my favorite food joint and all of a sudden I got knocked out from behind. Hours later, I woke up here in a stupor."

"Was it Van Faye that you owed?" I ask.

"Nah, I don't reside in Shogun. I owed Boss Gorilla Rugi of Katana Village. That's about one hundred miles north of Shogun."

I guess Van Faye isn't the only one involved in the action.

"I wonder if different bosses of different cities are working together," I say. "I mean, we're from two different places, but we're both here for the same reasons."

"It's a pretty broad reason. Just about everyone who owes the leaders credits are bound to get their comeuppances," he says apathetically. "This is ours."

"Then why didn't they just kill us?"

"Well, maybe they're not the ones interested in us. Maybe they're working with a common third party."

"The Collector?"

"Oh, so that's her name? I didn't even catch it."

"Her? It's a her?"

Odd. Though briefly, I saw The Collector with my very eyes, but under all that armor, I wouldn't have guessed it was female.

"So you know what she looks like?" I ask.

"Of course, why wouldn't I?" he responds.

"Wasn't she wearing a mask? Didn't she have the black armor on, just like when she captured you?"

"I don't know what you're talking about. Like I said, I got knocked out by some goons and when I woke up, I was here. When I saw this, um, Collector or whatever, she wasn't wearing any mask or anything."

"And you're sure she's the one that captured you?"

"She has to be. I mean, she's the only one that I've seen since arriving here. She's like the boss of this place, walking around, checking on us, feeding us, and taking us away. She doesn't talk much, and when she does, it's usually pretty brief. She reminds me of a robot. It appears to be a one woman operation."

"And where are we exactly?"

"I have no idea."

Interesting information.

"So since you've seen her, The Collector is human, right?" I ask.

"Um, something like that," he says hesitantly.

"What does that mean?"

"I'd say she's more of a chimp, kind of."

His half-assed answers don't inspire a lot of confidence. I'm starting to wonder if he's been lying the whole time.

"*Kind of* doesn't mean anything," I say. "Is she human or is she a chimp?"

"I can't really describe it," he says. "You'll have to see for yourself."

I'm confused by his answer and decide to switch the topic. Once again, I observe the empty chambers.

"So is it just you and me locked up without the key, huh?" I ask. "All the other cells are vacated."

"Yeah, we're the only ones, at least for now," he says.

"For now?"

"Indeed. Animals have been coming and going. Some stay here for a few hours, some stay here for a few days. I'm surprised I've been kept this long."

"And where do they go?"

"I don't know. Once they get escorted out of their cages, I never see them again."

"And you have no idea what happens to them? Or what The Collector wants? Why so many cages? Why so many animals?"

"Like I said, I don't know."

Mack appears to be irritated with my assault of questions. I suppose I'm asking a lot, and his ignorance frustrates him. Or perhaps he doesn't want to talk about it because he's mulling his own fate.

"One more question," I say. "How long do you think we'll be held?"

He doesn't answer immediately and is hesitant. That can only mean the answer isn't good.

"I think forever," he says. "Either that or this place is our final destination."

"Why do you say that?" I ask as my voice quivers with fear.

"I haven't seen one animal come back after being taken away by the chimp-girl, or The Collector, as you call her. When she takes you, it's forever."

"But what does she—"

"Quiet! Someone's coming."

Our conversation ceases, and I hear footsteps approaching. They're heavy and swift, marching in perfect cadence as they draw closer. Then I hear a large creak. The sound bounces off the walls loudly, and after a few more steps, a figure approaches. I look up at the creature and am astonished by the sight before me.

I can see what Mack means when he says she looks kind of like a chimp, kind of like a human. The features are there. She has a shaggy face full of frizzed hair. It's on her cheeks, her forehead, even some strands on her chin. And her face itself has human features, the eyes, the nose, the lips, but they look deformed and exaggerated, like a chimp. Her nose is flat and broad, her mouth protrudes from her face. Her hair is long like a human woman's and she wears glasses for style. When I think of a chimp, I see her, but when I think of a human, I see her as well. It's unlike anything I've witnessed.

She wears a white lab coat and stares at a tablet. Her dress is proper and crisp. She moves stiffly and looks focused. I even sense a bit of neuroticism in her demeanor. It's much different from the warrior-like garb and body language I saw during the brief encounter with her armored alter ego.

But enough with the details. I need to jump into action.

"Hey, you!" I yell. "What's going on?"

The creature ignores me. Instead, it continues to mess around with its device.

"I asked you a question!" I yell even louder. "Where am I?"

"Cat subject hostile. Sedation possibly needed," she says. Her response has nothing to do with my questions.

"Did you even hear me? Answer my question."

"Don't even bother," Mack says. "Like I said, she doesn't say much, so don't expect anything from her. She's just going to make her notes and ignore you like most of the others."

"Condition good. Physically healthy. Bruises and tranquilizers minor. Subject ready for work as early as few hours," she says, taking note of her observations.

It sounds like gibberish.

"What work are you talking about?" I ask, looking directly at the chimp-woman's face. She doesn't even bat an eye. Her focus is completely on her device.

"Behavior disobedient," she says. "Unlike others, spirit intact. May want to expedite process for this subject."

"Expedite what?" I attempt another question.

"Van Faye quick with delivery," she says. "Satisfied with service. Unfortunate must drop elephant as supply source. Worked with several bosses. Van Faye was most reliable and ensured quality. But cannot be trusted."

"Source? Delivery? Are you talking about me?"

My tone morphs from angry and hostile to whiny and desperate.

"Will you quit it already?" Mack says. "You're giving me a headache with all the noise. Can't an old tiger get some sleep?"

"Shut up!" I scream at him.

"You're the one who needs to be quiet. It's useless."

"But I need to know! This isn't right. You can't just kidnap us. Someone's going to come looking for me. The authorities, my parents, someone. You think you can abduct us from the street and no one's going to notice?"

"No one will notice," she says.

I'm caught off guard. I'd gotten so used to her ignoring me that a simple response is surprising.

"Like hell no one will!" I say. "I have people that care about me! The authorities will be on the lookout."

"Incorrect. No one cares. All subjects degenerates," she responds. "Undesired in society. Illusion of personal affection maintains in subjects. Truth is obvious. Subjects have abandoned social bonds for some time."

It's a bit hard to decipher what the creature is saying, but the message is clear enough. The words hit me hard. I try to imagine an animal, any animal, that's worried sick of my disappearance. I close my eyes and think hard. Not one creature comes to mind. I've lived my life trying to make connections in Shogun, yet nothing has come from my efforts. I'm alone. I always have been.

It doesn't matter. I need to stay strong if I am to survive.

"You don't know anything," I say to the being.

"Know plenty," she responds tersely. "All subjects similar in backgrounds and motives. Cat subject not special. Not individual. Simply a social clone of others. In society, such beings easily disposed of."

"Well, the police will look."

"Authorities look in wrong place. Will investigate crime lords."

"And the crime lords will tell them about The Collector."

"Irrelevant. Collector's identity remains mystery. Police will chase phantom being."

"Someone will find out who you are."

"Unlikely. No witnesses left behind."

"What does that mean?"

The creature looks back at its tablet. It appears something has alerted it.

"Have wasted time talking," she says. "No further questions. Subject due for work later in evening. Will see you soon."

The chimp-woman turns around and walks in the other direction, out of my view.

"Hey, wait!" I yell. "You need to tell me more. You can't just leave us!"

"It's useless" Mack says. "You should be happy she actually talked to you. We're stuck here and that's that."

I cease my shouting and slump down. My body curls up. I try to find a safe place to go to, a place where I can run away from this horrible predicament. But it's useless. I find no solace. I lose my concern regarding the upcoming plans this chimp has in store for me. Instead, I dread seconds as they pass by.

"Hey Mack," I say, "have you seen any of these animals escape?"

"No," he says.

It's the answer I didn't want but expected.

Chapter 27 – Bastion

Reconcile

<u>March 13, 3061 11:49 PM</u>

I've had the past hour to contemplate my next move. I left Ivy's room feeling shocked and dismayed. I decided to walk back to my pod instead of teleporting there. It was a long trek, one filled with anger and confusion. Things have never been easy with my daughter ever since the divide happened, but I never would have imagined this. I know she loved her precious Aunt Lucy, but I can't believe she's plotting something with her behind not only my back, but Iris's as well.

The discovery hurt both my pride and disappointed me as a father. What has my parenting done to lead Ivy to this path? Am I that much of a failure that I can't even steer her in the right direction? She's willing to follow Lucy and help her with her sinister schemes despite all the warnings I've given her. Was the moral compass I tried to set simply a lost cause?

I think of the what ifs that could have made me a better parent. Perhaps I shouldn't have banished Lucy. Perhaps if I was more understanding, Iris wouldn't have kicked me out. So many possibilities flushed down the toilet. But the past is something I can only reflect on, not live in, and now I have to make tough decisions if I want to save what's left of this father daughter relationship.

Ivy Lawton. Sending progress. Schedule on track. Expect no delays. Prepare to leave soon.

That's the message Ivy received from Lucy. I analyze it over and over in my mind, but the last part is what gets to me. Prepare to leave soon. Ivy is planning to go somewhere, and based on her behavior in the last few days, it's somewhere far. I know she has the desire to leave this island forever. I'd say it's stronger than Iris's. If she does go, I'll track her down, but that's not the part that pains me. The part that pains me is that she didn't tell us. She's just going to leave her family without a whisper, make us both worried wrecks. She'll be a runaway, and there are no officials Iris or I can turn to. How could my daughter be so selfish? Doesn't she realize she'll hurt the ones she loves?

Even worse, she's running away to her, that chimp asshole. I'm so baffled. I thought banishing Lucy from this island would be a good thing, that the farther that bitch is from Ivy, the better. Yet it seems it's actually fueled Ivy's desire. But if I'd let Lucy stay, her influence would be stronger. Ivy might have abandoned us regardless. If only that dirty ape would have left me alone. I made the mistake of letting her live. I should've blasted her once my family was involved. I have no idea what Lucy is planning, but with her schemes of grandeur and Ivy's growing telekinesis, anything is possible.

I need to tell Iris. Or should I confront Ivy myself?

Perhaps telling Iris isn't the best idea. I'm the one who discovered her secret, and I feel it's my responsibility to keep Ivy away from Lucy. I'm the only one who truly knows how dangerous she is. I always knew, dating to the times when Lucy and I worked together at HORUS. Iris doesn't know what Lucy is capable of. She has always had a soft heart for the crazy hybrid, and if I tell Iris the predicament, she might actually side with Lucy. Hell, this could turn into another argument. I think she hates me so much that she'd consider pushing Ivy to Lucy just to scorn me.

Wait a second, what am I saying? I'm making crazy stories in my head again. How could I think Iris would put her friendship with Lucy over our daughter? These thoughts of paranoia are what's causing the friction. Iris may hate me, but she thinks the world of Ivy. Their mother daughter bond cannot be broken. It doesn't matter who the enemy is—me, Lucy—if someone is putting Ivy in danger, Iris will do whatever it takes to protect her. The idea that Iris would let personal differences interfere with her judgment is ludicrous.

Iris must know. She has the right. I can't keep secrets from Iris, especially when the news is about Ivy. To keep a secret like this from her would only strain our relationship further. For so long I've wanted to rebuild the bridge that has been burned to the ground. How can I pave the first piece if it's built on a foundation of lies? No, Iris will get the news, and we will talk to Ivy together.

It'll make things easier too. Ivy won't listen to me. She'll blow me off and push me away the second I bring up Lucy. We're already on borderline speaking terms. I get the feeling she only tolerates me. No, she needs to listen to a voice she's comfortable with, one that she accepts and loves. Ivy doesn't trust me, but she trusts Iris with her life. The voice that talks to my daughter has to be hers.

I'm actually surprised Ivy is keeping such information from Iris. I guess that's what disturbs me so much about the situation. Iris is Ivy's best friend on this island, her confidant, the one that holds all her secrets without judgment. Ivy tells Iris everything. Ivy must be doing something so atrocious that she can't even tell her own mother about it.

What is she plotting with Lucy? Perhaps the reason she doesn't want to tell Iris is because it has something to do with Iris. Iris and Lucy are friends, but I wouldn't put her above sacrificing her own friends for her needs. The chimp is cold like a snake in the wintertime. Her lack of empathy is legendary. She's changed a bit, I'll give her that, but no one truly changes, not even us hybrids.

Then again, Iris has changed, and now I sit in my pod with a communicator in my hand, ready to make the call, or not. Why is this so hard? It's just a simple call. I used to live with Iris, used to spend so many intimate moments with her. I remember a time when I thought we'd be together forever. I was supposed to be her protector, the one who saved her from her life of hardship.

Where did things go wrong? I've asked the question so many times, and I have so many answers to it, yet I can't find a resolution. It is my eternal struggle, and I feel it will linger with me until the day I die.

Bah! Enough of this. I've been trained to be a hybrid of action, not one that wallows and mopes. I have to set aside my melancholy. Ivy is the only one on my mind, and I can't dwell anymore.

I pick up the communicator and reach out to my love. My heart is racing with anticipation. What will Iris say? How will she react? Will she even pick up knowing it's me on the other line?

My communicator beeps and beeps and beeps, and I sit there nervously waiting for her to answer. A few seconds pass by, then ten, then a whole minute, and I don't hear her voice. Perhaps she's ignoring me after all. But I won't give up. I'll stay on the line as long as I have to for both of them.

But then reality sets in. Another minute passes and there's no answer. I'm confusing my persistence with foolishness.

"This is dumb," I say to myself. "Why would Iris pick up? We haven't talked for years. What makes today so different?"

"Hello?" I hear a familiar voice say.

Oh my God, she actually answered. My brain scrambles and I'm at a loss for words. It's been so many years that I second guess my senses and wonder if I'm dreaming. My mind can't even compute a response.

"What do you want, Bastion?" she says.

I snap out of my daze and get my mind straight. There's no video feed, it's just her voice. And it sounds a little fuzzy, garbled. It's kind of odd. Reception should be crystal clear on the island.

"Where are you?" I ask her.

"What do you want?" she repeats herself, disregarding my question.

She's already losing patience, so I have to make this quick.

"Iris, it's about Ivy," I say. "I think she's in trouble."

"What? What kind of trouble?" she says. Her tone changes immediately from annoyed to concerned.

"Well, she's been acting weird. I mean, she's normally pretty hostile to me, but lately she seems sad, worried about something. I think she's gotten involved in something bad, real bad. It has to do with Lucy."

"Lucy?"

She stops speaking. She sounds shaken by the mere mention of her name.

"How do you know this?" she asks. "What does Lucy want with her?"

Crap, I can't tell her I went snooping around her place. This conversation would be over.

"I don't know what Lucy wants," I say, ignoring her first question. "They're in league with each other, and that spells trouble. I know you got along with her, but you also know how Lucy is. With Ivy's powers and Lucy's influence, Ivy could be in real danger."

Once again, there's a long pause before Iris answers.

"And you're sure of this?" she asks. "You actually have some concrete evidence? This isn't one of your paranoid theories?"

"Positive," I say. "I have proof."

"And you actually know Ivy is in jeopardy? Or you simply think it?"

"Trust me, Iris, I know."

"Very well, then. This sounds pretty serious. I'll have to talk with Ivy, but I don't want to storm in and make it seem like a confrontation. Do you have the evidence on hand?"

"Yes."

"Then I want to meet to discuss this. I want to make sure I have all the facts before talking to my daughter."

She wants to meet? She wants to meet!

"Okay!" I say, barely able to hold in my glee. "We can meet and I'll tell you what I know."

"Fine, but don't get any ideas," she says in a threatening tone.

"When should we meet?"

"In a week, March twentieth at ten in the morning. I need some time to think about this and do some investigating myself."

"At my place?"

"No. Like I said, don't get any ideas. We'll meet at the cliffs, the ones that you and Ivy often spend time at."

"Sounds like a plan."

"I will see you in a week. And Bastion?"

"Yes?"

"Don't call me again."

She disconnects her communicator. The conversation was brief. I thought Iris would have more questions and concern, but she was cold about things. That may be because of me though. Her disgust hasn't wavered. Perhaps she's simply too shocked to rally a thorough response. Maybe she realized I was right about Lucy all along. I'm sure when we get together, she'll have much more to talk about.

Seven days, March twentieth. That's when I'll see her. I'm filled with anticipation. I didn't want to reunite under these circumstances, but then again, I'm thrilled that there's a chance to reconcile. Perhaps this is the start of a new beginning. It's been so long, and I know she'll give me a second chance. I have to prove my worth. I want to show Iris I'm a good father, a good partner, that the only way we can be safe is if we're a family. That's all that's ever mattered to me, family. I thought I had one with Lionel Changer and HORUS, but it was always lacking. Iris is my family, Ivy is my family. It's time to mend these broken bonds.

Yes, seven days couldn't come sooner.

Chapter 28 - General Rox

Collapse

<u>March 14, 3061 4:45 AM</u>

The sun is coming up soon and our team has made no progress. Silverwolf has been at it for over four hours, using its skills under our guidance, but the search has been cold. No scents, no evidence, not even a footprint. The Collector is out there somewhere, and it frustrates me to no end. Allen is tired. I'm tired. We desperately need to rest, but now is not the time to quit.

The only thing we have to go on are rumors. We've been gathering information from the locals concerning The Collector. Most of our investigations have been disappointing. The residents are more interested gawking at Silverwolf even though a famed general is talking to them on Silverwolf's holoscreen. Almost always, the conversation morphs into a question and answer session on how Silverwolf works, what my creation is made of, why the Alliance created it, and so on. I've only been able to attain bits and pieces of information. It's never a full story, and it's been extremely unproductive.

From what I've gathered so far, the creature is a mystery to the residents. It's a boogieman, a feared legend known for taking vagrants off the streets. None of the locals have ever seen it face to face. It's possible The Collector only deals with the bosses and isn't a citizen of Shogun or even Fan Zui Bin. With a personal teleportation device in hand, that's a likely assumption. Other than that, the intelligence I gained was minimal.

The occupants of Shogun are petrified to even whisper The Collector's name.

The night wasn't completely fruitless. The civilians weren't very helpful in our search, but the authorities provided something for us to work with. They received alerts of various supply depot security sensors going off. There weren't any reports of theft or loss of inventory, but they were still notified. They told us a rat or some small animal was the most likely culprit, but we were dead out of leads. This supply depot news was the only thing we had going for us, so Allen and I sent Silverwolf to investigate each one.

The Narukami, Shirogane, and Hanamura Supply Depots were the targets, and we were given access to each one. The Narukami Supply Depot was the newest and most used facility on the list, so it was the first one Silverwolf checked out. It was one of the cleanest, nicest, state-of-the-art supply depots I've ever seen. It was also one of the largest, stocked with every item imaginable ready to be teleported to anywhere in the world. The Collector definitely wasn't there. It would be too obvious.

Then Silverwolf went to the Shirogane Supply Depot. It wasn't as nice as the Narukami one, but it was still in good condition. It was smaller and in a more secluded part of town. I was certain we'd find The Collector there. It fit the profile of a nice getaway spot, plenty of supplies yet far enough from civilization to hide. However, Silverwolf scoured the area left and right, shining scanners, and found absolutely nothing. Another supply depot and another empty-handed search.

The last one is the Hanamura Supply Depot. Silverwolf currently stands in front of it. It's larger than the Shirogane Supply Depot, but also much older and decrepit looking. The paint is crusting off and there are several cracks running through the walls. The other supply depots were beautifully landscaped. Radiant shades of green surrounded their areas. Here it's different. All I see is brown, nothing but dirt and dead plant life littering the perimeter. The authorities said that the Hanamura Supply Depot was barely in use and had plans to be decommissioned. From the way it looks, that sounds about right. Meanwhile, a newer supply depot that would put the Narukami Supply Depot to shame is going to be built a few blocks away.

It's odd that the security alert got set off here because there doesn't appear to be a soul in the vicinity. If The Collector is here, it's either a tactical mistake or a perfectly set up trap. I feel it's the latter. A part of me even thinks The Collector is toying with us, like a hunter with its prey.

But that's okay. Silverwolf is prepared now. We've analyzed the data from the previous battle. We know The Collector's abilities and the tricks it'll play. We're ready. We are the hunters, not it.

"Command Silverwolf to enter the premise and start the search for clues," I say to Mark Allen. "Have him fish out any evidence that can be found."

"Yes, sir," he says.

Silverwolf begins to walk toward the musty building and enters through the front. Unlike other supply depots that usually have a lobby or office area, this one is basically a big warehouse and nothing more. Everything is off, from the machinery to computer systems. It appears that it hasn't been online for quite some time. The place is dusty, dingy, and pretty empty. Whatever goods were stored here have been sitting around for a while. And the supplies are quite sparse.

Silverwolf begins to scan the ground, looking for footprints, handprints, paw prints, whatever it can find. My creation looks at every inch of floor, cracking down on each corner in hopes of discovering a trail. And like all the other ones, there's nothing. No loose hairs or scales, not even a spec of saliva. The supply depot has lived up to its reputation. No one has been here for some time. And I mean no one—not thieves, not crime bosses, not the homeless, and definitely not The Collector.

"Have Silverwolf look around a little more, but honestly, I think this is another cold lead, just like the others," I say to Mark Allen. "We're done for now. I'm going back to my quarters. Once Silverwolf completes his search, you may rest too, and we'll start again around noon. Understood?"

I start to walk back, too exhausted to wait for Allen's confirmation. But even as I approach the door, he still doesn't answer.

"Allen, did you hear me? Is that understood?" I repeat myself.

No response.

"Allen!" I bark.

"Um, sir, um…" he finally spits out. "You have to look at the communication link."

"What now?"

I peer into Silverwolf's feed to see the wall he faces cracking. The fissures travel slowly at first, like water trickling down the side of a bucket, but soon the crevices expand violently. They break and tear as loud crunching noises erupt from their direction. One crack rips through the wall in a matter of milliseconds. Rubble falls like snowflakes from an unkempt roof. I've only seen this happen once, but the events stay fresh in my mind.

"Crap, it was a trap after all," I say.

And with those words, the wall that was in front of Silverwolf splits apart from the building. It careens toward the wolf in seconds like a bullet train smashing into traffic. We hear a smack echo through the depot and his feed scrambles upon collision, temporarily going blank while Mark Allen and I can only hear what's going on. The sound of swooshes followed by a large, earth-rumbling crash. Metal crunches and rubble bounces. Thousands of tiny pitters echo as debris falls to the floor.

And then silence.

"Get Silverwolf's visual link online now!" I yell at Mark Allen. "And give me a damage report!"

The prisoner-scientist quickly gets to work fiddling with every control, keyboard, and device he has.

"Rebooting the communications systems," he says. "Damage report currently being processed."

A holoscreen pops up while a percentage flashes on it. It's quickly climbing its way to one hundred.

"Visual feed is back online," Allen says.

The screen is completely black, but I see faint traces of light. Silverwolf must be caught under some loose rubble. As the creature gets back on its feet, the debris slackens and collapses, falling to the ground, while the visual feed gets clearer. Silverwolf appears functional, standing on its four feet sturdily.

"The assessment is done," Allen says.

"How much damage has Silverwolf sustained?" I ask.

"Surprisingly very little. Reports show a few cracks in the armor, but other than that, everything is fully functional. Weapons systems are online, and mobility capabilities are a full go."

"The Hanamura Supply Depot is old, making the wall weak and thin. The impact to Silverwolf must've been like a twig hitting a hovercar."

"The air is still dusty, but I think a target is approaching."

Allen doesn't have to tell me who it is. I already know. The black figure rises as the dust settles. The Collector has come to finish this. I should've known a creature as elusive as The Collector couldn't be found so easily unless it wanted to be. This was an obvious trap, but my obsession with finding the being made me disregard that fact. But I've had a few hours to prepare my strategy. Silverwolf is ready.

"Have Silverwolf engage!" I yell.

But The Collector beats him to it. Just as before, the being levitates objects with its mind, palms opened to each one. Scrap metal, empty containers, junky supplies, and other items float in the air. Then the creature hurls them at Silverwolf with a swift movement of its arms. They fly toward my canine at unbelievable speeds.

It doesn't faze me. I've learned.

"Bioshields initiate!" I scream into the command module.

Immediately, the translucent shield encompasses Silverwolf. The objects collide and deflect from it.

"Put up the communication link," I tell Mark Allen. He does so, and a holoscreen with our feed faces The Collector. "You're going to have to learn some new tricks."

I know I shouldn't gloat, but when I'm prepared, I never lose a battle. The Collector is in for a challenge.

"Fire the cannons!" I tell Mark Allen. "Full assault!"

Every one of Silverwolf's turrets sprout from its armor. Cannons, blasters, grenades, the works are primed and ready to fire. All this firepower would level tens of enemies, and we're using it just on one.

But The Collector opens its palms at Silverwolf and closes its hands into fists. It then twists its wrists and the cadre of weapons turns with it, contorting from their base in Silverwolf's armor and rotating in an unnatural fashion. I hear metal and gears snapping and grinding. Sparks fly and parade my visual feed.

"What's going on?" I ask Mark Allen.

"It appears The Collector has damaged the cannons and turrets directly," he says. "They're now deformed and offline. The targeting system has also been impaired."

"Damnit!"

"Always with your guns," The Collector says as we watch from the screen. "You need to learn some new tricks as well."

"Projectiles are disabled," Mark Allen says. "What should Silverwolf do now?"

"Engage physical combat," I say.

"General?"

"Just do it, Allen!"

"Yes, sir."

Silverwolf gets the order and instantly charges toward The Collector. Two energy whips spurt from its back. The Collector actually looks surprised with the strategy. The moment the wolf started its charge, The Collector's body tensed and its arms shook. But it quickly gets itself ready, moving into a fighting stance while it anticipates the oncoming collision.

Silverwolf powers forward, and a split second before making contact, it fires its boosters for an extra push. The Collector ducks to the right and easily dodges Silverwolf like a matador with a bull, but it forgets about Silverwolf's energy whips, which trail behind. One of them latches onto The Collector's ankle and the momentum carries it. The Collector falls face forward, landing with a painful-sounding thud.

Silverwolf then retracts the whips and pulls The Collector toward it, launching the black-armored menace into the air. My creation then gets its jaw ready, hoping to snatch The Collector in the sky like a ragdoll. But The Collector recovers in flight and stiffens its feet. It then pulls the rope to it. The whip fully retracts and Silverwolf is greeted in the face with a flying kick courtesy of The Collector. It causes my creation to stagger and release its hold. The creature lands softly on two feet and the enemies stare each other down once more.

The two circle each other, contemplating their next move. My wolf is thinking how to approach the enemy and I refrain from giving any direction. Relying on Silverwolf's instincts is a better battle plan than I can give. The Collector also takes some time to think of the next move. Mark Allen and I watch intensely.

The Collector acts first, unleashing its own energy whips from its wrists and lashing them at Silverwolf. My creation dodges the first one and catches the second one with its teeth. Silverwolf has a firm grip on it and starts to pull The Collector. All the creature can do is struggle to get free. Silverwolf gets closer and closer.

Thus, The Collector releases the whips from its wrists. The moment they hit the floor, the cloaked being starts its next attack. The Collector throws a roundhouse kick at Silverwolf's head. The wolf retreats to avoid the blow and then lunges forward, fangs first. Silverwolf's jaws are coated with the same metal alloy that covers its body. One bite could tear off an enemy's limbs.

The Collector takes notice and retreats just as Silverwolf did. But my canine maintains the assault, snapping its fangs continuously while all The Collector can do is back off. Step by step the wolf sends The Collector in the other direction, until finally, we have the creature cornered. The Collector's back presses against the wall. Nowhere to run this time.

Silverwolf sets and jumps forward with its jaws wide open. But before Silverwolf gets there, The Collector raises its arm and in unison, two pieces of wall split apart from behind. The creature then clasps its hands simultaneously, and the slabs come together on Silverwolf. The bioshields are off. My creation gets the full impact. It stumbles to the floor while a rain of debris falls on the wolf's head.

It's the same move The Collector pulled on Sai. Except the walls are weak and my wolf can take it. Silverwolf quickly recovers without sustaining any serious damage from the previous blow. Its durability is quite remarkable. So far the wolf has survived being thrown from a building, getting blasted by grenades, having walls smash into it, and endured more telekinetic shots than any other animal could possibly handle. Yet here it is, still standing, ready for battle. Silverwolf is indeed the perfect soldier, and it's only a prototype.

"Give it up, you fool," I say tauntingly to The Collector. "Silverwolf cannot be taken down. It'll take anything you dish out."

"Is that so?" The Collector says.

The floor vibrates around Silverwolf. Pillars shake, containers fall down, and a window shatters nearby. Pieces of dust float from the ground, spreading a light fog of dirt. Is it an earthquake? No. It's the work of The Collector. Throughout all the tremors, my wolf maintains its eye on the prize, and to our astonishment, we see The Collector launch into the air, floating above us like an unholy spirit. The Collector flies without the use of boosters or anti-gravity tech. It's all natural.

I shouldn't have been so arrogant. The Collector raises both arms high above its head, and the floor shakes even more violently. It's gone from a mild earthquake to full-on seismic activity. At first it isn't so bad. A few light fixtures plummet from the ceiling. They crash on the floor and explode into millions of pieces. Stacked containers topple over. But that's as far as it goes.

However, a few seconds later, a support beam collapses. Then a piece of the roof drops and free-falls like deadweight. Several windows burst and shatter, causing a rain of glass. One of the walls crumbles into millions of pieces. Now I'm worried. This supply depot won't last very long if things continue to get destroyed left and right. The Collector is bringing the place down, literally.

The view from Silverwolf's eyes becomes as shaky as its surroundings and within seconds, it becomes one giant blur. It's still clear enough to see that within the next few minutes the roof will crumple on top of Silverwolf. He'll be buried alive if he doesn't get out of there.

"This building is going down," I say. "Allen, engage the boosters. Silverwolf needs to escape!"

Silverwolf engages flight mode and the rockets begin to flare. He starts the launch, but The Collector spots the wolf and sticks a palm to the wolf's direction.

"Not so fast," I hear The Collector say.

A metal beam goes flying across the room and swats Silverwolf like a fly. He plummets hard to the ground. His visual link goes down momentarily, but when it recovers, it's too late. A wall of rubble and scrap metal fall upon Silverwolf, hitting him like a tsunami. Mark Allen and I see nothing but a blanket of dust and darkness approaching my armored soldier. It's massive. Even The Collector is gone from our view.

And then it hits my wolf. The screen goes completely black, not because his feed is down, but because too much stuff obstructs the camera. We hear a mix of sounds. Metal clangs, winds roar, wires snap, pipes burst. It only lasts a few seconds, but it feels like an eternity. And then the sound subsides. We hear nothing but eerie silence. The building has fully collapsed, and Silverwolf is trapped beneath it.

"What's the damage?" I ask Mark Allen.

"Surprisingly, nothing is critical," he says.

"Hot damn, outstanding work! You really have made an indestructible soldier! He must have had at least two tons of weight fall on top of him. Any normal being would've been crushed! But not my wolf! Command him to continue with the pursuit."

Mark Allen fiddles with the controls, but there's no response. He does so again more fiercely, but nothing.

"It appears Silverwolf is stuck," Allen says.

"What?" I say. I'm flabbergasted. "How is that so?"

"Silverwolf is durable, but it's not invincible. The weight is simply too much for Silverwolf to get out of."

"Damnit! There has to be a way to get up."

I spoke too soon. Right after the words leave my mouth, a piece of debris that was on Silverwolf flies into the air, clearing up Silverwolf's vision link. Then another piece rockets off of my wolf. Then another. And another. And another.

"What's going on?" Mark Allen asks. Can't he tell? It's obvious. I thought he was supposed to be smart.

The Collector stands in front of Silverwolf. The creature lifted some debris off my creation, leaving parts of the wolf's body exposed.

"Can he get out now that the load is lighter?" I ask Mark Allen.

"Negative, it's still too heavy," he says.

"What is The Collector doing?"

But then I see it with my own eyes. The Collector points its palms at Silverwolf and concentrates. Its arms shake a bit, but after a few seconds of focus, The Collector's hands pull back and pluck something that was embedded in Silverwolf.

"He just ripped out the bioshield activator!" Mark Allen says.

"What?"

The Collector raises its hand again, pointing at a different area on Silverwolf, and does the motion again. This time a small microchip has been ripped out.

"Now the muscle power core is disabled!" Allen says. "Silverwolf is immobile without it."

The Collector does it again.

"The systems monitor is damaged now," Allen says. "I can't read Silverwolf's vitals."

I realize The Collector is disabling Silverwolf piece by piece. It picks a target and dismantles my creature. I suppose this is different than telekinetically hurling scrap metal or pieces of wall. This requires precision, accuracy. The Collector needs the target to be still, which explains why the creature pinned down Blackwolf earlier to rip off its mask. The same goes with Silverwolf, except this time it used a whole supply depot instead of some energy whips to restrain my canine.

The Collector stops its assault and walks toward Silverwolf, looking directly into the visual link.

"This is a message for you Alliance cronies," the creature says, speaking to Mark Allen and me. "I'm taking Silverwolf back. He's done working for you.

You've seen what I can do. If you don't want additional problems, I suggest you leave me alone."

And with those final words, The Collector raises its hand one last time and rips out the communications controls. Our holoscreen shuts down. Silverwolf's feed is gone and there's no way for either of us to know what will happen to him.

The battle is over. I've lost.

Chapter 29 – Iris Lawton

Farewells

<u>March 14, 3061 4:59 AM</u>
Bring this place down. I need to bring this place down.

I've already messed up my execution. I was supposed to be quick and hop over those energy whips after avoiding Silverwolf's booster power. Unfortunately, I didn't get the timing right, and one of them latched onto my ankle. I did a total face plant to the ground. Not one of my proudest moments.

Getting the wolf to the supply depot in the first place was simple enough. I foresaw how to do it in a vision, and I followed the directions to a tee. My precognition told me my victory would be in a supply depot. The stage needed to be set. Hacking into the supply depot security network was a breeze. If my sister, Candy, did it many years ago, so could I. Setting up the trap was easier. All I needed to do was lay down a few juicy breadcrumbs for the Alliance to follow, and then they'd send their weapons my way. That's always been their M.O.

Now it's just Silverwolf and me, one on one. So far I'm on the losing side. I disabled his weapons, but I should have known that I couldn't best him in a physical fight. The only thing keeping me afloat is Bastion's many years of training. I suppose that's one good thing he's done for me.

The Alliance has done their homework. They've made Silverwolf indestructible. Even with my telekinesis, it's an impossible task. Blackwolf was different. In her past life, she was always the weaker of the wolves. She never matched up to Silverwolf physically or mentally. Her armored self was the same way. That's why I targeted her first. But with Silverwolf, it's a different kind of beast. Even my visions tell me the odds aren't in my favor. Every attempt I've seen to take him down leads to my demise. I've only seen one way to defeat him.

Bring this place down. I need to bring this place down.

I've been sloppy. Other than the tripping incident, I've made plenty of other mistakes. First of all, the battle shouldn't have lasted this long. I was supposed to humor my enemy for a bit, then unleash my fury. But I missed the window my vision told me to take, and I've been playing catch-up since. I hope these actions don't alter the future I anticipate. I don't have time to reassure myself with another vision. I'll have to improvise.

My back is against the wall. I'm cornered and running out of options. Ah, but wait, Silverwolf's bioshields are inactive. And he's looking to finish me off with those powerful jaws. I can use his overzealousness to my advantage. Time to use the good old rock clap. It worked on Sai, it'll work on Silverwolf.

The moment he leaps, I rip two slabs from the walls and with my clap, they come together to crush Silverwolf. He goes crashing into the floor, and for a moment, I'm hopeful that I won't have to use the final attack. But he quickly recuperates and gets back on his feet. No matter what I throw at the wolf, he recovers and comes back fighting. But for this brief second, his attack has stopped. I have a new window to do what I'd planned all along.

Bring this place down. I need to bring this place down.

I use my hands to direct the energy. I close my eyes and focus. I mentally locate each part of this depot I want to attack. Everything—the walls, the floor, the roof, the storage bins, everything. Each image flashes through my mind as I simultaneously concentrate on the individual items. I feel the energy flowing from my body to every corner. The ground slowly shakes and the walls echo the vibrations.

I concentrate harder, and the shaking becomes more violent. If I don't move, I'll lose my footing to my own powers, so I raise my arms and levitate myself in the air. I open my eyes and unleash more force. Soon, portions of the roof come plummeting to the floor. If I'm not careful, a piece may land on top of my head. Thus, with a thought of my mind, I create a telekinetic bubble that encases and protects me. Falling debris that would've landed on me deflects off my shield and falls to the floor.

The Alliance has now caught on. They're ordering Silverwolf to escape. I see him preparing his boosters. But it's too late. I use a metal beam to bat him down and he comes crashing back to Earth. Escape plan destroyed. The building has almost fully collapsed, and the wolf becomes buried under the rubble.

When I first got this power, this telekinesis, I was scared. Lionel Changer had always hypothesized that my foresight was only the beginning, that I had the potential to grow. And as much as I hated him, it appeared he was right.

I was already a hybrid, a halfkind, an abomination. Then I became a freak among freaks, one that could look into the future. Many have hunted me, not only because of what I am, but because of the power I wielded. I felt like my precognition was a curse. I didn't want to know what was going to happen to me before it happened. That kind of knowledge could drive the mind insane. And I didn't want to be a target for anyone. This power made me feel like I was always going to be used, a pawn to a player, for the rest of my life.

I was terrified that my telekinesis would carry the same burden. But then I was given a chance to control it. Lucy helped me harness my potential, just as she did with my precognition. For that, I became even more grateful to my friend. And when this control came, I realized the usefulness of my abilities. They were no longer a curse, they became a gift. I understood what I never could before, that I could shape my destiny. And from that moment, that's exactly what I set out to do.

My power did the opposite of what I feared. I was the player, not the pawn. No longer will I run in fear, no longer will I be hunted. I will fight back, like a caged animal tired of its jail. But my battle is not reactionary, it's a plan. I've calculated every action, looked into several visions, and now the time is right. Now I will make my move. It's time to start the long quest to obtain what my fallen family has always wanted—freedom.

And my gifts will pass on to the next generation. My daughter has the same talents that I possess. I'm hopeful she'll eventually grow as powerful as me. So far she can only lift cups and pillows, light items, but one day it'll be mountains. The potential is there. I will help her develop her skills. She may even surpass me. When the climax comes and freedom is within our grasp, I would want nothing more than to have my daughter by my side. She knows my plans and has voiced her support ever since I told her about it years ago. Ivy is my loyal daughter. I am a proud mother.

The fight for my kind's freedom will be fought one battle at a time. And this one is about to end.

The building is completely leveled, and I shut down my telekinetic shield. I release the hold I have on myself and fall gently back to the ground. My attack is over. No more shaking, no more loud rumbling. I am on open ground, standing on a pile of ruin. I only hear a faint breeze blowing and feel the cool morning air softly caress my face. I look around to survey the damage. The dust is still thick, so I lift my hands and it quickly separates. Not a single pillar is left standing.

I don't see Silverwolf anywhere, but then again, I already know he's buried under all the debris. I locate him and lift up the pieces that cover him, removing enough to expose his head and parts of his body but leaving enough to keep him trapped. Now it's time to dismantle the creature.

Lifting and flinging objects is a lot different than picking off specific things. The latter requires concentration and a still target. It's hard to get a grip if what I'm trying to get a hold of is moving. I had to shackle down Blackwolf in order to get a handle of her mask. Silverwolf is no different. I know what I need to take out to disable the wolf and cut its feed to the Alliance, but now I can actually do it. Bringing down the depot was the only way I could tie him down. Sometimes I wish I could control living bodies, but it's much too difficult. My powers only work on inanimate objects.

I want to take out those pesky bioshields, the power core, the tracking module, and of course, the communications device. Simple enough. I merely aim my palms at their location on Silverwolf, concentrate a little, and there they go, popping out of the armor like firecrackers. It only takes a few seconds. Most devices are unplugged. Before I rip out the communications feed, I say some parting words to the Alliance.

"This is a message for you Alliance cronies. I'm taking Silverwolf back. He's done working for you. You've seen what I can do. If you don't want additional problems, I suggest you leave me alone."

Then I disable the link. The Alliance is out of Silverwolf's system forever. They've done enough to the poor guy. They mutilated his wonderful body. He doesn't belong to them anymore. No, now Silverwolf belongs to me, where he always should have remained.

I remove my mask to get a better look. I then rip out Silverwolf's mask with my telekinesis. His face is badly scarred with burn marks. His beautiful fur is no longer there. His eyes are completely white. He has a hallow look on his face. Behind his once magnificent eyes is nothing—no mind, no soul, no life. He is a ghost of his former self.

And as I stare into the face of my friend, I can't help but cry the tears I've waited years to shed.

"Oh, Fenrir, what have they done to you?" I say softly.

I continue to sob a little. I've already seen this moment so many times in my visions, but I have a difficult time comprehending it as it plays out in real time. Experiencing things is so much harder than looking at them.

I lift the wreckage that covers his body and set it to the side. Carefully, I dig my arms underneath Fenrir's and hold his head close to me, wrapping him in an embrace that I wish could last forever. In the distance, I see the sun starting to rise, and it reminds me of the moment I met him so many years ago.

That was just a memory, and soon this will be too.

Once again, I look into Fenrir's eyes. They appear to twitch. He barely moves a muscle, but that twitching tells me the story. It's his way of yelling out, begging me to end his pain.

Don't worry, old friend, I will.

I hold him closely one more time and then delicately lay his body back to the ground. Then I levitate a nearby rod and take a final look at the wolf I loved.

"I'm sorry, Fenrir," I say as the tears continue to flow. "I wish I would've known how things were going to be."

And with those last words, I send the rod hurling into Fenrir's head. I end things quickly. He's suffered enough. I put the personal porter on Fenrir and teleport him back to base, just like I did with Blackwolf. Then I activate my own porter. It's time to go home.

Chapter 30 – Fenrir Snow

Armor

<u>January 2, 3043 3:13 AM</u>

It's been quite a celebration. The year 3043 is upon us. The winter has been brutal, but our cabin is quite cozy, and I'm already psyched about the months ahead. Spring will be coming and hunting season will be back. We'll have a fresh supply of meat and the flowers will be blooming. It's what Iris looks forward to.

The holidays have been quite fun as well. I never really experienced a true human holiday season before. We wolves don't make a big deal out of it. However, every December Iris insists on celebrating. I suppose her human mother raised her and her family to cherish the holidays so it brings a certain sense of nostalgia for her. It was a big deal to them and remains a big deal to Iris. When she got me a Christmas gift during that first winter she spent alone, I was skeptical, insulted almost. But at the same time, I appreciated the gesture, and now it's become a tradition. I suppose it isn't about the gifts or the history behind the holiday, it's about appreciation for friends and family. Iris is the only family I have these days, and whenever December rolls around, I have to admit I look forward to it.

She cooked me a nice dinner and we opened gifts on Christmas morning. Then when New Year's Eve came around, we had a small party. We ate our meal and watched the live streams of animals celebrating in the street. Sometimes I can tell Iris wishes to be part of that crowd. She says it with her eyes. They're yearning and filled with curiosity. But at the same time, I think she's happy in this little cabin. We've carved a home together and both of us are at peace. I hope it lasts.

I haven't had the time to reflect on the past year during the festivities. What a year it's been. I've been a fugitive for quite some time, and I've adjusted fine. I must admit, though, I don't think I would have made it if it wasn't for her. I take great pride in being an independent creature. I have the skills to do it. My training with the Brotherhood has always kept me prepared to battle any physical hardship that may come my way. But it never trained me to handle the emotional trials.

I've always underestimated that part of surviving. After Eve, I felt it was a luxury, that in order to survive, all you needed was to keep your body alive. I ignored the pain and suffering that took a toll on my emotions. It was a mistake to do so. That's why I need Iris. As much as I like to say she needs me, I need her more. She is the one creature who helps me keep my soul intact. I was lost before her and then weary to let her in, but now she is the only one in my world. She is the reason I live.

What a strange year it has been. I've cut ties with everyone from the Brotherhood, even my own family. If anything, I should feel alone, sad, and depressed. But I feel none of those things. I feel fulfilled. I feel like my life has meaning now. Iris's companionship is more than I'll ever need in any lifetime. Sometimes I see her and think about what she's endured. She remains optimistic, cheery. I could never do that. She probably doesn't even think the way she carries herself is a big deal, but it has made me respect her more than ever.

And not only that, but I feel loved by her.
Sometimes, life takes a strange course. We started off as enemies for reasons I can't even quantify. I killed her brother without purpose. If anything, she should've hated me, and I should've killed her. But time has passed, circumstances have brought us together, and I sit here in this cabin grateful to the gods for letting things turn out the way they have.

I used to think I was cursed, that tragedy followed me like a wolf to its prey. But now I think quite the opposite. I recognize life isn't always easy, but if you persist, if you remain hopeful, one day things will work out. It may not happen in the way you expect, and you might be resistant to the change, but with an open mind, peace will come. That is what happened to me.

I hope things will stay this way for a while. I hope one day I will grow old with Iris. I used to hate the relationships dogs had with humans. Even after they gained their intelligence, I still saw dogs as slaves to their master, treated as the inferior being. Now here I am, a canine with a half-human companion. I'm not Iris's slave, but she will always be my master. Dare I say it, but I love this halfkind.

Iris is asleep, but I am awake. We are still on the lamb, and there are still those who look for us. I must stay awake and vigilant, not only this night, but every night, to ensure that my love is safe. I am trying to teach her the ways of combat so one day she won't have to rely on a crusty old wolf.

But until then, I must be the one who keeps her from harm. I am her armor, impenetrable, tough, and strong, to stop her attackers, to keep her alive. Our pursuers may come in dozens, even thousands, but I do not care. I'll take the hits. I'll absorb the damage. The Alliance, the

Brotherhood, whoever can send anyone they want. But when they chase Iris and see me standing in between them, they will know what it means to face death. They will know what love can do.

The winds blow harder against or cabin, and Iris tosses a little. I wonder what dreams she dreams. I don't have use for dreams anymore. I'm already in one. It is now I can finally say the future is coming, and I am hopeful for what it brings.

Chapter 31 – Adachi Konoe

Extraction

<u>March 17, 3061 11:11 AM</u>

I'm tired. I think it's been a few days since I came to this place, but it's hard to tell. Hell, I don't even know what time of the day it is. There's no sunlight, no windows, nothing that would let me know. All I've had to look at are these stupid grey walls and the crappy view from the cage door. It smells like shit thanks to the bucket I've been forced to do my business in. I smell horrible. The only thing I can do is lick myself as my primitive ancestors did. I never thought I'd be reduced to this.

Mack is gone. I was sleeping when it happened. I woke up to the sound of roaring and arguing between him and the chimp freak.

"What the hell are you doing?" Mack bellowed.

"Time for extraction," the chimp-human responded.

"No, it's not time for that! I know what that means. Please don't do it. I've seen others go the same way. I'm not ready."

Mack's voice had a violently desperate tone to it. Listening to his pleas sent chills down my spine. I tried to see what was going on, but from my vantage point, the two were out of view. I could only listen.

"You are ready," she responded.

"No, I'm not! I have so much I want to do, so much to see," he cried. "I'm begging just let me go! Let me-"

His petition was interrupted by a sharp sound. I heard a thud and then some gears moving. A few moments later, the door shut, and the room became quiet once more. That was the last time I ever heard Mack's voice. In fact, it's just been me in the cells. I'm the last new arrival.

Unfortunately, I've seen that chimp freak plenty of times since. I have to get fed, after all, and she appears to be the only one running this operation. Every day she comes with food and water, and I get served like a pet. It's enough to keep me alive but also little enough to leave me wanting more. She also scans me during her visits and checks my vitals to make sure I'm fit. I guess keeping me healthy is high on her priorities.

Whenever she stops by, I try to get something out of her. I ask her questions, demand answers, even yell insults.

"When are you letting me go?"

"I want to know why you're keeping me here!"

"You bitch! Set me free!"

But it's all in vain. Nothing gets to this mutant, nothing. All she does is focus on her devices, like a robot. Even when she speaks, it's monotone and unexpressive. From her appearance, I suspect she's half human, but from her actions, I question what she truly is.

And that's how the day goes. I sit in this cage and watch the hours go by. There's nothing but time on my hands. Time to sulk, time to think, time to regret.

That's the word that stays on my mind: regret. When I look back on my life, I realize there's not much to look back on. I've tried to hustle my way to the top, but now I'm forced to face the truth. All I do is lie, and the cat I lie to the most is myself. A week ago, before all this happened, I would look into the mirror and see a cool cat.

I'd see a hustler, a moneymaker, a top-notch player in the city of kings, Shogun. Now, if I could look in a mirror, I'd see a bottom feeder, a lowlife, a cat full of excuses, the lowest card in a hand played by the puppet masters of Shogun. I was a loser when I got to the big city, and I'm still a loser as I sit in this cage.

I should've listened to my parents. They warned me about how dangerous Shogun was. They told me my plans were foolish. I didn't listen. What did they know? They were just silly farm folk who feared the power Shogun could offer. I wasn't afraid. I welcomed the opportunity. While they saw the big cities as havens of crime, unregulated Alliance-free zones, I saw them as the place to make my bones. I was too damn proud and eager to see otherwise. Even when times grew tougher, my ego was too big to admit they were right. I thought I was the shit even though I had nothing to back it up. I guess arrogance is different from confidence.

Nevertheless I continued to grind that hustle because I felt my time was coming soon. I did it because I had big dreams. Achieving your goals is what life is about, right? I didn't have the skills or brains, but I had the ambition. How could you deny that to a youngster? My folly was that I was shooting for the wrong stars.

This is what happens when you aren't honest with yourself. My capturing by Van Faye and the predicament I'm in now is a culmination of all the mistakes I've made chasing the magic dragon. I knew I was doing things that would only dig me deeper into the hole. I started to owe bosses, made empty promises, all the while acting like there was nothing to worry about. The storm was coming, but I ignored it because I thought I was unbeatable. If only I hadn't, it could've all been avoided.

I'd do anything to have one more chance. If I could, I'd take the first teleporter back home. I'd walk to the farmlands, tell my parents I was sorry, and hope they would accept me back into their lives. They'd invite me in, and it'd be like old times again. I can taste my mom's soup just thinking about it.

But as I stare into the view in front of me, I realize it's only fantasy. I'm stuck here, and the only thing that comforts me is the frantic calls for help from my former cellmate as they replay in my memory. I will meet the same fate soon.

An opening door breaks me from my thoughts. I hear footsteps approaching and look up to see the abomination, the chimp. She appears as stone cold as ever. I look around and see her armed with a gun-like weapon and a small gurney contraption. She's not here to bring me a new cellmate, she's here to take me away.

So this is it, huh? It's time for things to end. I wonder if I should scream my heart out. What's the point? It's not going to do anything.

But I have to say something. I have to have the last word. Our eyes meet, and I stare piercingly at her.

"Fuck you," I say sternly.

And with those last words, she points the gun at me and fires. It's not a bullet that comes out of the barrel, it's a dart. I feel a stinging sensation hit my neck. I'm not dead. I thought I'd see darkness, but I don't.

Instead, something much worse happens. I collapse to the cell floor, hitting my head on the ground. I try to move my paws, but I can't. Hell, I can't even move my face. I'm completely paralyzed. I'm aware of what's going on. I can smell, I can hear, I can see, but as hard as I try, I can't control my body.

The chimp opens the cage. My instincts tell me to jump out and make an escape, but my instincts do nothing. A drone enters and lifts my body, placing it gently on the gurney that hovers in the air. As if I weren't immobile enough, belts eject from its sides and strap me down securely.

Though I'm paralyzed, I now finally have a chance to see my surroundings from outside the cage. The chimp woman leads the way, and the automated gurney follows her. We exit the holding cells and walk into a hallway. The bright lights hit my eyes. It's a huge change from my previous holdings. The walls are a light hue of pale blue. The color is so soft it looks white. We pass by some doors, but everything is closed. I also think we're underground because I don't see a window anywhere. The corridor is quite long because we've been traveling through it for a while. The chimp woman remains apathetic and quiet during the entire walk. Her silence makes me nervous.

Finally, we enter another room. This one is dimmer, but a beaming glare shines from the center. I can't move my head, so I try to maneuver my eyes to get a proper glimpse of the setting. I see a lot of machines. I don't recognize many of the instruments, but from what I can tell, they're monitoring devices. Holoscreens litter the place, displaying percentages and stats.

It appears harmless, but that's when my eyes see something else. Next to the equipment are various medical tools. I see an industrial strength syphon and several cutting instruments. There's also a large needle device and a hose looking contraption attached to it. To the side are a bunch of gadgets I've never seen. But they all look sharp and I can smell traces of blood emitting from their direction.

Lastly, I notice a waste bucket labeled "biohazard" and from it hang several bloody rags. I look closer and see the cloths have pieces of fur of different colors. They belonged to someone, and I can only imagine what these poor saps' fates were. Is that what's going to happen to me?

My heart is racing. No, it can't be. Is this chimp going to murder me? Is she going to experiment on me? The evidence I see gives me the obvious answer, but it can't end like this! I'm going to go out fighting.

But it's useless. I can't even move my legs or show my claws. My fight is over before it even began.

The chimp woman approaches me and sticks something in my side. She looks as detached as always. The prick pinches my torso and the pain shoots across. I then feel a little dazed. My mind starts to drift into unconsciousness and my vision becomes hazy. My eyelids grow heavy, and as much as I try to stop it, they shut and send me into darkness.

I think of my life one last time. It is now that I realize we truly have one life to live, even us cats. I wish I would have lived it differently.

Chapter 32 – Lucy

Friend

<u>March 17, 3061 12:05 PM</u>
Completing latest extraction. Have dissected necessary vitals. Now cleaning up parts for storage.

Cat specimen was in excellent condition. Much better than tiger specimen Kirijo. Surprised Van Faye procured such creature. Usually subjects from Van Faye in bad shape. Bought low. Excellent payoff in end.

Process completed. Not much left of subject Konoe. Harvested everything. Will dispose of remains in incinerator. Program drones to clean blood, entrails on operating table. Syphon tool old, must purchase new one. Have gutted creature of organs and bones. Also extracted strands of fur. Anything with DNA must be collected. Yet must not hoard. Only take what needed. But requirements many.

Extraction phase serving purpose. But must move to creation phase soon. Have gathered what needed. Goal to recreate Changer's work on schedule. Collection and deals with bosses better idea than prostitutes. Less loose ends. Control own supply and sources. Changer's method risky and unnecessary.

Am close to unlocking method for artificial splicing. Birthing implants will be obsolete. New method safer for all involved. Leaves less trail to follow. Have learned from Changer's mistakes. Now time to conduct trial runs.

Feline samples have been prime target. Have produced extraordinary beings. Iris Lawton, Ivy Lawton, to lesser extent Bastion, all proven worthy specimens. Feline and human combination provides potential for great power. Not limited. Will use various animal types. Combinations necessary. To unlock secret behind combination is to unlock perfect specimen. Creatures will dominate inferior creatures. Only way to end unnecessary conflict, only way to unite front, only way to kick start evolution.

Friend and I have same views. Both believe hybrids are future. Must start anew and preserve species. Alliance tried to crush new species. Alliance foolish. Does not realize altruism behind goals. Alliance only plays political games, does not think of greater good. World too shortsighted.

Iris Lawton has own missions to complete. Will need to communicate with friend to check status. See her a confidant, as leader. Only one willing to help me understand self when self could not understand. Did not expect anything out of relationship, but now see value of friendship. Lawton also has desire. Supports me in work. Lawton understands need for our species to survive. Friend has lost much. But willing to fight battles to take back what taken from her.

Also fond of Ivy Lawton. See her as protégé. Extremely smart. Has caring mother. Did not think self would be caring of young ones. Was uncomfortable with idea of teaching young Lawton. But as sessions continued, grew to be fond of little one. Angry at Bastion for having to leave her abruptly. No matter. Lost time recovered. Future is next. Will continue mentoring under eye of Iris. Hope Ivy will assist when creation phase begins. Looking forward to working with her.

Time to reach Iris. Pick up communicator. Wait for answer.

"Lucy?" Iris Lawton answers. Sounds tired.

"Iris. Latest specimen done with extraction," I respond.

"Good, good."

"Okay?"

"Yes, just tired."

"How did reunion with Snow go?"

Moments of silence. Hesitates to answer.

"It was difficult. One of the toughest things I've had to do in a long time," Lawton says. "Saying good-bye to old friends is always hard."

"Unfortunate. Offer condolences," I say.

"Thank you, Lucy."

Silence once more.

"Changing subject. Inquiring on when to expect arrival to base," I continue.

"Soon," she says. "Ivy and I will be leaving this island for good in a few weeks. But there are a few loose ends I need to tie up before it's set in stone."

"Excellent. Am excited. Yearn for company at facility."

"Hang in there, Lucy. We're making excellent progress. We'll recreate what we lost. The hybrid species, our species, will be resurrected from the grave. The only way our kind will survive is if we fight for it."

"Agreed. Good luck on next task."

"Thanks, Lucy. I'll visit you once I'm finished. See you then."

Hang up communicator. Anxiously waiting for Ivy and Iris Lawton's arrival. Have feeling will be more to look forward to.

Chapter 33 – Mark Allen

Production

<u>March 18, 3061 4:03 PM</u>
The hard part is over. The demonstration of the prototypes is finished, and, for now, I've passed. We may not have gotten the bad guy, but General Rox was thoroughly impressed with what I've accomplished. Reimagining Lionel Changer's work for military purpose was never easy, but somehow I found brains I never knew I had, and I got it done.

Of course I couldn't have done it without Eli Winde's help. That chimp was essential in the development. I'm glad he stopped by to see the finished product.

I've been moved to a better cell in Arkady. I now have additional amenities to make my imprisonment more bearable. Streams, a bigger bed, better food, and a cleaner bathroom are just a few of the upgraded accommodations. Rox also insta-itemed in some new research equipment and tools so my creative juices will continue to flow. I have to say my opinion of the dog has changed since the mission. I was afraid of him at first, petrified. But I learned that he takes care of his own as long as you keep up performance. I think I've been deemed worthy in his eyes.

He's still in Arkady. I believe he'll be here at least another week while he compiles his report on the Alphas for his Alliance superiors. He says right now is the most important step. If his report isn't convincing enough, the Alliance may not appropriate enough funds for this project going forward. Converting Changer's work for military use is his baby. Without the budget to back it up, it'll be dead in the water. General Rox hopes to get interviews, feedback, recorded footage, and any other pieces of data that demonstrate the Alphas' capabilities and their use on the field. The biggest hurdle he'll have to get over is explaining why the mission failed.

He's actually supposed to stop by any minute to discuss the Alphas. It'll be the perfect time to ask about my possibility of parole. My improved holdings are nice, but nothing beats the taste of freedom. I patiently sit in my cell and look at the clock. All I can do is hope for the best.

The door opens and a handful of guards come into my cell and split apart in two separate lines. General Rox emerges from behind them and marches my way. Right off the bat, it's a good sign; he appears happy.

"Afternoon, Mark Allen," Rox says.

"Afternoon, sir," I respond.

"We have a lot to discuss today, so I'll go straight to the agenda. First on the plate is a summary of the mission. Here's my report so far."

He slides me a tablet with his nose. The document is neatly divided into different sections listing who was involved, how the Alphas performed, costs, and other various topics. I scan it while General Rox continues to talk.

"No need to read it right now," Rox says. "It's quite long, and I'm not even half done. I still need to compile your feedback and some additional statistics."

"What did you say about the mission?" I ask curiously.

"I highlighted the Alphas' performance and detailed our activities in Shogun. I also gave an extensive summary of The Collector and its capabilities. The Alliance will certainly be interested in what we witnessed."

"I see. So we're going to chalk this up as a failure, huh?"

"Unfortunately so."

General Rox looks understandably disappointed. Though the Alphas performed admirably, we were still bested even though we were so confident. Who could've foreseen an enemy like the one we faced? No conventional weapon could've taken on such a creature. Still, I feel like I've let him down.

"What's going to happen to The Collector?" I ask. "Are you going to launch a follow-up mission?"

"Perhaps one day I will," he says. "But I won't let it be my obsession. We weren't ready to face such a being. Next time we will be."

"Do you think we'll see more of the creature?"

"I doubt it. The little operation The Collector had has been exposed. Maybe we'll get reports of sightings here and there, but I'm not sure if it's worth the risk for the being. And with Van Faye in my pocket, I'll know where and when to strike. If The Collector is smart, it'll stay away from not only Shogun, but all of Fan Zui Bin."

"I see. So what happens now?"

General Rox has one of the guards set a video cube on the floor and activates it. Recordings of the Alphas in action play in the air.

"I want to focus our efforts on the next phase," he says. "As you can tell, I was very pleased with how the Alphas performed on the field. Their defensive capabilities were astounding, particularly Silverwolf. Even if only a handful of my soldiers were that resilient, the Alliance would be unstoppable. We wouldn't have to worry about a rebel uprising or one of the animal groups breaking away from Alliance control. We'd usher in a new police state in order to keep balance in this world. I've seen firsthand what your creations can do, and I am confident you can deliver."

"Thank you, sir," I say.

When I was young, I never believed in myself. I thought I would always be some lab flunky, spending my days following instead of creating. But here stands a high-ranking Alliance official, and he's singing praises of my work. I am truly touched.

"Of course, we'll need some improvements," he says. "You said Blackwolf wasn't as capable as Silverwolf because it lacked the natural ability. I'll want you to level up the parity. Any creature should possess the ability to become elite regardless of prior skill."

"But natural ability will always be a factor," I protest.

"Agreed, but let's minimize that. Also, though I was impressed with Silverwolf's durability, I'd like you to raise the bar on the next wave's offensive capabilities. If we are to take on creatures like The Collector, we'll need better weaponry."

"Got it, sir. I better write this down."

I get a nearby tablet and start writing.

"I'll need to get your notes when I'm ready to present my case," he says.

"To the Alliance uppers?" I inquire.

"Yes. A bit of convincing will have to be done on my part."

"You don't think they'll finance your future endeavors?"

"I'm not sure. The world is changing. There's less focus on military funding these days. When I first obtained Lionel Changer's data, I saw a goldmine of potential. In every device he crafted, every blueprint he left behind, I saw a weapon that could be made. However, the Alliance masters saw different. They see medical advances, technology that could help bring this world back to the age when humans created a utopia."

"Ah, yes, the days before the Ark Project."

"Yes. That's their goal. But I think it's foolish. Those days are long gone. There's too much civil disruption, too many species clashing with each other. This world will never be how it was. That's why we need weapons like the Alphas. Our advances are the only things that will keep the world safe from itself."

"Well then, I'll start right away."

I say it eagerly. I'm excited to work on this project now. I feel like my life has a bit of purpose. I think of improvements in my head. Stronger armor, bigger cannons, better mobility. The possibilities fill me with glee. Now that I know it can be done, I can start producing in no time. But then, I think of something else, something that will be a roadblock to future development.

"Sir, I just realized there are no more wolves to use. We'll need new specimens to build off of," I say.

"You're right," General Rox says. "But don't worry, I'll procure some."

"How?"

"We'll find some stragglers in the Wolf's Den. Maybe trick a mercenary into volunteering."

"But the Brotherhood of Wolves won't like that."

General Rox's demeanor suddenly becomes irate.

"Who cares about them?" he says. "Wolves, nothing but a bunch of ungrateful assholes. They don't hold a candle to their superior canine brothers, my kind, the dog. Relations with the Brotherhood have always been icy within the Alliance. I could care less if they get pissed off over a couple of strays."

"So you're just going to take some wolves off the street?" I ask. "It's the same thing The Collector is doing."

"This is different. These are just wolves, and unlike The Collector, we're the good guys."

"I could always use a different animal."

"Don't bother. You built your first prototypes off wolves, and the next few runs will be the same thing. I want you to perfect your craft before deviating away from what you know. It will be wolves, and that's that. Is there an issue?"

I disagree with what General Rox proposes, but I'm not willing to risk the opportunity.

"None at all," I say.

"Excellent," General Rox says. "You're a team player, Allen. You've demonstrated your worth and I'm looking forward to what's next. As a reward, I'll be filling out your parole documents."

My eyes open wide and a large smile shines on my face. It is what I've been waiting to hear for years.

"Thank... thank you, sir!" I exclaim. I can't hide my excitement. "I don't know what to say."

"It's no big deal," General Rox says. "Your parole should be easily granted, provided you agree to its terms."

"And what are those?"

"With my influence, you'll leave this dreaded Siberian wasteland known as Arkady and reside in a place of your choosing. But in exchange for your freedom, you'll have to report to an office, and it's a task I will oversee personally."

"Sounds reasonable, not a big deal."

"And you'll be working for the Alliance. You'll be an official Alliance scientist and will head the Biomechanical Advanced Military Project."

"That's the name you chose?"

"Indeed. Those are the terms. Understood?"

He barks it out as if it's an order, but in my head, it's more of a promotion. A paid job working as a director of a military project? Sounds like a dream.

"Understood!" I say enthusiastically.

"Good to hear," Rox says. "The short-term goal will be for you to create more prototypes. After a few more test missions and experience, we'll stop production on the comatose canines and concentrate our efforts on live testing."

"What do you mean, sir?"

"Building on top of half-dead creatures is fine for now. I controlled the Alphas like sentinels. But eventually, I'll need to have your implants installed on real soldiers, ones that can think for themselves and utilize the experience they've gained on the battlefield. I don't intend to make glorified drones forever."

"I see. Do you think anyone will be willing to undergo the process voluntarily?"

"I don't see why not. Who wouldn't want such power?"

I shoot him a skeptical glance. He responds with a smile.

"Don't worry, Allen, my soldiers will want the implants," he says. "Besides, I already have someone in mind."

Chapter 34 - Iris Lawton

Exodus

February 13, 3056 4:21 PM

"I want you out of here," I say sternly. Bastion and I have been arguing for the last hour. Well, it's not so much an argument as it is a tirade against him. Over time, ever since Lucy left four years ago, I have grown to hate him in a way that I've grown to hate those who persecute my kind. He is like them. He oppresses me. I live on this island as his captive, forced to live his way. I am not free here. I am a prisoner to an obsessive, unreasonable hybrid.

That's his reasoning, after all. The word "safety" gets thrown my way so many times that it has lost its meaning. Who am I safe from? I used to think he protected me from the Alliance and their military boogiemen, but after living with him for so long, I begin to think he's the one I need protection from. His paranoia has gotten worse. He believes the Alliance can come down on us any minute, that they can blindside us in an instant and send us to our graves. He even fears that there are threats on the island already, and imposed stricter curfews on both Ivy and me, despite my protests.

For obvious reasons, communication of any sort is barred, and he regularly checks on our messages and compcube activity. Even though I want to, I haven't spoken with Lucy in years because I know he'll find out. I don't even know where she is or what she's up to.

He says he does it out of love, because he cares about Ivy and me. I believe his sincerity, but he's also an idiot. He doesn't know what true love is. Love is about trust and understanding, not terror and suspicion. It's about compromise, not tyranny. It's about doing things for your loved one, not telling them what to do. Love is free. This is not. He fools himself into thinking what he's doing is love, but I've experienced love once and only once. When I was with him, with my wandering wolf, I knew it was a wonderful experience, not this hellish nightmare that I'm bound to. Even though they were long ago, and even though they didn't last long, I miss those days greatly and yearn to live like that once more. But the longer I live with Bastion, the more it seems those days have passed.

I unwillingly live with Bastion's restrictions because he has the skills to keep me tied down. He may be a vile creature, but I recognize the talents he has. Bastion often says there's nowhere he can't find me, whether it is this island or the ends of the world. And sadly, he's right. I believe him, so a part of me stays here out of fear.

But that is dissolving. He may have his prowess and physical abilities, but he forgets I have a power greater than him. I can see the future. In fact, I can see how our current conversation is going to play out. It ends with him leaving and me keeping my daughter in our home. It's one future out of many. My precognition gives a window to upcoming events, but in order for them to be true, I must precisely execute the correct actions. If I do, the future I choose will be the future that is reality. I've perfected this process. When I want something to happen, I use my visions to guide me on how to get there. I can only go as far as a month into the future in terms of visions. Also, sometimes, it takes a while, as there are millions of outcomes and I can only view so many visions. But if I'm persistent enough and I really want something done, it'll happen.

That's what I did before I had this confrontation. I wanted to ensure that Bastion would be out for good. Ivy is away in her room, just like in my vision. I sent her before I talked to him. It's almost thirty minutes until five, just like what I saw. I even match the smallest details. There are two forks on the kitchen counter, the water is off, and one cabinet door is open. I meet every single idiosyncrasy because even the smallest wrong detail could change the future and play out a different vision that I might or might not have seen. It's tricky business, and I'm far from perfect every time. But at least now I clearly understand how the system works so that I can exploit it.

I'm done with him and done with all of this. It's time for him to leave Ivy and me alone, for me to truly be a mother, for me to stop living in his shadow. I should've done this earlier, but I suppose I've been mustering up years of bravery to stand up to my greatest enemy.

"You want me out of here?" he says in a perplexed tone. I suspect part of it is an act because he must have surmised that this moment was coming.

"Yes, I want you out," I say. "You can't control me anymore."

"Control you? You think that's what I'm doing. I don't know how many times I have to say it, but I'm doing this for—"

"Don't say it!"

I grab the pistol that I concealed in my pocket, grip it firmly, and point it at him. Unlike before, he looks completely stunned. His eyes open wide, and his jaw drops as he looks at me, stiff as a board.

"Iris, what are you doing?" he says with a shaky voice. "You're confused right now. Put the gun down and—"

"Shut up!" I scream. "Don't tell me what to do anymore! You've been doing this the whole time we've been here. It's always been your rules, your laws. I'm tired of it. I'm tired of being someone's prisoner. This is the last time. I've listened to you out of fear, for Ivy's wellbeing, but never because I wanted to. Well, now it's time to stop listening. Stand the fuck back from me!"

I hope I'm a good actress because it's not the first time I've spoken those words. I've been practicing that speech ever since I saw it in my vision. It looks like I'm convincing enough because he listens to my order and takes a step back. But then he realizes what he's doing and stays still, as if he's making a stance. I've already seen that happen too.

"Iris, I know you're emotional right now, but you need to calm down and think about things," he says in a peaceful voice. "I'm here to help. I love you. I wouldn't let any harm come to you. You know I do it because—"

A blast echoes throughout my quarters. I've fired a shot from my gun, and it hits the ground right in front of his feet. He jumps back with astonishment and disbelief.

"What the hell, Iris?!" he yells.

"I'm tired of hearing your speeches," I say. "I've been listening to them for ages, and it's time to put a stop to this. Just leave. You can worry about your things later. I'll drop it off for you, but I don't want to see your face around this home. There are plenty of pods for you to live in, just not this one."

His eyes narrow and anger rises in him.

"So that's it, huh? Just like that you're going to kick me out?" he asks. "After all we've been through, after all I've done for you."

"You've done nothing for me! Nothing but given me misery and resentment," I say coldly.

His demeanor suddenly switches. Instead of boiling with rage, my words have caused him to look sad, sullen.

"But, Iris, I can't live without you," he says. "I need you. You need me."

I knew he would say those words, and I know the words I must say. But his last statement irritates me, makes me livid even. I can't help but go off script to express my fury.

"I don't need you, and it's never been clearer to me that I never needed you!" I scream. "I am capable on my own. You may not think so, but you underestimate what I can do. I should be the one in control. I'm the one with power. You're just an over-glorified acrobat. You know nothing! Don't tell me what I need."

I let it all out and make myself calm down after the outburst. I wasn't supposed to say that, according to my vision at least. I quickly close my eyes and look at the current future to see if my words have caused a different path to emerge. It has not, thank goodness.

I reopen my eyes and see Bastion now on the verge of tears. He knows he's lost this battle and is about to throw a feeble desperation question to salvage what he can before I dismiss him completely. I can hear it already.

"But what about Ivy?" he says pleadingly. "You can't take her away from me. She's my daughter too."

"She is," I say. Right on cue. "I've already spoken to her and she agreed to stay with me. She can see you when I permit. But I am no longer yours."

He looks around. So quickly his world has crumbled before his eyes, so quickly have the tables turned.

"This is just a game, right? You can't be serious?" he says, almost laughing the words out hysterically. His eyes are swelled with tears, his breathing is heavy.

"I am serious. You will leave now. Walk east, walk west, walk north, walk south," I say, echoing the words my brother Tiago had once told me. "Just make sure it's away from here."

"But…"

"Go."

I put my finger closer to the trigger, this time aiming straight at him, ready to fire. The tension is thick, and he takes a few seconds to think it over, but he relents and leaves.

He may be back to plead his case, to clear things up on the Ivy situation, but he is gone for now. I breathe a sigh of relief. Even though I knew what was going to happen, that was intense.

As for the future, my visions tell me to stay here for the sake of my daughter. But one day I will leave this place, one day I will be free from him. It may take one year. It may take five, but I will wait as long as necessary to ensure my future plays out the way I want it to. I have the power and I will use it.

Chapter 35 - Bastion

Reunion

<u>March 20, 3061 10:02 AM</u>

The day is here. Time to see her again. I can hardly contain my excitement. We've had such a difficult, complicated relationship that I thought it would never recover. She's been bitter, hostile, angry, and hateful toward me, but now it seems her opinions are easing up. That's why I look forward to our meeting because it shows me there's a chance. I know I shouldn't be too head-over-heels as this is simply a meeting to discuss our daughter, but this means something. She wouldn't have even entertained the idea a few years ago. Things change. I know it.

More importantly, we're working on Ivy together. For a long time, I felt that our separation made me abandon Ivy. I've always wanted to be the best father I could be, but she pushed me away. I suppose Iris had much to do with that, but I wished that we could've set aside our differences to at least make it work for our daughter. A child cannot grow up with parents isolated from each other. It needs to be a team effort. And now, finally, we're starting to do that. Even if Iris hates me, I'm glad at the very least we've gotten to the point where it's not about us, it's about Ivy.

I hope we can do something about her. She's lost her way, taken the beaten path. It'll be through our united efforts that she'll find the right one. This is what I've always hoped for, that the family I once had would be regained. It's something that has kept me alive when I thought there was nothing left to live for. Now I'm closer. The three of us, talking about our problems, this reunion, that's how I'll get back my dream.

I arrive at the cliffs, and there is Iris. Her back faces me and the wind blows her hair gently. She's looking out into the ocean and seems deep in thought. She doesn't even notice I've arrived.

"Iris?" I say.

She turns around and she's more beautiful than I remember. Living apart from her almost made me forget how lovely she is. Her eyes are large and beautiful, her nose is dainty and petite. And she's in great shape. I'm actually really surprised. Iris must've been working out a lot because she looks extremely fit, more fit than I've ever seen her before. She's amazing.

"Iris, you look wonderful," I say.

"Thank you," she responds.

She doesn't say it with much of a tone. No enthusiasm, but also no anger. It's indifferent, almost cold. But perhaps she's feeling the same mixed emotions I am and doesn't know how to react about the situation. She's probably just concerned about Ivy and wants to get straight to business.

I take a quick moment to look over the cliffs. The horizon is blue and wonderful. The sun shines on both of us. This was our little spot back in the day. Ivy, Iris, and me as one family looking at what lay beyond the sea. Hopefully with what I'm about to tell Iris, life will be like those days once again.

"I understand you're probably worried," I say. "Well, as I said when I spoke to you earlier, I have some news that you might find troubling. You see—"

"Hold it," Iris says, cutting me off. "You don't have to say anymore. I already know what you're talking about."

At first, I'm confused by her interruption, but I take a few moments to think and I realize what she's getting at.

"Ah, your powers," I say. "Well, yes, you've probably already seen what I'm going to say, but you should still hear me out."

"Don't bother. I know you think Ivy is in cahoots with Lucy and that they're planning something. You want us to intervene and break Ivy away from Lucy. And I didn't even use my visions to get this info."

"What?"

I'm floored. How did she know without her visions? Unless...

"Did you know this all along?" I ask her. "You knew that Ivy and Lucy were communicating with each other?"

"Yes, I did," she says.

"Why didn't you tell me?! Why is it always secrets with you? Ivy is my daughter. I deserved to know. Yet I had to find out on my own. You know how dangerous Lucy is and you didn't tell me anything! I know you hate me—I've known this for a long time—but you could've at least told me this! Why Iris? Why?"

I'm heartbroken. I feel like I've been played, that I've been out of the loop in everything. I don't know who Iris is, I don't know who Ivy is. I'm completely in the dark to the hybrids I love.

"I didn't tell you because I want her to talk to Lucy," she says. "She's my friend, and you have no right to tell me what to do."

"You want Lucy to influence her?" I ask.

I think about what Iris says and it hits me. The plans and scheming that I feared Ivy was doing with Lucy… it wasn't her.

"It's you," I say. "You have something planned with Lucy. Ivy's not the one working with her. You are."

"Yes," Iris says. "But why so surprised, Bastion? It's not like you know me. We haven't talked or seen each other for ages. What do you think I've been doing all these years? Twiddling my thumbs?"

"But what are you planning? What are you doing?"

"It's none of your business. Just know that we're planning to leave this island soon."

"We?"

"Who else would I be talking about?"

Ivy. She plans to take Ivy!

"You're not taking her away," I say. "She is my daughter!"

"Don't kid yourself," Iris says mockingly. "She hasn't been your daughter for years. She's mine and mine alone. You're as much of a father to her as that tree over there."

"Shut up! You can't take her! I'll find you, Iris. I'll follow you to the ends of this universe if I have to. I've done it before and I'll do it again. You think you can hide somewhere from me? I'll do anything to make sure my daughter is safe from the Alliance, from Lucy, even from you."

"I don't doubt that. That's why right now I'm going to make sure that doesn't happen."

"What?"

She levitates a heavy looking rock and hurls it my way. I quickly duck my head to avoid getting smashed. When I recover, I can only stare at Iris, completely stunned by what has transpired. That blow could've knocked me off this cliff and sent me to my death. And it wasn't a warning shot either. Had I not reacted, it would've connected.

"How dare you do!" I scream. "You attacked me! All those years I've kept you safe, kept you from harm, and this is how you want to play it out?"

That's when I realize all of this has been premeditated. Her powers make everything planned. She knew what was going to happen and how it was going to go down. Her intentions are clear. Iris wants to kill me. I suppose the threat I volleyed against her threw her off the edge, but I suspect it's more than that. The years of staying on this island and the grudge she's been building have culminated to this day. That dream of being reunited is dust. She's always hated me and any shred of doubt I had is gone. I need to protect myself. I won't protect her anymore.

"I'm done with this too, you ungrateful bitch!" I holler.

But how do I fight a foe who knows what my next move will be? The combination of her telekinesis and precognition have made her an opponent I can't match.

Iris lifts another rock and throws it my way, but once again, I'm able to dodge it. I wonder how I'm able to evade what she throws. Shouldn't she know what's going to happen? Shouldn't she know what to do to end me? She can see the future, after all. She can anticipate my moves. And then I realize that is where she's vulnerable. Knowing things can help, but it doesn't matter if she can't execute what she sees.

That has always been the flaw in her powers and now it's my advantage. I've known Iris better than anyone else on this planet. I understand the nature of her powers. She can look into different futures, alternate timelines that branch off depending on her actions. However, these timelines will only be true if she's able to act. If her plan is to smash me with a rock because she saw that's the way I have go, that's great for her. But hitting me with that rock isn't so easy.

And with every miss, the future changes course, and she'll have to look into another vision to find a way to correct her mistakes. But she doesn't have the time to see, not when I'm around, not while I'm on the attack. She may have the upper hand in so many ways, but the future isn't set, and I have a chance to defeat her.

The hybrid I loved doesn't exist anymore. She's been replaced by this vengeful monster. Time to end this.

Iris recognizes I'm prepared to do battle, so she lifts a boulder this time and gets ready to fire. Perfect. She releases her hold on the rock and it comes crashing forward, bulldozing everything in its way. Instead of running away, I sprint toward it, and right before it slams into me, I jump as high into the air as I can. My gamble pays off, and I soar above the boulder, briefly landing on it. Once my feet touch the rock, I instantly push off, using it as a steppingstone for another more powerful leap.

I travel in the air and lock my sights on Iris. As I get closer to her, I clench my fists and prepare to strike her with a flying punch.

When I land, I strike, swinging with all my might. However, she ducks it just how I dodged those rocks earlier. It appears my own training has made her as equally physically gifted as myself. If she didn't have her powers, she'd still be a tough adversary to take down. But as I recover from my swing, I look at her face. She's startled. Perhaps she wasn't expecting me to still be alive, at least according to her vision. Her sudden lack of confidence boosts my hope and fighting spirit.

If I want to win this match, I need to be unpredictable. She no doubt knows the possibilities, so I'll have to do something that breaks the norm. I hate to fight dirty. I grab some dirt on the ground and throw it at Iris's eyes. It's a desperate move, but also something I wouldn't normally do.

She dodges it like my punch. Damn, she's quick. But her instinctive response has left her legs vulnerable. It's the kind of opening I was hoping for. I throw out a low sweep with my right leg and it actually connects. Iris falls to the dirt. She lands straight on her back and her head bounces on the ground.

There's not a moment to waste. I quickly leap on top of her, pinning her down while she's dazed from her fall. I look at my hands and hesitate just a little. Flashbacks and memories flash through my mind. I remember all of it—the good times, the bad times, the moments with her. But this is my life, and I do everything in my power to remind myself that those days are gone.

I plunge my hands to her neck and start to strangle her. I squeeze tight, pushing her neck hard to the ground, and bury my hands into the muscles. Realizing what's going on, she snaps out of her stupor and her eyes open wide. Her hands grab onto my arms and she struggles to pull them off their grip. But it's no use. I'm using every ounce of strength I have to maintain my hold. It's so strong that if I keep it up for another minute or so, her neck will surely be crushed and this conflict will be over.

I tighten my clench and the strangulation becomes more intense. Iris starts to cough loudly. Her hands no longer hold me. Instead, they flail wildly as she loses control over them. I try to not look into her eyes, but it's difficult. They're red and bulging. I'm such a mix of feelings and emotions that all I can do is stare into the desperation on her face. She looks terrified and though I don't relent on the choking, I'm dying inside. I feel no pleasure in this, no satisfaction in my actions. This is a crime that I will regret for ages.

Just as I think the deed is done, something blindsides me. An object pounds my head with great power. I instantaneously let go of Iris and fall to my left, but I'm able to stop the fall with my arms before my face hits the ground. I look around to see what the culprit is and notice a rock rolling on the ground. Damn her telekinesis. I'm stunned, but the adrenaline courses through my veins and I hop back to my feet.

But once again, I'm blindsided by another flying object. This time it's a large branch and it smacks my back. A stinging sensation erupts from my spine and it spreads across my body. My other senses dull, the only thing I feel is the pain. I fall forward and writhe on the ground, clutching my lower back. I'm exhausted.

No, I won't give up. Once again, I rise to my feet. I have to keep going. I have to live. I need to keep Ivy safe, away from her crazy mother, away from this madness. She's my daughter! It's my responsibility!

I can't though. Iris is just too powerful. Iris clenches her fist and punches upward. Simultaneously, a column of dirt morphs from the ground in front of me and collides right into my stomach.

I gasp when it makes contact and it knocks the wind out of me. My legs become shaky. They give in and I fall to my knees. My eyes bulge and I heave in another deep breath to try to recover. It's too much. My body simply cannot go on. I sit slumped in anguish, not only in my defeat, but in the whole situation. My heart has been betrayed and I only feel the devastation.

"How could you do this to me?" I say weakly with my head hanging low. "All you ever did was use me for Ivy. You wanted a child. I get it. But it wasn't like that for me. It was genuine and real. I... I..."

"Don't say it," she says authoritatively.

"I love you."

Her eyes narrow and she lowers her head to mine. She's fuming.

"You don't know what love is!" she shrieks. Her eyes are watery as she fights to hold back her tears. "Love is a two-way street. Love is sacrifice. Love is not only about protecting your partner, but making her happy. You did none of this! Only he did! I know what true love is, and it wasn't with you!"

She doesn't have to say his name. I already know whom she's talking about.

"It's always been about that stupid wolf!" I scream. "Even now, it's about him. I gave you everything, but I could never match up to his ghost. How dare you! You didn't even give me a chance. You never loved me!"

Tears of desperation and anguish run down my face. I'm pouring my heart out to the hybrid I always loved. Years of loneliness and pain rain out from my soul and into my words. I feel drained and lost, a time bomb of emotions that's now finally exploding after so many years of build-up.

Even with this display of raw emotion, Iris stands there coldly. She doesn't even react.

And that pisses me off.

I lunge at her with a strong right hook in a final attempt to end this confrontation. But Iris ducks under it and kicks my leg. Immediately, I lose my balance and start stumbling toward the edge of the cliff. I do everything in my power to try to regain my footing, but I can't. This is how my life ends. I fall to my death. I close my eyes and accept my fate.

That's when she grabs my hand and stops me from going over. And then she pulls me in strongly and we embrace. It's something I've waited years for. I stand there, hugging her, and lose control of my senses.

"Thank... thank you, Iris," I say. I'm a sobbing mess.

I'm shocked but happy at the same time. She saved me. All the anger, all the paranoia, all the heartbreak gets washed away into the ocean. I'm so grateful for this moment, and all I can think about is how I wish it would last for an eternity.

She pulls her head closer to mine.

"Bastion, I have to apologize," she says. It's a curious statement. "You see, you're right. I never loved you."

I feel sharp pain pierce through my stomach. My eyes widen, and it feels like she's sucked the soul out of me. I try to break away from her, but she clutches me tighter. She starts shaking her hand, and the agony multiplies. With every movement of her arm, I feel my torso being ripped. I become weaker as the pain continues to overtake my senses.

Finally, she lets go. I instantly clutch my stomach and look down to see that my hands are covered in blood. In fact, everything is. My torso, my clothes, it's even trickled to my legs. And then I look at Iris and see the knife. It's not made of light. It's made of steel, and my blood drips from the tip.

She stabbed me in the stomach, but she really stabbed my heart.

I stumble backward. Blood starts to pour from my mouth, and I can't muster a coherent response. My back faces the edge of the cliffs where I've had so many memories with both Ivy and Iris. With my dying thoughts, I think of them. They were my world. I did everything I could to protect them. But in the end, it was my downfall.

I fall to my knees and shed one last tear, thinking about how things have ended. Oh how things could have been. If only.

I collapse, my face hits the dirt, and everything fades into darkness.

Chapter 36 - Ivy Lawton

Fathers

March 20, 3061 3:01 PM

I have a few boxes packed, but I'm done for now.
I'm in my room, lying on my bed, wondering about the
past and the future. I think about my father. He wasn't a
great dad, far from it, but he tried. I knew he loved me.
Isn't that the only thing that matters? We all make
mistakes. Are they unforgivable? Perhaps when you
make so many of them, one just can't find it in your heart
to accept any more apologies.

I don't know though. Does that mean he deserved
such a fate? Is it my call to make? Maybe it's out of my
scope. My issues with him didn't go as deep as the issues
others had with him. I struggled with being his daughter,
but that's about it. Others weren't so fortunate. I love
my mother, so whatever she's had to deal with because of
him caused this day to come. I shed some tears, but I
cannot forgive Bastion for all he's done to her. I trust my
mom's judgment more than anything in the world.

But…

…

…

…he was my father.

Suddenly, the door opens and in comes mom.

"You're home," I say.

"Yes," she says.

Mom looks tired and beaten. Her hair is a mess. I see
some small cuts on her face, and her neck looks roughed

and sore. Small bits of blood stain her light pieces of fur. I knew she was in for a struggle, but I don't know the fine details. My imagination can only fill so many blanks.

"Are you hurt?" I say as I touch her wounds.

"I'll be okay, nothing serious," she says gently. "I miscalculated a few moves. Guess I'll have to work on it."

"Are you sure you're okay? Those cuts look bad."

"Don't worry, my dear. I'll ask Aunt Lucy to take a look at it. But I'm one hundred percent sure I'm fine."

"Okay."

An awkward silence fills the air. There's only one thing we want to talk about, but neither of us have the courage to spit it out. We sit there, staring at the walls, wondering how to initiate the conversation.

Finally, I decide to speak.

"So how did it happen?" I ask.

"Just like how I told you it would," she says tersely.

"So he's...?"

"Yes... he is."

I don't follow up with any other questions. Once again, a tense silence fills the room. All day, I've been waiting to hear the words. When mom confirmed the truth, it was rather anticlimactic. I guess I went through this conversation so many times that I've become desensitized.

I don't have anything else to say at this point. There's nothing left to process. The deed is done. Bastion is dead. Am I a bad daughter? Perhaps I am. But was he a bad father? Perhaps he was. Does it really matter anyway? In the end, he couldn't make us his prisoners on this island anymore.

"So what happens now?" I ask my mom.

"We'll be leaving this island soon," she says.

"How soon?"

"In the next few weeks."

"And we'll be joining Aunt Lucy at her base?"

"You mean our base. You better get your things ready."

My mom looks around my room, surveying it. She's probably thinking of memories.

"The island is nice," she said. "But it's time to move on. We can't live here forever. We can come back from time to time. The facilities and pods will always be around, but it won't be our home anymore. The base that Aunt Lucy and I have set up isn't big, but there's plenty of room to grow. And I hope it will be temporary as well. Our permanent home will not be underground. Our permanent home will be free among the masses. That's what I envision for not only us, but all our kind. That is the future I want."

My mom looks like she's about to tear up. She's worked so hard for this day—the planning, the training, the constant visions—and now it's here. She's traveled far on her path, but her journey is only beginning. I know her plans. They're grand. They're wonderful. But I'm scared it's too much, that the weight will be too heavy for her weary shoulders. It must be hard. She's made so many sacrifices and endured so much grief.

I reach out and hold her hand.

"Don't worry, mother," I say reassuringly. "I'll support you every step of the way. I am your daughter, and I love you."

She looks at me and smiles.

"I'm so proud of you," she proclaims.

Mom makes her way to the exit.

"Stay here and continue to pack," she says. "I have to go out for a little bit, but I'll be back soon."

"Where are you going?" I inquire.

"To the Great North," she says. "I have to meet with Aunt Lucy."

Chapter 37 – Iris Lawton

Phases

March 20, 3061 3:32 PM

The flashing brightness stops and my eyes adjust to the dim lights of the room. I've just teleported into the arrival bay of our base. Lucy is here and greets me. She smiles, which is rare even though our relationship is solid.

This place will be not only mine, but my daughter's new home. Lucy and I have spent the past few years constructing this place out of nothing but teleported materials. We utilized Lucy's knack for ingenuity and some of Lionel Changer's old, shady contacts to get this place up and running. For the past few years, I've kept it a secret from Bastion. It's not like he really knew about my whereabouts anyways, and the modified personal porter that Lucy designed made leaving the island easier.

If he'd found out about it, he surely would have gone out of his way to stop us. I had to keep everything a secret from him. The only time he had an idea of my plans was when I deemed the time was right. I consulted my visions to see when I could strike.

When I finally saw an opportunity, I did what I needed to do. First, I had Lucy send that initial message to him, the one that mentioned Shogun. That would start to raise his suspicions. Then, I had Lucy hack and upload that news report to his stream to make sure he would see it. He needed a way to make the connection between

Lucy, Shogun, and Ivy so that he would have a reason to be paranoid.

After those pieces of evidence were set, I had Lucy send the final communication to Ivy to finish the set up and draw Bastion out. It was the only way I could get his guard down. This was the way to get rid of Bastion once and for all. It had to be through deception. Any direct confrontations would have led to my demise. My visions told me all of this.

Landing that final blow helped me release the years of rage I had in side. He was right. I never loved him. The only good thing he ever did for me was help me produce Ivy. I guess I owed him that much.

"How did confrontation go?" Lucy asks. It's like she can read my mind.

"Okay," I say. "I made a few mistakes. It should've ended sooner."

"Job is done. Should not worry. Fully understand powers. Should be proud of accomplishment."

Lucy is right. There's no doubt in what I can do. But it's not the precognition that I need to master, it's the execution.

"I was sloppy out there," I say. "Not only against Bastion, but against the Alphas as well. If I want the future to come true, I need to improve."

"Upgrade implants?" Lucy asks.

"Yes, in due time at least. If I want to become stronger, quicker, faster on my feet, I'll need to enhance my physical limits."

"Will work on it."

"Thanks, but that's not a priority. We need to focus on the rebuilding effort. What's the status? I understand you made another extraction recently."

"Yes, Adachi Konoe. Will update progress. Follow me. Going to lab."

I trail Lucy through the corridors of the facility. I've been here a few times, but Lucy knows this place like the back of her hand. She effortlessly navigates her way. The look and feel of the rooms and hallways is an amalgam between HORUS and the island. It's cold and industrial yet homely at the same time. That's good. Ivy and I will need some time to adjust, and having it feel like home will help expedite the process.

We arrive in the extraction zone. It is here where Lucy stores all her work and analyzes the samples she's extracted. Fancy equipment litters the area. Compcubes, high-intensity microscopes, and other tools that I don't even recognize are present. The items have all been funded by Lionel Changer's offshore accounts. On the walls, I see containers and canisters labeled with various species names and subsets. They're held in place by focused light, which also acts as a sterilization corridor.

"So this is what you've collected?" I say, pointing at the canisters. "I thought there would be more."

"Only sampling," she responds. "Most resources in storage."

"I see. And how is the collection phase going?"

"Almost complete. Focused on feline subjects. Harvested desired amount. Soon specimens not needed."

Lucy talks about those poor abducted saps like crops. I, on the other hand, will always feel remorse for my role in their deaths. Perhaps that's what we need in this partnership. Lucy will be the pragmatic one, the hybrid who sees things objectively. I will be the balance, the moral compass that understands that the sacrifices, though helpful to our kind, may not always be the right choices.

I'm glad this stage will be over. I've dealt with some shady people, and I'm looking forward to never having to work with them again.

"I cut ties with Van Faye," I say. "And now that the harvesting stage is almost done, I'll be cutting ties with others. These crime bosses are dangerous. The less I have to deal with them, the better."

"Agreed," Lucy says. "Van Faye betrayed you. Revenge option?"

"Not right away. But she'll get what's coming to her soon enough."

Lucy appears worried and changes the subject.

"Come. Show you work station," she says.

We walk out of Lucy's lab and into her research room. It's small, but I'm sure it'll get bigger as time passes. She has a few compcubes running and activates one to show me a simple diagram that outlines the next steps. I'm actually surprised. It seems Lucy has a little presentation for me.

"Currently on track with large scale plan," she says. "After collection phase complete, move on to design phase. Will modify Lionel Changer's abandoned plans for splicing. Changer deemed impossible to splice. I deem possible. Already have prototype process in place. Will use harvested animals as building blocks. Hybrid creation ultimate goal of splice. After initial splice subject created, will continue perfecting. Ultimate objective to create perfect hybrid, in turn making hybrid perfect species."

"That's the plan indeed," I say. "The Alliance may have almost wiped out our kind from the face of the planet, but we three—you, Ivy, and I—are survivors. With your ingenuity and my powers, we will reestablish the hybrid population. This is for our kind. This is for

everything and everyone we have lost. It's for my fallen
brothers and sisters."

I look at my hands and think about the things I've
been able to do with my powers.

"If we use some of my genetic makeup to splice this
new generation of hybrids, will they have my abilities?" I
ask.

"Unsure," she responds. "Most unlikely though.
Changer's research suggests genes you carry only passed
down by natural birth. Ivy's abilities support theory."

"I see. In any case, that won't be the focus. What we
need to concentrate our efforts on is mass creation. The
next generation will have to be created in droves. Large
numbers are needed to build what we need to win our
freedom."

"What is that?"

"An army."

"Is army wise path? Even with mass creation,
numbers small. Alliance too big, too powerful. Will
crush us."

"That's true. But at least there's still a chance. Look
at us now. We've been hiding underground all our lives.
If we want our freedom, if we want to live on our own,
we have to fight for it. The nonhumans did it when they
were given intelligence, and we'll have to do the same."

"If fight necessary, new implants needed. Strength
implants, armor implants, mental enhancement implants.
Many new possibilities after retrieving Alliance tech.
Have studied Alpha prototypes. Remarkable."

The "Alpha prototypes" as Lucy refers to them is
really Fenrir. I'm using his corpse to my advantage. Is
that right? Am I wrong to use my dead friend? Then
again, he was dead on arrival. The Alpha known as
Silverwolf isn't Fenrir. No, my dear wolf was killed long

ago. The only thing that remained was his soulless body for the Alliance to harvest. He became a monster because of them.

"Yes, they were impressive," I say. "And after you study and recreate their technology for our purposes, I can't wait to take it out on those Alliance scumbags."

"Reverse engineering should not be difficult," Lucy says. "Will replicate and refine technology of Blackwolf and Silverwolf. Will redesign for needs of hybrids. Impressive, yes. Alliance able to design blueprints from Lionel Changer. However, self is smarter. Self will win in implant arms race. Iris can expect implants that will make body as powerful as mind."

"I don't doubt that. You've already demonstrated your skills so many times. I mean, just look at the modified personal porters you made. Instant teleportation anywhere without the need of a station. It was the sole reason I was able to infiltrate so many areas and sneak away from the island. I was untraceable. And after I teleported Blackwolf to you, you studied her and was able to pinpoint all of the Alphas' weak spots and tell me how to disable their devices. I wouldn't have been able to take down Silverwolf without your knowledge. You are truly a genius, the smartest in the world."

"Thank you. One problem though."

"What is it?"

"To continue study of Alphas and understand technology, will need deconstruct. Means dissecting creatures. Understand Iris has emotional connection to one Alpha. Still wish to proceed?"

I think of who the wolves used to be the moment Lucy says the words.

"Do what you want with Fang," I say. "She got what she deserved."

"Agreed. Blackwolf ready for deconstruction. And Silverwolf?" she asks.

I get teary-eyed just thinking of him. As much as this will help us, I can't bear to see my love ripped apart like a science experiment once more.

"Harvest the armor, but leave the body," I say softly. "I wish to cremate him."

"Will do," she says. "One last thing. Discovered Alphas have recording devices installed. Found this in Silverwolf."

She digs a small device from her pocket and activates it. From it plays a holographic video of Fenrir's last moments as Silverwolf, right before I killed him. The images flash and I feel the same pain I felt when I ended his life. The fury and sadness come rushing back to me, and I can barely stomach watching further.

"Understand if Iris wishes to dispose painful memory," she says.

I snap out of my shock and quickly respond.

"No, I want you to save it," I say.

"Peculiar. Why?"

"It's the only thing I have left of him."

"I see. Will store in personal compcube. Observe that Iris needs time. Suggest Iris get fresh air."

"Thank you for your concern, Lucy. I think I'll take your advice. Ivy will come soon. I just want to say that I appreciate all those years you stuck by me despite the difficult circumstances. You are a true friend."

"Not a problem."

Lucy walks away and I get my personal porter ready to teleport to the surface. Sometimes I get worried that someone might see me port in, but I don't think I have to worry about that here.

A flash of light temporarily blinds me, but when I open my eyes, I look around to see I'm at the surface, hundreds of feet above our base.

The view is beautiful here. It's peaceful, relaxing. I look into the sky and think about the past years. When I created this Collector persona, I knew there would be no turning back. I would be committing reprehensible acts. But I've always done it with the future of my species in mind. I still wonder if what I've done, what I will do, will be the right thing. Some will view me as a monster, but I suppose all of society already thinks that of my kind. But to the ones who matter, I will be remembered as a freedom fighter, the one who rose up against oppression and saved the hybrid species.

I know things will never be so black and white. When I see my future, it will be grey. Yet I will remain vigilant. It is my destiny. I look up at the sky one more time. In the horizon lies that beautiful blue planet I've called my home all of my life. I now understand what my brother Tiago was desperately shooting for. Earth looks breathtaking. Excitement fills my body.

I think I'm going to like my new home on the Moon.

About The Author

Andrew Vu is a novelist who was born in San Jose, CA. He graduated from UC Berkeley in 2007 and currently resides in Oakland, CA. During his spare time, he enjoys movies, video games, and watching sports. He roots for his California Golden Bears, the Kansas City Chiefs, the Golden State Warriors, and the Oakland A's.

If you enjoyed the book, feel free to leave a review! Also, check out the Halfkinds wiki at http://halfkinds.wikia.com.